Based on the hit TV series

Sabrina

The Teenage Witch®

Millennium Madness

Will Sabrina ring
in the new year
as a mortal?

SUPER EDITION

AN ARCHWAY
PAPERBACK
PUBLISHED BY
POCKET BOOKS.

$4.50 U.S.
$6.50 CAN.
£3.50 U.K.

**I'm 16,
I'm a witch, and I *still*
have to go to school?**

**Look for a new title every month
Based on the hit TV series**

Available from Archway Paperbacks
Published by Pocket Books

"The dawn of a new millennium!"

Sabrina pointed up a bowl of Happy-O's. "We talked about Y2K last week in school. Mr. Kraft's nervous about it, but Aunt Hilda and Aunt Zelda said things should be fine."

"For witches, sure." Salem flopped over on his side. "But computers run the Mortal Realm now. Some people are afraid they won't be able to get money out of the bank after midnight on New Year's Eve. Or that airports won't be able to tell planes which runways to use. Or that hospitals will mix up medical charts and the wrong patients will get brain transplants!"

"Oh, Salem, people don't have brain transplants."

"They most certainly do," Salem replied. "What do you think this is, the bad-old good-old days of the twenty-first century?"

"Huh?" Sabrina blinked and looked around in astonishment.

What had just happened?

The kitchen looked entirely different. Where once wooden cabinets had hung, there were now sleek metal containers, each dotted with the hologram of a knob. Shiny silver counters floated above a gleaming floor that sparkled and danced with shifting colors.

"Salem? *We're in the future!*"

Sabrina, the Teenage Witch™ books

Available from ARCHWAY Paperbacks

Sabrina The Teenage Witch®

Millennium Madness

SUPER EDITION

Based on Characters Appearing in Archie Comics

And based upon the television series
Sabrina, The Teenage Witch
Created for television by Nell Scovell
Developed for television by Jonathan Schmock

AN ARCHWAY PAPERBACK
Published by POCKET BOOKS

New York   London   Toronto   Sydney   Singapore

AN ARCHWAY PAPERBACK *Original*

An Archway Paperback published by
POCKET BOOKS, a division of Simon & Schuster Inc.
1230 Avenue of the Americas, New York, NY 10020

ISBN: 0-671-02820-0

First Archway Paperback printing January 2000

10 9 8 7 6 5 4 3 2 1

Printed in the U.S.A.

IL: 4+

Contents

As Sand through the Hourglass
By Nancy Holder

"Morning, morning!" Sabrina Spellman cried as she rushed down the stairs of the Victorian home she shared with two of her aunts, Hilda and Zelda. "Wow! Have you looked outside? It must have snowed all night." Lucky for her, she had on a very nice new pair of snow boots and a beautiful new Norwegian pullover in addition to black wool pants.

She glanced out the front windows at the beautiful white blanket covering their lawn and the trees along the street. The house was festively decorated for the winter holidays. Garlands of holly and mistletoe were draped along the overhang and twined around the posts on the porch. The holly berries were dusted with soft white snow that glittered like sugar crystals.

Near the porch, a fat snowman sported a shiny

black top hat that Sabrina had found in the basement. Her aunts had kept many possessions from their centuries of living, and Aunt Zelda had told Sabrina that that very hat had once belonged to Charles Dickens.

A beautiful Christmas tree gleamed in the corner of the parlor, resplendent with ornaments Hilda and Zelda had been collecting for decades.

Despite the fact that Halloween was the favorite celebration of witches everywhere, the Spellmans had honored the custom of celebrating Christmas since long before Sabrina came to live with them.

Admiring the lovely tree and the Christmas stockings that hung on the mantel, Sabrina sailed toward the kitchen in a wonderful mood.

"I think I'll zap up some Happy-O's for breakfast," she said, zipping through the swinging door. "Too bad we aren't allowed to conjure up brand names. What are you guys having?"

But neither of her aunts was in the kitchen. Sabrina was a little surprised. The three of them usually had breakfast together.

"Make that the *four* of us."

Salem, the black cat, was curled up on the counter with the phone between his paws.

"So you're sure my investments will be secure?" he was saying into the phone. He saw Sabrina and gave her a casual wave of his tail. She waved back. "You're absolutely positive you've fixed the bugs?" He listened. "Oh, I see. Started over from scratch.

4

Well, that's impressive. So no bugs. All right. Thanks."

He disconnected and stretched. "Morning, Sabrina."

"What bugs?"

"Computer bugs," he replied.

"Oh."

While it was a little unusual that Sabrina's aunts weren't home for breakfast, it wasn't strange at all that Salem could talk. Salem, the American shorthair, was actually Salem Saberhagen, the warlock. As a warlock, Salem had raised an army and tried to take over the Mortal Realm. The Witches' Council had stopped him and, as punishment, turned him into a cat. For the duration of his sentence, the Spellman sisters had charge of him.

That wasn't unusual either, because Hilda and Zelda were witches. They enjoyed living in the Mortal Realm, making their home in the small town of Westbridge, Massachusetts.

Sabrina's parents were divorced, and both had far-flung interests. Her archaeologist mother was on a dig in Peru, and Sabrina had thought her father was in the foreign service. So it made perfect sense to her that her friendly aunts would invite her to live with them and go to Westbridge High.

Little had she realized that while her mother was a mortal, her father was a warlock. The night of her sixteenth birthday she had levitated above her bed in her sleep, proof positive that she had inherited witch powers from her father. The next morning, Hilda and Zelda had told her that she was a half-witch and that it was their job to teach her how to use her powers responsibly.

Easier said than done, Sabrina thought now, as Salem punched in another phone number.

"Westbridge Survival Supplies? Mr., ah, Spellman here. Have my twenty cases of Cat-tastrophe Cuisine come in yet?"

Intrigued, Sabrina cocked her head. *What on earth is Salem doing? First he calls to make sure his investments are bug-free, and now he's ordering Cat-tastrophe Cuisine?*

And just what is Cat-tastrophe Cuisine? Food that's free of bugs?

Ew.

Salem listened into the phone. Then he said, "Last Chance Chicken sounds just fine." His eyes widened. "Oh, you have Time's Up Tuna? I want the tuna. Nothing but tuna." He sighed. "Gobs and gobs of tuna."

He hung up and looked at Sabrina. "With any luck, in four days, there will be rioting and looting in the streets," he said eagerly. "Then I'll dine like a king." His eyes took on a dreamy, glassy stare. "King Neptune, in fact."

Sabrina frowned in puzzlement. "Salem, what on earth are you talking about?"

He cocked his head. "On the other hand, there's

no reason why I can't eat my Cat-tastrophe Cuisine even if we don't have the catastrophe."

"*What* catastrophe?" Sabrina pressed.

He swished his tail as he reached for the phone again. "Why, I think it should be obvious," he said. "The Y2K menace, of course. Today is December 28. Three more days until New Year's Eve 2000."

"Woo-hoo! The dawn of the new millennium!" Sabrina cried.

"And of potential disaster," he reminded her, "once we ring in the New Year."

She pointed up a bowl of Happy-O's and a glass of orange juice. As she sat down to eat, she said, "We talked about Y2K last week in school. I guess a lot of people are really worried that their computers won't be able to understand that it's the year 2000."

Salem nodded. "Exactly. Most software was developed to record each new year by changing the last one or two digits of the date—from 98 to 99, for example. But programmers neglected to prepare for a time when the first two digits also change, from the 1900s to the 2000s."

"Mr. Kraft's pretty nervous about it," Sabrina said. "But Aunt Hilda and Aunt Zelda said things should be fine."

"For witches, sure." Salem flopped over on his side and wrapped his tail around the phone. "But computers run the Mortal Realm now. They've completely taken over. Some people are afraid they won't be able to get money out of the bank after midnight on New Year's Eve."

"Some cats, too, I'm guessing," Sabrina said dryly.

He ignored her. "Or that airports won't be able to tell planes which runways to use. Or that hospitals will mix up medical charts and the wrong patients will get brain transplants!"

"Oh, Salem, people don't have brain transplants." Laughing, Sabrina started eating her cereal.

"They most certainly do," Salem replied. "What do you think this is, the bad-old good-old days of the twenty-first century?"

"Huh?" Sabrina blinked and looked around in astonishment.

What just happened?

The kitchen looked entirely different. Where once wooden cabinets had hung, there were now sleek metal containers, each dotted with the hologram of a knob. Shiny silver counters floated above a gleaming floor that sparkled and danced with shifting colors.

And Salem, while still a cat, was pure white, with speckles of what looked like glitter in his fur.

Sabrina herself was wearing a short slip dress of a lightweight silver fabric and high-heeled silver knee-high boots.

"Salem? *We're in the future!*" Sabrina cried as she jumped out of her chair, which was actually nothing more than a cushion hovering above the floor.

Then *poof!* they were back in the old kitchen of their large but cozy Victorian house. Salem was a black cat once more, seated in his customary place on the regular old counter, and Sabrina stood beside her chair dressed in her new Christmas clothes.

"Wow, that was trippy." Salem blinked and looked around. "Did we just travel forward in time?"

"That, or someone's playing a practical joke on us. Aunt Hilda? Aunt Zelda?" she called. "You can come out now. You got us."

There was no answer.

Salem said, "Wow, that was trippy." He blinked and looked around. "Did we just travel forward in time?"

Sabrina peered at him. "Salem, you just said that."

The big cat looked confused. "What? What did I just say?"

" 'Wow, that was trippy,' " she mimicked him. " 'Did we just travel forward in time?' "

"Mmm. That explains the strange feeling of déjà vu I have." He scratched behind his ear. "Furthermore, I'm guessing we didn't eat breakfast wherever and whenever we were, however many times we were there, because I'm starving."

"This is really very odd." Sabrina crossed the kitchen and began rummaging through drawers.

She opened the cabinet where the family kept their spell-casting supplies. "Did one of my aunts make a time ball?" She gave him a pointed look. "That you maybe 'accidentally' ate?"

Salem shook his head. "Not guilty. This time," he added guiltily. Once before, Sabrina had created a time ball, and Salem had eaten it. It had sent all of Westbridge back to the sixties.

Which is a nice decade to visit, but Sabrina wouldn't want to live there. Too much folk guitar music, for one thing.

"Is today some Other Realm holiday I don't know about?" Sabrina continued, quizzing the cat as she gave up on the drawers. "Such as Tease a Teenage Witch Day?"

"No. That's next Tuesday. Whoops. Ha-ha, just kidding."

"Well, I'll have to ask my aunts about it when I get home from the mall. Unless you know where they are," she said to Salem.

He shrugged. "Not a clue."

"Well, I hope they're having fun, whatever they're doing. Meanwhile, I'm due over at Valerie's. We're going to catch the after-Christmas sales."

Salem yawned. "You morning people are always so perky."

She grinned at him. "Perk, perk, perk."

"You're wearing me out." He flopped over on his side and closed his eyes.

"I thought you were starving."

"I'm just going to have a little pre-breakfast cat-nap," he told her.

He immediately started snoring.

Sabrina chuckled. Then she pointed up a dish of tuna cat food for him to wake up to, grabbed her little backpack purse, and headed for the front door.

Bracing herself for the cold weather, she threw open the front door and stepped across the threshold.

It was a beautiful warm day. There was no snow to be seen. No garlands of holly and mistletoe. No snowman, not even a puddle.

Stranger still, sunshine glowed on a stone urn full of colorful mixed flowers that Aunt Hilda had pointed there last . . . June?

"Salem?" she called, staring.

She walked outside. In her heavy sweater, she began to perspire. A warm breeze ruffled her hair.

She went back inside her house.

Only it wasn't her house anymore. It was a lush, verdant forest, with trees that towered fifty feet above her. The thickness of the branches and leaves hid the sky from her, and the rich smell of damp earth filled her nose.

"Salem?" she called again.

She walked into the forest. Beside her right foot, a ring of mushrooms glistened with dew.

She heard a titter. Another. As she watched, tiny, glowing fairies bobbed out from beneath the ring of mushrooms and flew up to greet her.

"Hello, hello!" they chirruped in musical voices. "Are you Sleeping Beauty?"

"Huh?" She blinked. "No. I—"

She looked down at her clothes. She was dressed in a velvet gown. There was a garland of wildflowers in her hair.

Salem, curled up in the crook of two tree limbs, gazed down at her and said, "What just happened? Are you working on a play for school or something?"

Just then a man with curly hair parted in the middle and a thick mustache stomped out from behind Salem's tree. "Young miss," he said, "may I ask you, please, if you have seen a hat? My best top hat seems to have gone missing."

"Mr. Dickens?" Sabrina asked in a shrill, amazed voice.

"The same." He looked pleased that she had recognized him.

He bowed and said, "I'm off to deliver a lecture on my novel *Great Expectations*. Quite suddenly I became aware that my hat was not on my head." He laughed quietly. "A most awkward predicament, don't you think?"

"Sure," she squeaked.

"I've looked everywhere." He gestured to the forest.

"Ask Frosty where your hat is," Salem suggested, gesturing with his head toward the front door.

"I beg your pardon. Did you just speak?" Dickens asked Salem.

Then the forest began to wobble, the way things do in dream sequences on TV. It blurred, grew faint, and then was gone.

Salem fell out of the nonexistent tree and tumbled to the floor of the Spellman parlor, which reappeared just in the nick of time.

"Whoa," he said.

"Don't say it's trippy," Sabrina begged. "Just help me figure out what's going on."

"Might I suggest a visit to the linen closet?" Salem said.

"Right." She nodded.

Together, cat and witch hurried up the stairs to the second floor. To their left was the linen closet, with the door closed. Besides actually containing sheets and towels, it was the Spellmans' portal to the Other Realm.

Salem hopped onto the bench beside it and said, "I'll just wait here."

"Don't you want to come with me?" she asked.

"Not really," he drawled. "If we get trapped over there or fall into a vortex or something, I won't be here for my shipment of Time's Up Tuna."

"Oh, I see. Well, it's good to see you have some perception of how serious this all is," she said dryly.

"I do indeed." He waved her toward linen closet door. "Besides, someone has to take care of our home sweet home. And I'm just crazy enough and brave enough to do it."

"My admiration knows no bounds," she informed

him. "Just make sure you don't turn into the Cheshire Cat while I'm gone."

"What do you mean?" he asked her.

She frowned anxiously at him as she opened the closet door. "From *Alice in Wonderland*. He slowly disappeared, until all that was left of him was his smile."

She walked into the closet. As she closed the door behind her, she heard Salem say, "Gulp. Maybe I'll come with you after all, Sabri—"

Rumble! Crash!

It was too late. Sabrina was already on her way to the Other Realm.

The streets of the Other Realm were deserted. On all the doors of the shops, including Witchmart and the Other Realm Beauty Supply, and on all the restaurants and homes hung signs: Gone to Emergency Witches' Council Meeting. Even Vesta, Sabrina's fun-loving aunt, had left her pleasure dome for the meeting.

But when Sabrina arrived at the Witches' Council chamber, the doors were barred. A sign stood on a metal stand: Emergency Session In Progress. No Latecomers. The council bailiff stood beside the sign, with his arms folded over his khaki uniform shirt.

As Sabrina tested the doorknob, he frowned at her and said, "Can't you read? No latecomers."

"What's the emergency?" she asked.

He rolled his eyes. "Kids today. You don't pay attention. You don't watch the news. Civilization is just another four-syllable word to you."

"Actually, it's a five-syllable word—"

"Plus you have no respect for your elders."

"We do too!" she protested. Then, as he narrowed his eyes, she added, "Um, sir."

"Well, you still can't go in. Everyone received a memo, and if you didn't bother to read it, that's just too bad."

"But I never saw the memo," she insisted.

"Hey, I don't make the rules. I only enforce them." He straightened his shoulders. "You'll have to wait until the session's over." He pointed over his shoulder. "The cafeteria's open, but there's no one there to serve you. They're all at the meeting. You'll have to use the vending machines."

"I'm not hungry," she said. "I just ate breakfast."

He gave her a look. "It's almost midnight."

"What? That's impossible!"

He shrugged. "If you'd read your memos—"

Just then the doors of the chamber flew open. Witches, warlocks, fairies, leprechauns, trolls, and other assorted spell-casters hurried out, discussing and arguing among themselves.

In the crowd, Sabrina saw her three aunts and waved. "Aunt Hilda! Aunt Zelda! Aunt Vesta!"

"Sabrina." Aunt Zelda was the first to reach her. She was dressed in a charcoal-gray sweater and a black skirt slit up to the thigh. A highly respected physicist in both the Mortal Realm and the Other

Realm, Zelda was the most intellectual of Sabrina's three aunts. She was also the most strict—the one most likely to say no to something Sabrina wanted to do and the first one to insist that she be grounded if she did that something anyway.

"We were so worried about you," Zelda said, waving at a couple of passing wizards in spangled cone-shaped hats. "Why didn't you come to the meeting?"

"I didn't see the memo," Sabrina told her. She tried to remember if she had checked the toaster that morning. That was how the Spellman witches received memos from the Other Realm.

"Well, you're here now, thank goodness," Hilda put in, as she gave a weeping pixie a gentle hug. The pixie wiped her eyes and darted away. "We need all the input we can get."

While Zelda was intellectual and conservative, Hilda was easygoing. She was much more likely to go along with Sabrina's plans and schemes, or to suggest semi-legitimate ways of using magic to get out of a predicament. Her round cheeks were usually dimpled into a mischievous smile, indicating that she was ready for fun. But at the moment she looked as worried and earnest as Zelda did when she was preparing a physics lecture.

Aunt Vesta looked worried too. She was flamboyantly dressed, as always, in a brilliant royal blue suit dotted with tiny black silhouettes of hourglasses and a matching hat shaped like a sundial.

Vesta said, "Well, this crisis certainly puts a kink in my weekend plans. I'll have to cancel my dinner date with the king of Mars."

"That's too bad," Sabrina sympathized. "What was the meeting about? What's the crisis? All this weird stuff has been happening at our house and—"

Hilda made a mopey face. "Let me guess. Shifts in the time-space continuum, holes in the fabric of reality, yada-yada-yada."

Sabrina nodded eagerly. "Yes. Exactly. Charles Dickens showed up looking for his top hat, and we kind of warped in and out of the future. Salem and I, I mean."

"See, it's leaking, just as they said," Hilda told Zelda and Vesta. The other two nodded.

"What's going on?" Sabrina asked.

"The Great Clock of the Other Realm has a flaw," Zelda explained. "On New Year's Eve it will stop working altogether."

"Which, I gather, is not a good thing," Sabrina ventured.

"You're not kidding," Hilda told her. "When the Great Clock stops, all witches everywhere will lose their powers."

"What?" Sabrina raised her eyebrows. "For how long?"

"Forever, Sabrina dear," Zelda informed her. "In fact, magic will cease to exist. There will be no magical beings anywhere or at any time!"

"Yikes." Sabrina bit her lower lip.

"Yikes is right." Vesta gently pressed her chin with the tips of her fingers. "For one thing, we'll all have the life spans of mortals. We'll start to grow old." She shuddered. "And their plastic surgery methods are so primitive!"

"I won't be able to use my laptop any more," Zelda added gloomily.

"And I won't be able to use magic to interfere with Willard's misguided romance with Zelda," Hilda said.

Willard Kraft was the vice-principal at Sabrina's school. He had initially been attracted to Hilda, but he was currently dating Zelda. For the life of her, Sabrina could not understand what her attractive, intelligent, and cultured aunt saw in Mr. Kraft. He was a bit of a buffoon, and he was the kind of dictator Salem would have been if he had succeeded in taking over the Mortal Realm. Mr. Kraft's territory consisted only of Westbridge High, but that was sufficient to make Sabrina's life miserable.

"My aging is far more serious than your inability to hassle Zelda and Willard," Vesta said.

"So we won't have any powers at all?" Sabrina asked.

Her three aunts shook their heads. "Absolutely none."

"Wow. And I finally got used to having powers." Sabrina frowned. "Isn't there anything we can do?"

"That was what the meeting was about," Hilda

said. "The Witches' Council formed a sub-sub-sub-committee to discuss the problem."

"That's all?" Sabrina asked, surprised. "But New Year's Eve is only three nights away!"

"Or less, if time speeds up," Vesta said, worriedly tapping her chin.

"Or more, if it slows down," Zelda observed. "The council has asked us all to suggest ways to repair the clock. I think we should go by, take a look at it, and see if we can figure out what's going haywire."

The four started walking. Sabrina said, "I don't think I've ever even seen the Great Clock."

"It's the same with all those other tourist attractions in your own hometown," Hilda said. "You've just never taken the time to see it. But it's pretty cool-looking."

"Cool-looking" is an understatement.

Sabrina stood with her aunts and gazed up at the Great Clock. It was an enormous sphere encrusted with jewels and set upon two columns at least a hundred feet tall. The twelve silver numbers on the face glistened and gleamed, and if one stared at it long enough, one saw a real face pass over the sphere once a minute. It was ancient and wise-looking.

"That's the spirit of Father Time," Hilda told her in a hushed voice.

"Wow," Sabrina whispered back.

A sparkly pendulum swung back and forth between the two pillars; and on the pillars were etched the words "Then" and "Now." As it arced, a *Tick-Tock-Tick-Tock* boomed like distant thunder.

"Hear that? That's the heartbeat of magic," Zelda said reverently. "If it stops, magic dies."

At the base of the clock was a bronze plaque. It read: "Time, time, time is on our side."

"Not for long," Sabrina murmured. She stared up at the magnificent clock. The air around it positively vibrated with golden beams of magic, and magic streams cascaded from it to billow and froth on the ground below until they soaked into the very soil of the Other Realm.

Sabrina asked, "What's wrong with the clock?"

"No one's exactly positive," Zelda said. "Some people think the main spring has sprung."

Hilda shook her head. "I agree with the ones who think the gears are worn out."

"It's the pendulum," Vesta said with authority. "You know that old song: 'It don't mean a thing if it ain't got that swing.' That song is actually about the Great Clock."

"That's true," Hilda agreed, nodding. "A warlock wrote that song."

"I've never heard that song," Sabrina said. "Are you sure it has something to do with the Great Clock?"

"Well, *something's* broken, and it needs to be fixed." Zelda gazed up at the clock and tapped her chin. "The problem is, we can't take the clock apart to see what's broken. That would make it stop."

"And if it stops, we'll lose our powers," Sabrina finished for her.

Vesta kept tapping her jawline. "What would we do without eternal youth and beauty?" she groaned.

"Age?" Hilda suggested.

Vesta groaned louder. Then she said, "I need to lie down. I always think better after a nap. I'm going to the pleasure dome for a siesta. And possibly a massage. I also invited an incredibly handsome movie star who shall remain nameless but whose initials are B.A.—all right, first name is Ben, second name is Affleck—to come over for dinner."

"It's wonderful to see how seriously you're taking this crisis," Hilda said, making a little face.

"I am," Vesta assured her. She tossed her auburn hair. "The Witches' Council has requested that we all try to think of a solution." She stretched. "It's a proven fact that one thinks more productively when one is relaxed." She smiled at Sabrina. "Isn't that right, Sabrina?"

Sabrina shrugged. "I wouldn't know. I'm a teenager."

Vesta laughed. "Oh, you are so funny! Why don't you come with me? We could brainstorm while we sit in the spa."

"Well, that's tempting, Aunt Vesta, but I think I should go back to the house and see if it's still a house," Sabrina told her. "Salem's there all alone."

Hilda and Zelda nodded in unison. "That's a good idea," Zelda said. "Hilda and I have to stay here and discuss possible solutions. We're on the sub-sub-subcommittee."

"Oh, pooh." Vesta waved her hand dismissively. "Those witches and warlocks will talk and talk, and nothing will get accomplished."

Hilda looked glum, as if she agreed. Zelda shrugged helplessly.

"Well, I'm going home," Sabrina told everybody. Now that she had an idea of what was going on, she was even more worried about Salem. For all they knew, he really had become the Cheshire Cat by now, with nothing of him showing but his smile.

"Okay, dear." Zelda grimaced and touched Sabrina's shoulder. "I'd tell you to be careful, but I don't think there's any way for any of us to protect ourselves. Until we get the Great Clock fixed, we're all in terrible danger."

Sabrina sighed. *Oh, for the good old days, when my major source of terror was math homework.*

She looked up at the clock.

Someone's got to fix this thing before time runs out. Literally.

When Sabrina walked through the linen closet door, she knew something had gone haywire again.

Because she didn't open the door; she simply walked through it.

"Hi," Salem said shakily. "The house keeps melting . . . or something." To illustrate his point, he put a paw against the wall opposite the door. His front leg disappeared up to his shoulder.

He burst into tears. "What if something happens to my Time's Up Tuna? What's causing this?"

"The Great Clock of the Other Realm is not working correctly," Sabrina said.

Salem pulled his paw out of the wall. "Maybe it has a Y2K problem."

Her eyes widened. "Of course! That's it!"

"Well, duh," Salem said, not meanly.

"Salem, you're a genius!"

"Well, duh."

"Okay." She started to pace. "How are programmers fixing the computers?"

"They aren't," Salem told her.

She kept pacing. "I don't mean the computers themselves. How are they fixing the bugs in the software? What are they doing to the computer programs?"

He shook his head. "Again I say they aren't."

She stopped pacing and stared at him. "They aren't?"

"Nope. They've written all new programs. They started from scratch and—"

"A new clock!" she shouted. "That's the answer! We can't stop the old clock long enough to fix it, so we need a brand-new one!" She raised her fists above her head and did a little victory dance. "Woo-hoo!"

"That's brilliant!" Salem said with real enthusiasm. "My genius is rubbing off on you!"

"Yes!" she crowed.

"So how do you make a new clock?" he asked excitedly.

She froze. "I have no idea."

They looked at each other. "Magic book?" Salem suggested.

"Magic book," she agreed.

They trooped into her bedroom.

The large jeweled book lay on Sabrina's desk. As Salem hopped up beside it, she bent over it and started paging through the entries. She paused at the *S*'s to see if her father was in, but he wasn't listed at the moment. She thought *Maybe he's on the sub-sub-subcommittee too.*

"Here we go." She took a breath as she began to read: " 'Timing of spells. Stitch in time to save nine. Steppin' time, *see* Mary Poppins. Parsley, Sage, Rosemary and Time—incorrect spelling, *see* Simon and Garfunkel.' " She sighed.

"Try 'Great Clock of the Other Realm,' " Salem offered.

"Okay." She paged back to the *G*'s. "Nothing."

"Clocks."

Sabrina leafed through the *C*'s. " 'Clocks, magical, maintenance and repair.' " She rubbed her hands together as she read. "Okay. There's a spell listed. I'll recite it, but wherever it says 'clock,' I'll say, 'Great Clock of the Other Realm.' "

"That sounds good." In his nervousness, Salem

wagged his tail wildly back and forth. "Go for it, Sabrina."

Sabrina silently read the spell through once more. Then she cleared her throat and said:

> *Tick-tock, what's up with my Great Clock*
> *Of the Other Realm?*
> *Can't tell the time with this Great Clock*
> *Of the Other Realm*
> *Of mine.*
> *Father Time, come with your powers*
> *So I can tell seconds, minutes, and hours!*

Nothing happened.

"That was pretty klugey," Salem murmured. "Maybe if you try saying it without adding all the extra—"

Poof!

In the middle of the room stood a middle-aged man in a white robe, holding a weed whacker.

"Father Time?" Sabrina cried. "Is it really you?"

"No." He looked around. "I'm Justin Time, his son-in-law. I'm the Timekeeper, actually. Since you reworded the spell, I showed up."

"Oh." Sabrina glanced questioningly at Salem. "Did you know there was a Timekeeper?" she whispered.

Salem shook his head. "Not for a second. But then, my career in magic was cut short by the Witches' Council," he sniffed.

"We need your help desperately," Sabrina told the Timekeeper. "The Great Clock of the Other Realm is winding down and—"

"And you need a new one," he said. "We time-types know all about it." He scratched his head with the weed whacker. "We've been wondering when you guys were going to get in touch with us."

"What?" Sabrina asked, bewildered.

"We sent a memo decades ago."

Sabrina stared at him. "You did? Maybe the Council didn't get it."

"More likely they misfiled it," Salem said. "Typical inept bureaucrats. This illustrates why it makes more sense to let dictators run things."

The timekeeper looked at Salem. "You must be Salem Saberhagen."

"You've heard of me?" Salem asked, preening.

"Sure. But I promised my wife I wouldn't repeat any of those jokes. They're *so* politically incorrect."

Sabrina giggled. Then she said, "Well, speaking of time, we don't have any to waste. How do we build a new Great Clock?"

"It's a little tricky," Justin Time told her, "not to mention time-consuming. You have to travel in time to twelve magical moments, collect a souvenir from each, and incorporate it into your new clock."

She brightened. "Oh, okay. Well, I'll go back to the Other Realm and tell everybody. We'll send twelve magic users to twelve places and—"

He shook his head. "Now that you've summoned

me, you have to collect the souvenirs alone—right now or the spell won't work. You don't have a second to lose, and believe me, I know from seconds."

Sabrina stared at him. "You're kidding, right?"

"Nope. I don't kid. Never had the time for it." He snapped his fingers. A large wooden hourglass appeared on her desk, next to her magic book. The top section, which looked like an upside-down triangle, was full of lovely sparkling crystals. None of the crystals were falling into the lower half, which resembled a right-side-up triangle.

"You have twelve hours from the precise nanosecond—which is a very, very small part of a second—that I snap my fingers again to complete your task. When you come back to this time, it will be exactly twelve minutes and twelve seconds before midnight on New Year's Eve 1999. You will have twelve minutes and twelve seconds to assemble the clock from your souvenirs. On your mark . . ."

He put his thumb and middle finger together.

"Don't snap yet!" Sabrina pleaded. "How do I know which moments to go to?"

"You don't. It'll just happen."

"But wait!" she cried.

Snap!

Sabrina was in an immense church, surrounded by women in long gowns with bell-shaped skirts of colorful satin and brocade. Their hair was swept up and held in place by gold nets studded with pearls and gems. Pretty starched lace collars stood stiff around their necks.

Best of all, Sabrina was dressed just like them.

In fact, everyone in the church was dressed up in costumes, the men in extremely fancy jackets, some kind of bloomers that ended at their knees, and tights. Jewels sparkled and shimmered in rings and earrings on both men and women.

The church was ablaze with hundreds of candles, and a choir was singing. There were no places to sit; everyone was standing, facing the center aisle, waiting for something to happen.

"Cool!" Sabrina said as she took in her surroundings.

One of the women turned and said, "Ssh! Her Majesty is about to make her entrance."

Her Majesty?

The choir voices swelled. There was a rustle through the rows of people. Just like everyone around her, Sabrina craned her neck to the left.

At the vaulted entrance to the church, a woman stood all alone. She was wearing a heavy robe trimmed with fur. Her red hair trailed over her shoulders like a veil. Between her pale hands, she held a single white lily.

Sabrina caught her breath. *What a regal lady! She looks like a queen.*

The woman began to walk slowly down the center of the church. Just then, Sabrina heard Salem muttering, "Who put the lights out?"

He was under her skirt! She pulled up the hem, and he popped his head out. He looked around and said, "Oh, wow, déjà vu."

"No, no, we haven't been here before," Sabrina told him. "This is new. Or rather, old. We're in the past. I'm not sure when or where. But we've never been here before."

"*I* have," Salem informed her. "It's 1558. This is the coronation of Queen Elizabeth I of England. And I was here the first time." He sighed. "As a handsome courtier. Nobody could play the lute like I could. Liz always said so." He looked around intently. *Probably looking for himself!* she thought.

"Oh." Sabrina looked at the woman walking all alone. "Why are we here?"

"Queen Elizabeth was the strongest monarch England has ever had," Salem explained. "Her reign was called the Golden Age. Surely that makes this a magical moment."

"Sssh," one of the ladies said. "Her Majesty approaches."

Sure enough, Elizabeth was drawing close. Sabrina smelled the lovely perfume the queen was wearing.

"I've just got to say hi," Salem murmured.

"No, Salem!" Sabrina hissed. But the cat disappeared into the procession.

As the queen walked past Sabrina, she jerked and looked startled. Her skirts swayed. At the very same time, Salem darted out from beneath Elizabeth's skirt.

Something was falling, a small, circular object made of gold. Salem deftly caught it in his teeth.

Sabrina immediately crouched down to retrieve it, realizing that as she did so, everyone around her was doing the same thing. Only they were bowing.

Anxiously she took the object from Salem's mouth. It was a locket. On it, engraved in the center of a rose, were the initials A.B.

"Um, excuse me, Your Royal Highness," Sabrina murmured, "I think you dropped this."

The ladies around Sabrina gasped. One of them whispered in her ear, "Are you mad? No one speaks to Her Majesty without her permission!"

Uh-oh. Well, too late now.

The queen smiled down at the locket. Sabrina saw now that she wasn't much older than Sabrina herself.

As the queen stretched out her right hand, Sabrina saw that her fingers were covered with rings, even her thumb. She looked tired and her hand shook a little. She was nervous!

Elizabeth took the locket and said in a very soft voice, "We thank you, lady. This is a most treasured talisman. It belonged to our mother, Anne Boleyn."

Then she peered curiously at Sabrina. " 'Twas said she was a witch."

"Oh, really?" Sabrina asked, trying to keep her eyes wide and innocent.

"Indeed." Then the queen smiled at Sabrina. " 'Twas said." She cocked her head. Then she looked down at the locket and suddenly handed it to Sabrina.

"Something tells me you need this," Elizabeth said. "I wish you well, sister."

Poof!

Sabrina and Salem stood in Sabrina's bedroom. In Sabrina's hand was the locket.

"Wow." Sabrina stared at it. "Salem, that was amazing!"

"I guess I forgot to mention that it was rumored Queen Elizabeth was a half-witch too," Salem drawled. "On her mother's side, that is. So her coronation was a doubly magical moment in history—the first witchly queen and the best monarch England ever had."

Sabrina laid the piece of jewelry on the desk. "Well, if this is all we have to do to collect eleven more souvenirs, this is going to be a cinch. We'll have that new Great Clock in no time."

The voice of the Timekeeper echoed through the room: "Don't set your watch to that thought."

The Man in the Moon
By Nancy Krulik

"**S**alem, I give up," Sabrina said with a frown as she sat on the couch, staring at the cover of her magic book. "I have looked at every single page of my magic book, and there is not one clue about what other items I'll need to build a new Great Clock. Maybe the Witches' Council was right— these kinds of things are better left to more experienced witches."

Salem rolled his eyes. "Teenagers!" he moaned. "They just don't stick with any—" Salem never finished his thought, because the doorbell interrupted him.

Sabrina jumped up and quickly hid the book under the couch cushions. She had to make sure that it was out of sight, because no human was ever allowed to see it. Sabrina had no doubt that whoever was at the door was a human. After all, witches never rang the bell before coming inside. They just sort of popped in—or at least they did before everyone's magic started going so crazy.

Sabrina walked across the room and opened the door. Harvey Kinkle was standing on the porch, holding her backpack. "You left this at the Slicery yesterday," he told her. "I thought you might need it so you can study, just in case we have a surprise test or . . . something, when we get back to school after vacation."

Sabrina had to laugh. How could she tell Harvey that she probably would have to "pass" many history tests today? Harvey was functioning on normal time. The Great Clock didn't affect his schedule one bit. For him, this wasn't even a school day.

Sabrina knew that she should go on looking for things to fix the clock, but she also knew that slamming the door in his face would hurt Harvey's feelings. And he'd been so sweet to bring her backpack all the way to her house.

"Come on in," she urged Harvey. "Are you hungry?" Sabrina didn't wait for Harvey to answer. It was a given that Harvey was hungry. He always was. She held out a hand for his jacket. "How about I make you a sandwich? We have some roast beef in the refrigerator." Harvey nodded, and started to follow Sabrina toward the kitchen. "Sounds great," he said. "I'll help you."

Sabrina rushed ahead and blocked the entrance to

the kitchen. She couldn't let Harvey in there. The way everybody's magic was going lately, there was no telling what was happening inside the kitchen. For all she knew the toaster could be popping up and down on its own, and the refrigerator could be skating around on Rollerblades. For now, at least, there didn't seem to be any weird stuff going on in the living room, so that seemed a much safer place for Harvey to stay.

"No, no, no. I'll make the sandwiches," Sabrina told Harvey. "You just sit and relax. You must be exhausted from carrying my heavy backpack all the way over here."

"Actually I drove it over in my dad's van," Harvey admitted.

"Whatever," Sabrina said, trying to keep her voice calm. "But I still want to make this sandwich for you. Think of it as my way of saying thank you." She waved her hand in the direction of the couch. "Sit down. I'll be right back with the eats."

Harvey shrugged and went over to the couch. He knew by now that there was no arguing with Sabrina when she got weird like this.

Sabrina breathed a sigh of relief as she walked into the kitchen. The coast seemed clear. There were no signs of magic having run amok.

Sabrina went to the cupboard and pulled out a loaf of whole wheat bread. Then she opened the refrigerator door and scoured the shelves, looking for the roast beef. Unfortunately, there was no meat to be seen. There was also no ketchup, no mayonnaise, no lettuce, no tomatoes, no fruit, no milk, no juice, no butter, no yogurt, no soda, and no mustard. The refrigerator was completely filled with cheese.

Sabrina pulled one package of cheese out of the refrigerator and opened it. The smell was putrid, and the cheese looked worse than it smelled. It was green!

Sabrina opened a second package of cheese. *Gross.* This cheese was green as well, and it smelled even worse than the first package.

Just then Salem padded into the kitchen.

"Salem, do you know anything about this stinky green cheese?" she asked the cat.

Salem went over to the refrigerator and sniffed. "Yuck!" he exclaimed. "I haven't smelled or seen that stuff in centuries—not since I was a warlock vacationing on the moon. Where did it come from?"

"I have no idea. It just sort of appeared." Sabrina said. She looked curiously at the cat. "So you mean the moon really *is* made of green cheese?"

Salem shook his head. "Nah, that's just an old ad campaign started by a cheese company with headquarters on the moon. But don't laugh—a long time ago moon-made cheese was considered a delicacy. In its heyday, the moon was the Wisconsin of the solar system."

Sabrina stared at the cheese for a while. "The moon, huh?" she said aloud. "Maybe I should go there to find a missing piece for the Great Clock."

She closed the refrigerator door and headed for her room.

"Is everything okay in the kitchen, Sabrina?"

Sabrina jumped at the sound of Harvey's voice. She had been so caught up in the green cheese that she'd forgotten he was still sitting on the couch, waiting for his roast beef sandwich.

Quickly, Sabrina dashed into the living room. "We're all out of roast beef," she told Harvey, handing him his jacket and ushering him toward the door. "So I guess you'll want to be going, huh?"

Harvey shook his head. "No, that's okay. I'll eat anything. Maybe just a cheese sandwich."

Sabrina gulped. How did Harvey know about the cheese in the refrigerator? "Cheese? What cheese?" she asked suspiciously.

"Any cheese," Harvey said. "American, Swiss, Brie, Gouda, even Cheez Whiz would be okay."

Sabrina pushed Harvey closer to the door. "Sorry, we're all out of those," she said quickly. "But I'll meet you at the Slicery tomorrow, and I'll buy you lunch, okay?"

Harvey shrugged again. "Okay," he said. "See you later."

Sabrina closed the door behind Harvey. Then she ran to the broom closet. Salem followed close behind her.

"What are you doing now?" the cat asked.

"Getting my vacuum cleaner," Sabrina replied. "I've got to fly to the moon."

Salem snickered as Sabrina hopped on her vacuum and turned the key in the ignition. The vacuum sputtered and then died.

"I could have told you that would happen," Salem said. "All Other Realm vehicles have been shut down until further notice. The Witches' Council is trying to conserve energy."

Sabrina climbed off the vacuum cleaner and scowled. "So how am I supposed to get to the moon?" she asked.

"Climb on a spaceship?" Salem suggested.

Sabrina shook her head. "Astronauts don't go to the moon anymore," she said. "They haven't gone there since the Apollo missions of the sixties and seventies." Sabrina smiled as an idea began forming in her head. "That's it! I'll go back in time and hitch a ride on Apollo 11, the first manned spaceship to land on the moon."

Sabrina cupped her hands over her mouth and began to shout as loud as she could. *"Justin!* Justin Time! I need your help!" She waited for Justin to appear. But he didn't.

"Maybe he's running late," Salem suggested.

Sabrina grimaced. "How can he be running late? He's the Timekeeper!" Sabrina ran to the couch, pulled her magic book out from beneath the cushions, and ran upstairs to her bedroom.

"What are you doing?" Salem asked as he raced up the stairs behind her.

"Time is running out, Salem. I can't wait for

Justin to decide to transport me back in time. I'll have to do it myself." She began scanning the index of the book for time-travel spells.

"I don't know, Sabrina. Magic has been a little— how shall I put it?—*undependable* lately," Salem said.

"I have no other choice," Sabrina told him as she turned the pages of the book. "Here it is, an incantation for time travel to the past."

Sabrina stood up, closed her eyes, and pointed her finger in the air.

1969 is the time I seek,
When bell-bottoms rule and hippies speak.
Among the stars I need to go,
So take me to the Apollo!

There was a flash of light, followed by a *ping*, and suddenly Sabrina felt herself transported to another time and place.

When she landed, a warm light was shining right on her face. She opened her eyes slowly, expecting to encounter three astronauts in a tiny space capsule flying through the universe. But that was not what Sabrina saw.

She put up her hand up to shield her eyes from the light. She looked out and came face-to-face with a huge audience of cheering people. And they all seemed to be staring at her!

"Here they are, the grooviest group on the block!"

an offstage emcee told the audience. "Let's have a real Apollo welcome for the Rhythm and Blue Notes!"

Grooviest group? A real Apollo welcome? Oh, no! Sabrina had sent herself to the 1969 Apollo all right. But not to the Apollo spacecraft. Sabrina had managed to transport herself to New York City's famous Apollo Theater!

The backup singers in the Rhythm and Blue Notes were staring at Sabrina curiously. They had never seen her before, and here she was, part of their act. Sabrina gave the singers a weak smile. There was no way she was going to be able to explain this to them.

The band started to play an old R&B tune that Sabrina had once heard her aunt Hilda sing in the shower. There was only one thing for Sabrina to do. She opened her mouth and started to sing along with the backup singers.

"Baby, baby, so sad," she sang as she did her best to mimic the complicated choreographed dance moves of the other singers. Sabrina smiled. *This is actually kind of fun,* she thought. *I could really get into this singing thing.*

Unfortunately, the other backup singers did not agree. Sabrina was more than slightly off-key. But, completely unaware of her musical shortcomings, she just kept on rocking!

Suddenly, she heard a loud *ping.*

* * *

Sabrina waited to touch down on solid ground after her magic transported her from the Apollo Theater. But that never happened. Instead, she found herself floating in the air inside a small spacecraft.

"Well, it's about time," Sabrina shouted into the empty craft, hoping Justin could hear her. She was now exactly where she had planned—inside the Apollo 11 command module. As she looked around the cabin, she was amazed at how much technology had changed since 1969. Today kids were carrying computers the size of notebooks. But the Apollo's onboard computer was huge; it would have taken up a great deal of the floor space in Sabrina's room.

As Sabrina moved around the cabin, she was careful to avoid being spotted by the various cameras and audio equipment placed onboard the space vehicle by NASA. She didn't feel like being picked up as a stowaway by Mission Control.

"I am about to make contact with this satellite that has orbited the third planet from the sun since . . . No! That's not right!" a man's voice declared suddenly.

Sabrina looked up. There, with his back to her, was Neil Armstrong, the man who would eventually be the first human to set foot on the moon. He was obviously working on the speech he would transmit to the earth as he walked on the moon.

"The work of astrophysicists has allowed us to

make physical contact with . . ." Neil Armstrong said as he made another attempt at his speech.

Sabrina was shocked. What kind of a sound bite was that? Didn't Neil realize that the words he spoke would be memorized by schoolchildren for centuries to come? He had to say something meaningful, exciting, and easy to recall on an exam. Sabrina had to help. But how? If she let on that she was aboard, Mission Control might call the ship back to earth before the mission could be completed. That would change the history of space travel forever. And as Sabrina had learned many times, changing the course of history could have dire effects.

Sabrina glanced around the cabin. Her eyes fell on the communications system, which helped the astronauts keep in touch with scientists on earth. That was it!

Sabrina closed her eyes and tried to concentrate. It had been a long time since she had transferred her voice to an inanimate object. Still, it was pretty basic magic, and she knew she should be able to handle it, despite her weakened powers.

"Neil, this is Mission Control," Sabrina said, throwing the deepest voice she could muster into the control panel.

"Roger, Mission Control," Neil Armstrong replied.

"Just wanted to tell you to be careful out there," Sabrina continued. "Just take *one small step*, my *man*. We don't want *a giant leap* or anything. You don't want to trip and fall. Remember all of *mankind* is watching you. Over and out."

Neil Armstrong thought for a minute after the transmission ceased. Then he let out a giant whoop of excitement. "I've got it!" he declared.

Just then Sabrina felt a series of hard jolts as the Lunar Excursion Module touched down on a part of the moon's surface known as the Sea of Tranquillity. Quickly Sabrina sneaked out of the LEM as Neil Armstrong prepared for his space walk. Having once skied on Mars, and even flown around inside a human body, Sabrina would have no trouble breathing in the oxygen-free environment. *Unless my magic acts up,* she thought nervously.

Sabrina hid behind a crater and watched as the astronaut prepared to take his first steps on the moon's surface.

"That's one small step for a man, one giant leap for mankind," Neil Armstrong announced to the world below.

Sabrina breathed a sigh of relief. Now *that* was a sound bite for the ages. As the astronaut dramatically placed the American flag on the moon's surface, Sabrina wandered off, trying to find something that might help her build a new Great Clock.

"There's nothing but rocks here," Sabrina grumbled as she looked at the dark, dusty surface. "The only other thing around is that American flag."

Sabrina raced over and picked up the flag. Suddenly a phone booth appeared. The phone inside it started to ring. Sabrina looked around. There was no one else in sight. "I'll get it!" she shouted.

Sabrina picked up the handset. "Hello?"

"Put that flag down, young lady!" a woman's voice ordered.

"Who is this?" Sabrina demanded.

"Betsy Ross, that's who. I made the first American flag. Can you imagine what an honor it is for me to have my flag, give or take a few stars, on the moon? Why would you want to destroy my happiness? There must be something else up here you can take home as a gift for your boyfriend."

"I'm not looking for a gift, I'm—" Sabrina began.

"Besides, don't you think future astronauts will notice if the flag is missing?" Betsy interrupted.

Sabrina nodded. "I never thought of that. Okay, you win. Look, I'm kind of in a hurry. Gotta go. Good—" Before Sabrina could even finish saying good-bye, the phone booth disappeared. Sabrina quickly placed the flag back in place on the moon's surface.

Phone booths on the moon? Magic is totally out of control now, Sabrina thought as she looked around for another item. Finally she picked up a moon rock. That had to be the answer. After all, it was the only object to be found on the moon. She popped the rock in her pocket and prepared to go back to the landing module.

"Where do you think you're going with that?" a male voice said, stopping Sabrina in her tracks. A small man with a big round face popped out from behind a crater and blocked Sabrina's path. "That's mine. Give it back."

Sabrina's mind was racing. Her history books didn't say a word about there being another human on the moon before Neil Armstrong—certainly not someone who wasn't wearing space gear to protect him from the lack of oxygen. That was when it dawned on her that he was not human. He must be from the Other Realm.

"Boy, am I glad to see you," Sabrina said to the man.

A huge smile came over the little man's huge pasty-white face. "You are?" he asked. "Why?"

"Because you're here to tell me what souvenir I need to build a new Great Clock of the Other Realm, right?"

The expression on the little man's face made Sabrina nervous. He seemed surprised to hear that there was anything wrong with the old clock.

"Oops," Sabrina said. "You, uh, didn't know anything about the Great Clock, did you?"

The man didn't answer. He just grinned wider. Sabrina didn't like the look of his smile. "Well, see ya! Gotta go," she exclaimed as she tried to bolt back to the Apollo.

But the little man was quick. He darted in front of her. "You're not going anywhere with that moon rock," he said. "This is private property, and you're trespassing."

Sabrina looked around. "I don't see any Private Property or No Trespassing signs around here," she said defiantly.

The man shrugged. "Okay, you got me on that one. Maybe I don't exactly *own* the moon. But for about two hundred years I've been the only one living here. That's gives me squatter's rights, doesn't it?"

"What do you mean you've been the only one living here?" she asked. "I had heard the moon was a hot vacation spot."

The man nodded. "It used to be," he agreed, "until the locals decided to allow gambling casinos on Saturn. Now everyone's off to visit the giant rings. Apparently, Saturn's the place to see, and be seen by, the beautiful people. The moon has gone downhill."

"So why are you here?" Sabrina asked.

"I might ask you the same question," the man said. "And since I'm the one who lives here, it's only right that you answer me. After all, guests first."

Something in the sound of the little man's voice made Sabrina nervous. She had a feeling that she'd better tell him the whole truth about why she was on the moon, or something awful might happen.

"Well, it's like this. There's this problem with the

Great Clock. And if I don't fix it soon, witches will become mortal," she said in one breath.

"The Witches' Council sent a little pipsqueak like you out to correct a problem like that?" the man asked incredulously.

"Hey! I'm not so little!" Sabrina defended herself, stretching her spine as straight as it would go. "Besides, they don't even know I'm here. It's just that I have this theory that if I can gather all the right parts, I can build a new Great Clock. And I think one of the parts is a moon rock."

"Well, you can't have one of mine," the little man said. "And they're *all* mine. So hand it over. Otherwise I'll make sure your astronaut buddies never make it home to the old blue marble."

Sabrina had no choice. She reached in her pocket and pulled out the rock. The man grabbed it from her hand.

"Aren't you from the Other Realm?" Sabrina asked the man. "If I solve the Great Clock problem, it will help you, too."

The man shook his head. "That won't help me. Your Witches' Council saw to that. They stripped me of my powers centuries ago. Then they sent me into exile up here."

"Whoa! That's a stiff penalty," Sabrina gasped. "Our cat was only sentenced to living one hundred years as a feline—and he tried to take over the world. You must have done something really horrendous. What was it?"

"I held the members of the Witches' Council hostage. They were not amused," the man said. "So now I'm the Man in the Moon."

Sabrina was surprised. She hadn't realized that there really was a Man in the Moon. She thought it was just an expression.

"Look, you seem like a nice guy," Sabrina lied. "I just need one rock. You have millions of them. Besides, you probably don't like having your privacy invaded by the astronauts and me. So just give me one little rock and we'll all be on our way."

"Forget it," the Man in the Moon told Sabrina. "It would serve all those big shot witches and warlocks right if they lost their powers. Let them see how it feels for a change. Besides, I kind of like having you around. It's nice having a friend to talk to."

Sabrina rolled her eyes. This guy sure had a warped sense of friendship. Someday she should fix him up with Libby. They deserved each other.

But this was no time to play matchmaker. Sabrina needed a moon rock, and fast. And she had to get it without risking the lives of the astronauts of the Apollo 11 mission. Maybe she could trick the Man in the Moon into giving her a rock. But how?

Sabrina stared at the small stone in the Man in the Moon's palm. It reminded her of a time she and Harvey had been shopping in town, and they'd seen some guys on the street playing a game with three cups and a stone. One of the guys had bet another five dollars that he couldn't guess which cup the stone was under. Then the first guy hid the stone under one of the cups and started moving the cups around really, really quickly.

The game had looked pretty easy to Sabrina; she was able to keep track of the stone without any problem. But when she'd suggested to Harvey that they try to win at the game, he warned her not to.

"The game's fixed," Harvey had warned Sabrina. "Those three guys are all in on it together. They're just waiting for a sucker to come by and offer to play with them. Oh, sure, they'll let you win once or twice. But by the third time, one of those guys is going to do something to distract you, and you'll lose all your money. It's an old scam."

As she remembered that date with Harvey, a big grin came over Sabrina's face. Now she knew exactly how to get her hands on that moon rock.

"Okay, you win," Sabrina told the Man in the Moon. "I'll stick around—for a while, anyway. But I'm going to have to leave when the astronauts take off. I won't have any magic powers by then, and they'll be my only lift home."

The Man in the Moon sat down on the edge of a crater. "Sounds good," he told Sabrina. "So what do you want to do?"

Sabrina pretended to think about it. Finally she suggested, "Why don't we play a game?"

The man in the moon rubbed his hands together with glee. "Ooooh," he said. "I love games. How about charades? I'll go first. This is the sign for movie . . ."

Sabrina shook her head. "Boy, you *have* been up here a long time," she said. "Nobody who is *anybody* plays charades anymore. The big game these days is the guessing game."

"You mean like I Spy?" the Man in the Moon asked her.

"Not quite. You'll need more skill to play this game. You want to try it?"

The Man in the Moon nodded. "Okay," he said. "What do we do?"

"Well, first, I need a few things," Sabrina replied. She took a deep breath and prayed that her magic would work. Then she waved her finger in the air.

Magic, help me if you're able.
Give me three cups and a table!

Instantly a table appeared. Beneath it were three tiny cocker spaniels.

"Woof! Woof!" the littlest one barked nervously.

"I said *cups,* not pups!" Sabrina exclaimed, waving her finger once again. This time the puppies disappeared and three small paper cups took their place.

"Okay," Sabrina said as she set the three identical cups upside down on the table. "Now I need a stone. That one in your hand will do nicely."

"Hey, wait a minute," the Man in the Moon argued. "Is this some kind of trick? Are you going to disappear the minute I hand you this rock?"

"Of course not," Sabrina replied. "I said I would stay and play a game, and I will. I never go back on my word."

The Man in the Moon held up the little finger on his right hand. "Pinky swear?" he asked.

Sabrina nodded and hooked her little finger onto his. "Pinky swear," she agreed, rolling her eyes. Sabrina hadn't pinky-sworn about anything since the second grade. But if it would make the Man in the Moon happy, so be it.

Obviously, the Man in the Moon was convinced that Sabrina was really going to play a game with him, because he handed her the moon rock.

"I place the rock under this cup," Sabrina said as she slipped the stone beneath the middle container. "Now I'm going to move these cups around and around the table. Keep your eye on the one that's hiding the moon rock, because when I stop, you have to tell me where the rock is. If you can do it, you win."

The Man in the Moon stared intently at the cup that hid the stone as Sabrina moved all three cups around and around. She was careful to move the cups slowly enough for the Man in the Moon to follow, but at a fast enough speed so that he wouldn't catch on. Finally she stopped. "Okay, where is it?" she asked.

The Man in the Moon pointed excitedly to the cup on the far left.

"Let's see," Sabrina told him. She lifted the cup from the table, and sure enough, the stone was there.

"I won! I won! I won!" the Man in the Moon shouted excitedly. "Can we play again?"

Sabrina nodded in agreement. Once again she placed the stone beneath the middle cup. "Here we go," she announced as she began moving the cups. After a few seconds, Sabrina stopped. She looked up at the Man in the Moon. "Well?" she asked him.

"I know! I know!" the Man in the Moon declared. "It's in that one. The one on the right."

Sabrina lifted up the cup the Man in the Moon had pointed to. Once again the stone was right where he had thought.

"You're pretty good," Sabrina said. "Too bad we're not on Earth. You could make a fortune doing this."

"I could?" the Man in the Moon asked curiously.

"Oh, yeah," Sabrina assured him. "Lots of people bet on this game. You're so good at it, you would walk away with the bank."

The Man in the Moon pondered that idea for a while. Then he looked Sabrina straight in the eye. "There are things we could bet for up here," he said slowly.

Sabrina looked around. "Like what?" she asked.

"Like that rock you need," the Man in the Moon suggested.

"Okay," Sabrina agreed. "But what would I bet? I don't have anything with me."

"Here's an idea," the Man in the Moon suggested. "If you win, I give you the rock. But if *I* win, you agree to stay on the moon with me for a year."

Sabrina gulped. A year was a long time. And this was no sure thing. What if Harvey was wrong about how the game was fixed? He'd been wrong about things before.

Then Sabrina thought about the thousands of witches who were depending on her to save their magic. She had to take the chance.

"Well, all right," Sabrina said nervously. "But just for one year, right? Then I get to hitch a ride with whatever astronauts come up here."

"It's a deal," the Man in the Moon agreed.

Once again, Sabrina set up the cups and slipped the stone beneath the middle one. "Ready, set, go," she said as she started to move the cups around and around, a little faster this time.

After a few seconds she looked out into the distance. "Hey!" she called out. "Isn't that Neil Armstrong coming this way?"

The Man in the Moon turned around just for a millisecond. But that was all the time it took for him to lose his concentration. By the time Sabrina stopped moving the cups, he wasn't at all certain where the stone could be.

"Okay, where's the rock?" Sabrina asked him.

The Man in the Moon stared at the cups. Sabrina could tell that he had absolutely no clue as to where the stone was. Finally he pointed to the middle cup. "It's there," he said, sounding less than confident.

Sabrina crossed her fingers for luck. She just hoped that by some weird coincidence, the Man in the Moon hadn't chosen the correct one. Slowly she lifted the center cup from the table. Then she breathed a heavy sigh of relief. The moon rock was not there.

Sabrina turned all the cups over and grabbed the stone from beneath the cup on the left. Then she smiled triumphantly at the Man in the Moon. "I won!" she declared as she grabbed the moon rock and tucked it in her pocket.

The Man in the Moon opened his eyes wide. "That's not fair!" he insisted. "You tricked me."

"A bet is a bet," Sabrina told him as she ran off toward the lunar module.

By the time Sabrina arrived back at the LEM, Neil Armstrong had returned from his stroll on the moon. But if Sabrina remembered her history correctly, it would be four days before Apollo 11 splashed down on earth. Sabrina could not wait that long. There was only one thing to do: she would have to use her magic to move time along.

When no one was looking, Sabrina sneaked over to the ship's calendar. She concentrated with all her might and waved her finger. The calendar pages flipped quickly, until they reached July 24, 1969, the day the lunar module splashed down safely in the Pacific Ocean.

"Whoa!" She was thrown off balance as she and the astronauts inside the capsule hit the water. Sabrina was thrilled. This time her magic had worked without a hitch.

As the astronauts were greeted by the crew of their recovery ship, the USS *Hornet,* Sabrina used her powers to pop herself into the crowd of cheering visitors who had gathered to congratulate the astronauts on their safe return.

Sabrina noticed that people in the crowd were staring at her curiously. At first, she thought someone had seen her land with the astronauts. Then she realized that people were simply staring at her clothes. Sabrina made a mental note to dress more retro the next time she took a time-travel excursion into the late 1960s.

The man beside Sabrina was listening to the news on an oversize transistor radio. "Hey, it sounds like our guys got out of there just in time," he told his wife. "According to this newscaster, NASA's instruments are registering a huge volcanic eruption on the moon's surface."

Sabrina shook her head. She knew the Man in the Moon had been angry with her—but a *volcanic eruption?* That kind of tantrum was ridiculous. Obviously, no eruption had really happened. Time and magic were being messed with again.

"It was only a game," Sabrina said to herself as she patted the moon rock in her pocket. "Some people take things so seriously."

She popped back to her bedroom and looked at the hourglass.

Time was literally running out!

Peace, Love, and Revolution
By Cathy East Dubowski

"I see you've been to the thrift shop," Salem drawled as he lounged across Sabrina's bed.

Sabrina scowled at Salem's catty remark. "Ha-ha. I can't believe you're so out of it." She twirled in front of the mirror, admiring her colorful outfit. She was wearing faded bell-bottom blue jeans that had several colorful patches sewn on; a purple, green, and yellow tie-dyed tank top; a string of love beads; and two buttons—one that read "Ban the Bomb" and another that said "A Woman without a Man is like a Fish without a Bicycle." Handmade leather sandals graced her feet.

"These are vintage clothes," Sabrina told Salem, "from the golden age of freedom, creativity, and self-expression."

"You mean the Renaissance, of course," Salem interrupted.

Sabrina rolled her eyes. "Do I look like Voltaire here? I'm—"

Salem interrupted again. "Voltaire was the 1700s. The Renaissance was the 1500s—"

"I'm talking about the sixties!" She picked up a faded denim jacket from her bed and held it up for Salem to see. The back had been hand-embroidered with colorful flowers and curling vines.

"I'm surprised these clothes aren't in the Smithsonian Institution in Washington, D.C.," Sabrina said.

"I'm surprised they're not in the rag bag in the laundry room," Salem replied dryly.

"Well, I think they're cool," Sabrina replied as she slipped two more strings of love beads over her head. "And, as I just learned, it's important to look the part."

"So what's the occasion?" Salem asked, leaping onto her desk and pawing her calendar. "Halloween's come and gone."

"Salem, how can you joke when the world as we know it may come to an end in only a few hours?"

Salem batted a string of hippie beads dangling from Sabrina's desk lamp. "Running around the room and screaming hysterically won't fix anything. Besides, I tried that already."

"You're right," Sabrina replied. "But maybe what I'm about to do now will help." She checked her backpack for cash, just in case, then shrugged into the denim jacket. "I'm headed for one of the most magical moments in history."

"My birthday?"

"No, silly! Woodstock—the famous three-day political rock concert that took place in August 1969 and defined an entire generation."

"Woodstock?" Salem exclaimed. "You've *got* to be kidding."

Sabrina wrapped a thin leather headband across her forehead and tied it in the back. "Hey, I figure if I've got to save the Other Realm from destructive millennium forces, I might as well have a little fun doing it. I mean, if I fail . . . and all the magic dies . . ." She paused a moment, her blue eyes shimmering at the thought, as she gazed at the other magical items she'd collected so far: Queen Elizabeth's coronation locket and a moon rock.

She had no idea how all these items would fit together, or what they had to do with a clock.

"Well, Woodstock is one place in time that I've always wanted to visit. This might be my last chance."

With a flick of her finger, she zapped a small TV-video combo onto her desktop, shoved in a video, and pushed Play.

"This will help me locate the place and time I'm aiming for." Aunt Hilda's copy of the documentary *Woodstock* began to play somewhere in the middle.

"But what about Justin Time?" Salem asked,

curling up in front of the tube. "Isn't he supposed to cast the spell that sends you back in time?"

"I thought so," Sabrina replied. "But look around you. He's late for my next appointment, and I can't wait—I don't have much time left. I've got to at least try to take matters into my own hands."

Sabrina fast-forwarded to the part where clouds dumped drizzle on the crowd. Rather than let the rain spoil the festival, dozens of young people made a game of it, running and sliding in the mud as heavy rock music played in the background.

"Whiskers, but that was fun!" Salem cried.

"What?" Sabrina stared at the cat, who never failed to surprise her.

Salem shrugged. "I've been pulling your leg, Sabrina. I know all about Woodstock." He looked at the video. "Whoa, whoa, whoa, wait a minute, rewind it just a little—there!" He pointed his tiny black paw at one corner of the TV screen. "That's me—Salem Saberhagen—when I was a cool cat, not a black cat!"

Sabrina studied the screen, which showed a sea of people bobbing, weaving, dancing, and grooving to the music. "Where? I don't see you. . . ."

"The guy with the long hair and beard covered in mud—see?—standing next to the girl in the tie-dyed halter top, the one with long hair parted in the middle."

"But they're *all* covered in mud," Sabrina pointed out. "All the guys have long hair. And all the girls are wearing halter tops and long hair parted in the middle!"

"Hmm, you're right," Salem muttered. "So much for the sixties myth of individuality."

Sabrina squinted at the video. In one corner of the screen a tall, shapely, auburn-haired woman was dancing like mad near the stage. She wore a long tie-dyed dress and had flowers woven into her hair—and she was the only person in the whole gyrating mob who was *not* covered in mud and soaking wet! "Is that . . . Aunt Vesta?"

Salem rolled his eyes. "She was such a groupie back then!"

A clock in the hall chimed, reminding Sabrina of her urgent mission. "Salem! Gotta go! Gotta find the magic moment and bring back a souvenir! If you see Justin Time, tell him I couldn't wait!" She slipped on some rose-colored granny glasses. "Wish me luck, Salem!"

"Hey, enjoy the party," Salem purred.

Sabrina quickly made up a spell:

Find me that magic moment in time,
I want to hang with the antiestablishment
  gang,
When talk of the war was on everyone's lips,
A place of love, where freedom rang.

"Oh, wait. I forgot something!" Sabrina dropped her backpack to the floor, darted to her dressing table, and dug quickly through her jewelry box.

"Yes! Here it is!" She slipped a long silver chain over her head, then held up the ornament that dangled from it, a shining symbol of a generation. "Mom's old peace-symbol pendant. I used to play with it when I was little, so she finally gave it to me." She closed her eyes and raised her face toward the ceiling. "I promise I'll take care of it," she murmured. Her mother couldn't hear her, of course. "Wish I could take you with me, Mom."

But that was a wish for another time, one that could come true only if she retained her magic. Only if she was successful at the task before her. Only if she could find an object magical enough to help repair the Great Clock of the Other Realm.

With new determination, she opened her eyes and grabbed her backpack two and a half seconds before the magic of the incantation began to whirl around her.

Sabrina shivered and closed her eyes again. Her powers were unpredictable right now; she hoped this journey would go more smoothly than her last trip.

She tried to relax and let the magic wash over, around, and through her, spinning her like a toy in a tornado. Traveling like this made her a little carsick. But she knew the feeling wouldn't last long. Would her magic work? *Yes!* she told herself. It had to. She was running out of time!

Seconds later her world stopped spinning and she dropped her backpack, staring down at her feet as she tried to work through the dizziness that had overcome her. The cold winter weather of Westbridge was replaced by heat and humidity. The temperature had to be close to ninety, which was a good sign. Was it August 1969?

As the winds died down and the dust cleared, she held up the two fingers of her right hand in the famous V-shaped peace sign of the sixties. She wanted to blend in with the crowd.

"What's happening, baby!"

Right on! A real live hippie! Sabrina thought, delighted that she'd hit her mark. She whirled around, but the words "Feelin' groovy!" died on her lips as she came face to face with . . .

Salem the cat, his head poking out of her backpack—with three strands of colorful love beads added to his usual cat collar.

"Sock it to me, baby!" he called out.

"I'd love to!" Sabrina exclaimed, glaring down at him. "Salem, who said you could come?"

Salem peered at her over his own pair of rose-colored granny glasses. "Lots of hip cats at a three-day psychedelic party with some of the greatest musical moments in the history of rock and roll. What's the question here? I'm digging this scene, baby. I hope I'm in time to catch Jimi Hendrix blowing everyone's mind when he performs his solo electric guitar rendition of 'The Star-Spangled

Banner'—yeah, baby, it was out of sight! You didn't just hear it, you felt it in your bones. It was probably the most moving political statement of the antiwar movement. Besides, there's this chick named Janis I need to look up and get down with."

"Oh, stop it," Sabrina said. "You sound like a bad guest character on *The Brady Bunch!*"

"Thanks! As a matter of fact, did I ever tell you about the time I met Marcia Brady?"

Sabrina rolled her eyes. She didn't have time for this. She had a universe to save!

"Uh-oh!" Salem said suddenly.

"What?"

"Here come da judge!"

"Huh?" Sabrina looked around.

"That guy looks important."

A heavyset old gent wearing a white shirt beneath an unusual dark suit was riding by in a sedan chair carried by two men. From beneath a black tricorner hat, long gray hair hung to his shoulders. He was wearing tiny wire-rimmed glasses, too. But he was no sixties hippie.

"Nice glasses," the man said with a smile as he passed them by.

"I wonder what's wrong with his foot," Salem said.

"Gout," Sabrina told him.

"How do *you* know?"

"Because," Sabrina replied, "that's Benjamin Franklin!"

"Get out of here!" Salem looked again. "Hey, he does look familiar."

"During the time of the writing of the Declaration of Independence, he was nearly crippled from terrible gout. So he preferred to travel this way. It didn't jostle his foot as much as a horse-drawn carriage would have."

Sabrina, her aunts, and Salem had actually met Benjamin Franklin before, when he was magically—and accidentally—transported to modern-day Westbridge. But since he was back in his own time now, he wouldn't know that he had ever known her.

"Whoa! Ben was at Woodstock?" Salem exclaimed. "I totally missed him the first time I was there."

"No, Salem, that's the point," Sabrina said. "He *wasn't* at Woodstock."

Salem gagged as if choking on a hair ball. "But that means . . ."

Sabrina took a moment to survey her surroundings.

There were no crowds of denim-clad hippies hanging out and groovin' to the music. In fact, Sabrina didn't even hear any music. Just the clip-clop of horses' hooves on the cobblestone streets.

"What's happening?" Salem asked. "And I'm not talking slang here. Where are Jimi Hendrix, Janis Joplin, Richie Havens, the Who . . ."

"Salem," Sabrina said, picking up her quivering

cat and hugging him tight, "I think we're in downtown Philadelphia—the City of Brotherly Love—in the summer of 1776!"

"Don't tease me like this," Salem begged.

"I'm not kidding! Look!" Sabrina pointed. "There's Independence Hall—see the redbrick building with the big clock on the tower? It was called the State House back then. That's the building where the Continental Congress met. I went on a field trip there once with my eighth grade class!"

"Boo-hoo-hoo!" Salem sobbed. "It's not fair! I was going to get an original Woodstock poster, autographs, a whole bunch of souvenirs. Then I could have sold them for a whole bunch of money when I got back to our time," he sobbed. "It was my back-up in case the Y2K bug destroyed my stock portfolio!"

Sabrina stroked the blubbering feline. "Sorry, Salem."

But how could this have happened? She thought back to her spell:

Find me that magic moment in time,
I want to hang with the antiestablishment
  gang,
When talk of the war was on everyone's lips,
A place of love, where freedom rang.

Sabrina groaned. "I get it. The antiestablishment gang I wanted was made up of *hippies*. The antiestablishment gang I got was the revolutionaries of early American history. Everyone's talking about war with England, not the Vietnam War. It's a place of love—William Penn named this place Philadelphia, the Greek word for 'brotherly love,' because he was a Quaker. And the 'freedom rang' part? That must refer to the Liberty Bell."

"That's great, just great," Salem complained, wiping away his tears with the back of his furry paw. "What's so magical about a boring old history lesson?"

"How do you think I feel?" Sabrina said. "Like I've been there, done that, taken the tours. Bought the copy of the Declaration of Independence and the little Liberty Bell pencil sharpener."

"Maybe you could try again for Woodstock?" Salem pleaded.

Sabrina sighed. "No time. And if my magic is this far off, how can I be sure we'll land in the sixties? Who knows where we might wind up?"

Salem growled. "Do you think Justin Time had anything to do with this?"

"Who knows? Maybe there's a reason I wound up here. An important reason . . ."

Sabrina noticed that passersby were starting to stare.

Oops. Standing on Chestnut Street in old Philadelphia wearing blue jeans and other hippie artifacts and talking to a black cat is definitely not the way to blend in!

She grabbed her backpack—and Salem—and ducked behind a neatly trimmed privet hedge.

Blue jeans, sandals, tie-dye, and beads,
Return to my closet this minute.
Send me a dress fit for a colonial girl,
And hurry—put me in it!

Instantly her sixties outfit was replaced by a proper ankle-length dress with a fitted bodice and a very feminine full skirt. It was made of blue flowered fabric with lace trim around the square neckline and the three-quarter sleeves. A pretty straw bonnet was tied with a jaunty blue silk-ribbon bow beneath her chin. She felt as if she were dressed for a school play.

"Ugh, these petticoats are scratchy!" she complained. "How did they stand to dress like this in all this heat!"

"But you look bonnie indeed, miss," Salem proclaimed, and Sabrina had to laugh.

"Here, give me those silly glasses—and those love beads," she instructed him. As she leaned over to tuck them into her backpack, she realized she still had on her mother's peace-symbol pendant. As she quickly tucked it inside the front of her dress, she wondered why the spell hadn't sent that home too.

She didn't want to have to explain what it meant to anyone. The Revolutionary War was yet to be won, and it would be years before these people would know peacetime; the Vietnam War would be beyond their comprehension.

"Better do something about this, too," she said, and quickly zapped her backpack into a tiny beaded purse on a chain.

Bong! . . . Bong! . . . The clock in the tower began to chime the hour. She watched as an old man came down the steps, checked his pocket watch against the great clock, then went back inside. Sabrina knew from her school tour that this was Andrew MacNair, the doorman who had kept unauthorized people from entering the meetings of the Continental Congress while the representatives debated the serious issue of revolution.

Was that the real time or just the time she'd landed in? *Never mind,* she told herself. *Just hurry, find whatever it is you're supposed to find, and get home as fast as you can!*

But where should she go? What was she supposed to get? "It would be nice to have a little bit of instruction here," she mumbled, wishing Justin could hear her. But she knew she was on her own.

Suddenly a short, stern-looking man in a powdered wig bustled past her. "Pardon me, miss," he said as he hurried toward the State House steps, a small green cloth satchel in his hand.

"Salem," Sabrina whispered, "I think that's John Adams!"

"How can you be sure?" Salem whispered back.

"Remember when Harvey and I went to that concert in Boston last week? We stopped at a diner on the way, and they had these paper 'Presidents of the United States' place mats. Mr. Adams looks *exactly* like his picture!"

"Quick! Get his autograph!" Salem whispered back. "It'll be worth a fortune when we get back home!"

"Shhh! Look!"

A tall, slender man—he had to be over six feet tall—also strode toward the State House, his long legs covering twice as much ground as Adams's quick, urgent steps. In his hand he carried a small hinged wooden box.

"That's got to be Thomas Jefferson!" she whispered. "When he went to the sessions of Congress, he always carried a portable writing desk that he designed and made."

Sabrina was surprised by the sudden prickle of excitement she felt at seeing these two famous men. It was like spotting celebrities, only these were people that no one of her time could ever meet.

Well, Aunt Zelda might have met them, Sabrina thought. *She did seem to know quite a lot of important people during the past several hundred years.*

Sabrina picked up her skirts and hurried along the sidewalk toward the State House. She couldn't help herself—she *had* to peek into that room and see what was going on! Maybe it held a clue to the item she needed to take back for the new clock.

Looking up at the State House tower, she wondered if it had something to do with that clock! She obviously couldn't take it with her. But maybe . . .

"Good morning," she said to the doorman as she started to go into the State House.

The old man politely stepped in front of her. "I beg your pardon, miss. But you are not allowed to go in."

"But—" *Now what? I have to get inside that room!* "I . . . I have a message! Yes, that's it. A message for Ben!"

Mr. MacNair's eyebrows shot up.

Hmm, Sabrina thought. *Maybe a young lady in Revolutionary America wouldn't call a man like Franklin by his first name.* "What I mean to say is, it's for the Honorable Mr. Franklin." There. That sounded much more formal.

Mr. MacNair held out his hand. "I'll take it, miss."

"Um, no," Sabrina said. "I mean, thank you, kind sir. But I'm supposed to deliver it to him—in person."

Mr. MacNair clucked his tongue and chuckled. "As old as he is—and the young lasses still chasing after him!" He shook his head. "He's old enough to be your grandfather! Now run along, young lady. There's serious business going on inside that room this morning. This is no place for a woman."

Sabrina immediately bristled and started to respond to such a sexist remark, but Salem hooked his claw in the hem of her dress and yanked. She looked down, and he growled at her.

Oh, yeah. Women aren't allowed to participate directly in government in this century. Heck, they won't even get the vote for almost 150 years!

Besides, she didn't have time to debate him. Too bad she wasn't wearing her button that read "A Woman's Place Is in the House—and in the Senate." That would have made him think! Of course, they didn't actually have a House of Representatives or a Senate yet.

"I'll—I'll give it to him later, when he's finished with his meeting," Sabrina said with a quick curtsy. "Thank you, kind sir." With a ladylike smile, she turned and walked back down the steps.

Salem snorted with laughter. "I wish Zelda and Hilda could see you. They'd be awfully impressed! Hey, maybe you could work as a tour guide for the Westbridge Historical Society when you get back."

"Quiet, Salem!" Sabrina said. "I've got to get a look at that room! It might hold a clue to my mission here."

She waited till she was certain no one was watching, then slipped around the side of the building and peeked in a window.

"What do you get when you cross James Bond with Betsy Ross?" Salem whispered.

"What?" Sabrina asked impatiently.

Salem snorted. "You—spying on the Continental Congress!"

"That is so lame," Sabrina said. "Now be quiet and help me look."

Salem leaped up onto Sabrina's shoulder so he could see. "What are you looking for?"

"The assembly room," Sabrina explained. "That's the famous room where the Continental Congress, made up of representatives from the thirteen colonies, met to decide whether to remain loyal subjects of King George the Third of England or to break away and form a new nation."

"Gosh, what did you do, tape-record that eighth grade tour?"

Sabrina shrugged. "I like history. And that makes it easy to remember."

She peeked in the next window and tried not to squeal. "Look, Salem," she whispered. "There's Franklin with his foot propped up on a chair. And Jefferson sitting right beside him. See—Jefferson is the only one taking notes." She surveyed the room, studying the other men—men who had no idea how famous they would one day become for what they were doing here. "And there's Adams, across the room."

"Boy, does he look cross," Salem commented.

A beautiful cut-glass chandelier hung from the ceiling in the center of the large white room. Two walls had tall windows, but they were opened only a crack at the top.

"Whew, it's only a little after nine o'clock in the morning," Salem said, flicking his tail, "and the temperature's got to be in the eighties already. How can they stand the heat in that room? There's not even a fan. Why don't they open the windows?"

Sabrina remembered from her eighth grade tour. "Revolution is serious business," she said. "It's an act of treason against King George, punishable by death. These guys don't want anyone to know what they're doing till everything is signed, sealed, and delivered. Even in this hot weather, they only open the windows a tiny bit from the top so no one can hear what they're saying."

"Great, just enough to let in the flies from all the horses in the streets!" Salem remarked.

It was true. Sabrina couldn't hear what anyone was saying, but she could see that the men were hot and uncomfortable, squirming in their seats and slapping at the horseflies that buzzed around their heads. Most of them looked as cross as Adams. A few actually dozed in their seats.

"I say let us wait!" she barely heard one man shout as he stood up to make his case. Adams scowled as if he'd drunk vinegar. Around the room men argued and shouted. Through it all, Jefferson seemed almost lost in a daydream, never uttering a word.

It was not quite the stately, dignified "fathers of our country" image usually depicted in paintings.

They're just people, Sabrina realized, watching them. Human beings who had no idea whether what they were doing was a fabulous idea, the right thing to do—or a disastrous course of action that would result in their own execution. Sabrina remembered that Franklin had said: "We must all hang together, or assuredly we shall all hang separately."

Suddenly Sabrina noticed something strange. Across the room, at one of the windows, something besides horseflies was coming in through the crack at the top of the window.

She and Salem exchanged a startled glance.

"Flying little redcoat guys?" Salem gasped.

Sabrina looked again. Two dozen or so tiny magical creatures dressed in the red coats of the British army were now flying around the room.

"They all look like Prince Charles," Salem remarked.

"I don't know about that," Sabrina said. "But look what they're doing! And how come nobody's reacting?"

Indeed, it looked as if none of the Founding Fathers even saw the Tiny Redcoats swarming through the room.

"Hey, wake up, dudes!" Salem hissed. "The British are coming! The British are coming!"

"I don't think our guys even see them," Sabrina said. She watched, horrified, as the tiny magical creatures did their best to disrupt the meeting.

They put itching powder down several men's collars.

A couple of them herded even more horseflies into the room.

One tiny guy sprinkled sparkly dust around Franklin's eyes, and soon his loud snores filled the room.

A dozen of them actually built a fire in the fireplace and began to fan the heat into the room—a fire that all of the men seemed unable to see, hear, or smell. But feel the heat they did.

"By Jove, if it gets any hotter, the State House will go up in flames!" Sabrina heard one of the men near her window complain.

The men in the room began to itch, fidget, fan themselves, mop their brows, and squirm. Some got up and walked around. The disorder was startling. How could they get anything done this way? Heated arguments broke out around the room. Obviously not everyone was ready to split with England.

"It's a shame we can't hear exactly what these guys are saying," Sabrina whispered.

"I'd love to be a horsefly on the ceiling of that room," Salem said.

"Who are these guys?" Sabrina said. "And what in the world are they doing?"

"They're Loyalists," Salem said, "and they're trying to break up the meeting."

"But why?" Sabrina said. "If they break up the meeting, our forefathers will never get around to voting to start the revolution, and . . . Oh." She and Salem exchanged glances. "I guess that's what they're trying to do—stop the revolution. But we've got to stop them!"

"But how?" Salem asked.

Suddenly Sabrina and Salem felt something strange happening. They stepped back from the window and looked around.

The world began to wobble. Then the images before their eyes began to whirl like fruit-smoothie ingredients in a blender. Then the whirling sped up to frappé.

"I hate it when that happens!" Salem cried as he and Sabrina hung on to each other in the center of the confusion.

The time-space continuum was freaking out again. "Salem!" Sabrina cried. "Hold on!"

The next thing they knew, it was nighttime. Sabrina felt as if she hadn't moved a step, and yet she and Salem stood on a different street in Philadelphia—the corner of Market and Seventh. The streets were empty, but candlelight still shone from nearly every window.

"What are we doing here?" Salem asked, shivering, as he looked around.

"I don't know, Salem," Sabrina said. "But I have to find out."

In an upstairs window she saw someone light a candle and sit down at a desk. It looked like . . .

"Salem, I know why we're here."

"Why?"

"That's Thomas Jefferson up there," she replied. "This must be the Graff House. It's a boardinghouse where Jefferson stayed while he was writing the Declaration of Independence! He must be up there working on it right now!"

"Maybe we should leave him alone, then, and go find some dinner," Salem suggested.

Sabrina sighed. "Maybe you're right . . . Oh, no! Salem—look!"

The Tiny Redcoats were back, hovering around Jefferson's window. Then the man got up from his desk, came over, and—"Don't!" Sabrina cried— opened the window to let in the night air. As soon as he sat back down, the Tiny Redcoats zoomed right in.

"Oh, no. What are they up to?" Sabrina said. "Salem, we've got to stop them!"

"Me? No, thanks. I'm scared of tiny little things that fly, especially when they look like Prince Charles!"

Sabrina tried to snap herself up to the room, but her clicker seemed to be on the blink. "Come on. We'll have to do it the old-fashioned way, by using the stairs!"

Sabrina hurried around to the front door and peeked in through the window beside it. No one was around. She tried the door. It was unlocked. Slowly she opened it, wincing when it creaked.

Salem leaped from her arms onto the brick sidewalk. "I'll wait here and be your lookout."

"Fine." Sabrina went inside and closed the door, then tiptoed up the steep wooden stairs. But when she reached the top, she wondered what she should do. She couldn't just barge in on Thomas Jefferson without an explanation.

Her stomach growled, suggesting her excuse. She'd pretend to be a serving girl and take Jefferson some food.

Mr. Jefferson must be starving
After his long and busy day,
So send me some food from City Tavern
Set out on a fine pewter tray.

Instantly a tray bearing a teapot, a mug, and a steaming chicken potpie appeared in her hands. Sabrina sighed with relief, grateful her magic had worked for once. Carefully shifting the tray to one hand, she knocked on the door.

"Come in!" Mr. Jefferson called.

Trying to keep her hands from shaking, Sabrina opened the door and stepped into the room. Jefferson was dressed as before, but he'd removed his coat and powdered wig, and his shirtsleeves were rolled up to his elbows. He had a tiny smudge of ink on one cheek. Several sheets of paper covered with scribbles lay on his desk. One had drifted to the floor. Jefferson looked surprised to see her.

Sabrina made a tiny curtsy. "Cook thought you might care for some nourishment," she said, trying to sound like a girl from the seventeen hundreds—

then frantically thought, *I hope this boardinghouse has a cook!*

"How thoughtful," he said. "Thank you."

Whew! "Where shall I put it?" Sabrina asked.

"Um . . ." Jefferson looked around, then cleared the papers from a side table. "Here would be fine."

Sabrina set down the tray. "I'll pour your tea and be gone, sir. And please don't let me interrupt. Go on about your work."

Jefferson chuckled softly. "Ah, yes. Well, that's not going too well, I'm afraid." He splayed his hands on the desk and leaned over his work, staring down at the scattered papers, his eyes shadowed with dark circles. "It is so important," he said, more to himself than to Sabrina. "Every word must be just right." He ran a hand through his hair and sighed. "I don't know if I can express . . ." He picked up a sheet, scanned it, then crossed something out.

He looked as discouraged as Sabrina sometimes felt when she was trying to finish an essay for English class the night before it was due. *But Jefferson definitely needs to bag an A on this one!* "A spot of tea will get you back on track," she said encouragingly, then picked up the teapot and poured.

Thick black liquid filled the cup. "Coffee?" she said, confused.

Jefferson reached for the cup and grinned as he held it up, as if in a toast. "The official drink of the revolution."

Of course. The Boston Tea Party had taken place in 1773. Colonists disguised as Native Americans had thrown a shipload of tea into the harbor to protest the British tea tax—ensuring an American future filled with lattes, mocha cappuccinos, and a Starbucks on every corner.

Jefferson took a sip of the steaming black brew as he sat back down at his desk. He dipped his quill pen in ink, then began to write once more. A moment later he seemed lost in his thoughts, the pen scratching noisily as he quickly filled the page.

Wonderful, Sabrina thought. She'd poured the coffee and encouraged Thomas Jefferson to keep writing. *Now for a little housecleaning . . .*

Sabrina looked around for the Tiny Redcoats. She spotted a couple flying toward Jefferson's desk. It was amazing—he couldn't see the magical creatures at all.

Oh, no! They were going to—

Sabrina reached out, but it happened so fast!

The two Tiny Redcoats knocked over the inkwell, splattering thick black ink across the paper-strewn desk.

Jefferson jumped up, muttering curses.

Sabrina grabbed a cloth napkin from the tray and hurried to the desk. *Boy, am I glad I was born during the age of paper towels!* she thought.

Jefferson took the cloth and mopped up the spilled ink. "How clumsy of me! And it's the second time tonight. That was my last bottle of ink, as well. If this keeps up, I'll never finish my writing!"

Never finish! Sabrina thought. *That would be terrible!*

"Excuse me, miss," Jefferson said, shrugging into his suit coat. "I have no more ink, and the shops are closed till morning. I must go and see if I can borrow a bottle of ink from one of the other boarders."

Sabrina just nodded and watched him go.

Perfect! she thought. *A chance to be alone with the Tiny Redcoats.*

As soon as the door closed, she put her fists on her hips and glared at the magical mischief makers. "Okay, who are you? Why are you doing this? And how come nobody else can see you?"

All of the Tiny Redcoats stopped and looked at her in astonishment, then one of them stepped forward. "You can see us?"

"Of course I can."

"Ahhhh," they all murmured.

"Then you must be a magical being of some sort," said another.

"I'm a witch. Well, half-witch, actually." *At least for now,* she thought, worrying about the time. "But never mind that now. I'm from the twentieth century, and I'm here on a mission. There's a . . ." How much should I explain to these little men? "Let's just say there's a problem at the end of the millennium. I'm here on official business, and you're interfering with some pretty important stuff."

"Ignore her, Harold," one of the tiny men called to the redcoat who seemed to be their leader. "Come on. Let's burn all his paper in the fireplace!"

"Stop!" Sabrina said, throwing herself in front of Jefferson's desk. "Why are you doing this?"

"Well, miss, *if* it's any of your business," Harold said, "we're here on official business, as well—official business of the *king*. And I'd say that would overrule any business you might have. We're here to make sure that Mr. Jefferson never finishes that draft of the Declaration of Independence. And that these power-crazed rebels get so mad they all pack up and go home. Can't have these daft men declaring independence and mucking things up. King George rules!"

"Right on!" a tiny guy in the back called out.

Quick! Sabrina told herself. *Think of something.*

"I—I have an important message from the future," she said. "I think you might like to hear it. If you'll leave Mr. Jefferson alone and come outside with me, I'll explain everything."

"Hmm," Harold said. "I should like to hear this message from the future." He scratched his chin, then said, "Come on, boys. Let's take a break and hear what the wench has to say."

"Hey! That's Sabrina to you. *Miss* Sabrina," she added for good measure.

"All right, *Miss* Sabrina. Can you fly?"

Sabrina didn't want to reveal that some of her powers were a little dicey right now, so she simply said, "I feel like walking. I'll meet you down-stairs."

"Suit yourself, miss." And with that Harold led all the other Tiny Redcoats out through the window.

Sabrina ran down the stairs to meet them. She gasped when she saw them. They shone like fireflies in the night.

"Cool," Salem said, batting at them.

"Call off your cat!" Harold shouted. "Or we just might— Hey, did he just talk?"

"The name's Salem Saberhagen, former warlock, temporarily unavailable for projects involving magic."

"Blimey, I never met a talking cat!" one of the tiny men exclaimed. "Magic or otherwise."

"Maybe cats talk in the future," another one said. "I wonder if dogs do, too?"

"So what's this message from the future you were speaking of?" Harold asked impatiently.

How could she phrase it gently? And quickly? "Listen, here's the deal. I'm visiting here from 1999, and I live in the United States of America."

All the little men gasped.

Sabrina continued. "Adams, Jefferson, Franklin—they're all going to declare independence, everyone's going to fight about it, but it's no use. The colonists are going to win their independence from England and start a brand-new country."

"Treason!" a Tiny Redcoat shouted. "Hang her at dawn!"

Sabrina gulped, and her hand flew to her throat. "Listen, it's true," she insisted. "You guys fail to change history. So why don't you all be nice and go home. Leave Mr. Jefferson and Mr. Adams and all the others alone."

An excited murmur rippled through the crowd of little men.

"She's lying!" someone shouted.

"It can't be true!" another cried.

"God save the king!" a third proclaimed.

"Wait," Sabrina said. "I can prove that the colonists win!" She opened her tiny purse. "Yes!" The cash she'd put in her backpack was now in the purse. Perfect! She took out a dollar bill with George Washington's picture on it and held it out for Harold to see. "Look. An American dollar. See? It says Federal Reserve Note. The United States of America. That proves it!"

"Blimey, if it isn't old Georgie Washington," Harold said, studying the bill. "He don't look too happy, does he? Why isn't he smiling if everything turns out as you say?"

"I hear he has bad teeth," one of the other men said, peering over his shoulder. "He probably didn't want to smile for the portrait."

Harold shrugged and handed the bill back to Sabrina. "So maybe you're telling the truth, and maybe you're not. But even if what you say is true, we're still here in time before it all happened. So who's to say we don't still have a chance to change the outcome? Come on, boys! Let's fly over to Ben's house and jump on his sore foot!" With that, they flew off into the night.

"Well, I guess I blew that," Sabrina said. Thinking quickly she tried to conjure up a box to trap them in.

Nothing happened.

"Salem, my magic's not working at all now," she said. "I wonder what time it is back home. Maybe it's all over. Maybe it's past midnight, and I failed miserably, and now there's no magic left anywhere in the entire universe. And we're stuck here!"

"Now, now, calm down," Salem said. "Think about it. If all the magic were gone, if all witches had lost their powers, the Tiny Redcoat guys wouldn't be able to fly and make mischief."

"Oh, yeah. Good point!" She glanced up at Jefferson's window. She could see him back at his desk, his head bent over his work. "Go, Tom, go!" she cheered softly into the darkness.

Then she started walking.

"Where are we going?" Salem asked.

"I don't know, exactly," Sabrina replied. "But I can't just stand here. I've got to do something!"

Two steps farther down the cobblestone street she felt it happening again—the world shifting beneath her feet, time spinning forward on its own to another time. Would they stop in a time after the Tiny Redcoats had worked their magic?

When the winds and roar of time travel faded,

Sabrina found herself standing down the street from the State House again with Salem clinging to her skirt. She swayed a little, catching her balance, then glanced up. Judging by the blazing sun's position in the sky, it was afternoon. But *which* afternoon?

Sabrina plucked Salem from her skirts, then went up to a lady walking by with a market basket over one arm.

"Excuse me, madam," Sabrina asked. "But could you please tell me the date?"

The woman looked at her as if she'd been out in the sun too long without a bonnet, but answered, "Today is the twenty-eighth of June."

"Thank you, ma'am!" Sabrina said with a slight curtsy. Then she whispered to the black cat in her arms, "Come on, Salem. We've got to hurry. We've got to do something! Today's the day that the final draft of the Declaration of Independence is to be read aloud to the Continental Congress!"

Just then she saw Jefferson hurrying down the sidewalk himself, his portable writing box under his arm, as usual. Suddenly he was surrounded by a swarm of Tiny Redcoats, buzzing at his ear, flying around his ankles. Finally they managed to trip the man, and his portable desk went flying to the ground. Papers flew out along the street. Sabrina ran after them and managed to grab a single sheet, but it was blank. There was no way she could catch them all, not with the Tiny Redcoats still able to fly.

Suddenly she saw something new—another band

of tiny men flying through the air. But these men didn't wear red coats. They were dressed in simple clothes made of plain dull-colored fabrics.

No one else seemed able to see these guys either.

Sabrina reached for another sheet of paper at the same time one of these new little men did, too.

"Who are you?" she asked him.

"What?" the little man gasped. "You mean you can see me, lass?"

"Let me cut to the chase," Sabrina said. "I'm a witch from the future. I can see you. My magic's not working too well, and I'm trying to stop those Tiny Redcoat guys."

"Then you're one of us!" the man said gladly.

"One of you? Who *are* you?" she asked warily.

"Well, the king's men call us traitors and rebels," he said. "We call ourselves patriots in the fight for freedom. My name's Patrick, by the way. We're from down in North Carolina. Just heard about these British twits trying to muck things up here in Philadelphia."

"Nice to meet you, Patrick. I'm Sabrina."

"Nice to meet you, miss," Patrick said. "You say you're from the future?"

"Yes. And let me tell you the good news: I'm from the United States of America. We won! Or at least we're *going* to win—if these Tiny Redcoats don't mess things up."

Patrick's eyes glistened with tears. "Are you telling me the truth, girl?"

Sabrina nodded happily.

"Woo-hoo!" Patrick exclaimed.

"I couldn't have said it better myself," Sabrina said with a grin.

"Excuse me, Miss Sabrina, while I trounce some redcoats!" he waved to the others. "Come on, men. Let's go!"

He flew off with his ragged band of fighters, and Sabrina could only stand and watch, amazed, as a tiny Revolutionary War took place—right over the head of Thomas Jefferson.

As he bent down to pick up his papers from the cobblestone street, the two bands of magic men shot sparkling bolts of magic dust at each other. They wrestled and zapped one another with magic as red, white, and blue sparkles erupted in the air like Fourth of July fireworks.

Sabrina wished Mr. Jefferson could see it.

And she wished she could help.

She looked at the Tiny Redcoats and the Tiny Patriots. It was a shame to see them fight, when two centuries later people would travel freely between the United States and England, work as allies in the struggle for world peace, and pay high ticket prices to get into concerts performed by rock groups from one another's country. If only she could show them what it was going to be like . . .

Suddenly Sabrina felt a burning sensation. She

put her hand to her chest and pulled out her mother's peace symbol. It was glowing slightly and warm to the touch.

Bizarre, Sabrina thought. *But maybe, just maybe, I can use this.*

> *I need to hold Congress*
> *With these pixies I've found,*
> *So make Jefferson temporarily deaf*
> *To Sabrina's sound.*

She winced at the awkwardness of the verse, wondering if her magic would work. "Hello, Mr. Jefferson. Can you hear me?" she called out.

Jefferson didn't answer. He just kept chasing his papers.

Thank goodness, Sabrina thought. *At least some of my magic is working. Maybe this next trick will, too.*

"What's happening?" Salem asked.

Sabrina laughed. "How appropriate for you to ask like that," she told him. "Just watch."

She waved her hands in the air. "Hey, guys! Guys! Over here." She checked to see if Jefferson was paying attention.

No. He didn't even look.

But the tiny combatants stopped fighting long enough to look at the crazy blond girl jumping up and down in the middle of Chestnut Street.

"What is it, Sabrina darling?" Patrick asked. "We're kind of busy at the moment."

"This is important," she said. "Can you all come here? I have something to show you."

There was some grumbling among the tiny men, but Patrick and Harold ordered their armies to fly to Sabrina.

"Out with it, then, girl," Harold said impatiently.

"Would you give the girl the freedom to speak?" Patrick snapped.

"Listen," Sabrina told them. "I want you to see something special, something that might end your fight."

"Is this some kind of patriot trick?" Harold asked.

"Just try it. If it doesn't change your mind, then by all means go back to what you were doing."

The Tiny Patriots and the Tiny Redcoats looked at one another.

"I promise—you won't be sorry," Sabrina added.

At last the tiny soldiers agreed.

Sabrina took off her mother's peace symbol and held it out. "This is a symbol of peace from the future. Everyone, put one hand on the chain."

Harold rolled his eyes. "What game is this, then?"

"Please?" she asked as nicely as she could.

"Come on, guys," Harold said. "Let's do it before she starts crying or something."

One by one each tiny man placed one tiny hand on one link of the chain, the Tiny Redcoats along one side and the Tiny Patriots along the other.

"Blimey, it's warm!" one of the redcoats said.

As the necklace glowed with magic energy, she stepped back and whispered,

Go together, quarreling brothers,
Forward to a magic moment in time,
When talk of peace is on everyone's mind,
And Brits and Americans get along fine.

Sabrina knew her magic was working even before it happened. Maybe it was the magic in the necklace or the sincerity of her spell. But whatever it was, moments later the necklace and all the tiny men disappeared in a flash of sparkling light.

"Hey, where'd they go?" Salem asked.

Sabrina grinned. "Take a guess."

"Woodstock?"

"Uh-huh."

"Oh, man! Why didn't you tell me?" Salem pouted. "I could have gone with them."

"Sorry, Salem. I didn't think." She glanced across the street. Jefferson had apparently picked up all his papers and was now hurrying toward the State House. She was awfully sad to lose her mother's pendant from the sixties, but happy with the results.

Thomas Jefferson would get to read his famous document at last.

But what if that necklace was also the souvenir she needed from a magic moment in time? What if she'd lost it forever?

Sabrina sighed and picked up Salem. She needed a hug. She was tired and worried and wondering if she should try to travel back home. Her magic seemed to working for the moment; maybe she could use it to get back to Westbridge.

"Uh-oh, here we go again!" Salem yelped as time whirled around them again. He snuggled against Sabrina as they watched the world spin before them like a video being fast-forwarded—one day, two days, three.

Then they stopped again in the same place.

"What was that all about?" Salem asked with a shiver.

"I think I know," Sabrina said. She shielded her eyes against the sun and stared up at the building that would one day be renamed Independence Hall in honor of what went on there. "The Continental Congress read Thomas Jefferson's Declaration of Independence on Friday, June 28, 1776. But they did not vote to approve the Declaration itself until the following Thursday.

"July fourth," Salem said.

"Right. The day they voted on it." Sabrina tapped a woman on the shoulder. "Excuse me, but can you tell me what day it is?" she asked.

The woman turned around and stared. It was the same woman she'd asked the date of once before.

"July fourth," the woman replied. "And might I suggest you find yourself a calendar, my girl?"

Sabrina blushed as the woman hurried on her

way. Then she heard a commotion at the door of the State House.

Sabrina watched as the Founding Fathers of the United States of America filed out of the building onto the street. And she knew at once.

They had voted in favor of the Declaration of Independence.

The world would never be the same.

But the men who came out weren't whooping and hollering joyfully. They looked pleased but tired. The decision they'd made seemed to weigh heavily upon their shoulders. A brave struggle lay ahead. And many who worked for independence would not live to see the colonies free.

Sabrina wished she could tell them that they'd done the right thing, that everything would turn out okay, that the country they dreamed of would one day be the strongest nation on earth.

As Thomas Jefferson walked by, Salem jumped into Sabrina's arms and called out, "Mr. Jefferson! May we have your autograph?"

"Sa-lem!" Sabrina hissed, but when Mr. Jefferson looked at them, the only thing she could do was hug Salem tight and paste a cheery smile on her face.

"You'll pay for this, Salem," she whispered through gritted teeth.

"Ugh, not so tight!" Salem whispered, his face turned away from the famous statesman and author.

Since Sabrina stood there alone with her cat, Jefferson smiled at her, thinking she was the one who had called out to him.

Sabrina swallowed. She was so mortified that it took all her willpower not to snap her fingers and disappear on the spot. But she didn't want to totally freak out Mr. Jefferson. It might have ruined his otherwise momentous day.

Relax, she told herself. *He's just a man. One of the greatest men who ever lived, true, but still just a normal human being.*

"Well, hello there! I am pleased to see you again, miss. I did not get to thank you properly for bringing me that excellent meal the other night. It restored my spirits."

"You're quite welcome, Mr. Jefferson."

"But, dear, why would you want my autograph, pray tell?" The thought seemed to amuse him, and the tired lines in his face eased somewhat.

Then she said what came from her heart: "To remember this day."

Jefferson smiled like the Mona Lisa—a smile filled with a million emotions, his hope for the future, his fear of the rough months ahead. "Yes, my dear. One way or another, I believe this is a day that many of us will remember forever." He held out his small portable desk. "Would you mind holding this?"

"No, not at all!" She held the box that was destined to become a priceless historical antique while Jefferson opened the hinged lid and removed a piece of paper, an inkwell, and one of several quill pens. He slid open the top of the inkwell, dipped in his feathered pen, and with a calm, steady hand wrote his signature on the piece of paper.

"The date!" Salem whispered in Sabrina's ear.

"The date?" she said out loud, then covered her mouth.

"The date—yes, an excellent idea," Jefferson said, scribbling once more. Then he replaced his things, took the box from her, and handed her the sheet of paper.

Eagerly Sabrina read it.

Thomas Jefferson
July 4, 1776

A strange shiver shot through her. It was a moment she would never forget. "Thank you!" she breathed.

"You are most welcome," he replied warmly. Then he stroked Salem's head. "What a fine cat you have, miss."

Salem preened.

"Thank you," Sabrina answered for them both.

"Well, I must be on my way," Jefferson said, and with a slight bow, he took his leave.

Sabrina just stood there, clutching Salem and the slip of paper, watching Thomas Jefferson walk away, trying to memorize everything about him before he disappeared.

And then he turned at the next corner and was gone.

"Yes! I got his autograph!" Salem exclaimed, pumping his little black paw in the air. "I'm gonna be a millionaire!"

"*We* got it," Sabrina reminded him.

"Hey, if I hadn't shouted at him—"

"Which, by the way, *totally* embarrassed me—"

"Yeah, but look what happened, thanks to me."

Sabrina opened her mouth for another comeback, then shut it. She had to agree. She sighed and glanced down. "Hey!"

Something lay on the ground at her feet.

She stooped to pick it up. "His pen! Oh, my gosh, Salem, Thomas Jefferson dropped his pen!" Setting Salem on the ground, she scooped up the pen. With the pen and her skirt in one hand and her hat in the other, she ran after Mr. Jefferson, with Salem right behind her.

But when she got to the corner, Jefferson was nowhere in sight.

"Salem! Where is he?" she cried.

Bong! . . . Bong! . . . The clock in the tower began to ring again, reminding her that time was her enemy.

"Maybe this way," she said, turning down another street.

But then suddenly she felt something happening. "No, wait—" she cried out, scooping Salem into her arms.

But she couldn't control the magic.

Once again she was swept into the maelstrom of magical time travel.

"I think I'm going to throw up!" Salem said as they hugged each other tight.

"Hang on," Sabrina reassured him. "It'll be over soon."

And with a thud, she landed on the floor of her room.

Sabrina's colonial clothes had disappeared, replaced by old jeans and a Polartec sweatshirt. It was kind of nice to be out of the July heat.

"Salem, are you all right?" she asked, holding him up to her face.

Salem opened one eye. "Do me a favor. Remind me to mind my own business the next time you go on an adventure."

Sabrina laughed, then gasped. "The pen, the paper—where are they?"

She felt in her pocket. "Here's the signature. Where's the pen?"

"There it is!" Salem showed her where it lay on the floor a few feet from where she sat. "It must have fallen from your hand when we hit the floor."

Sabrina picked up the pen and held it out so she could see it. And then—was it her imagination?— she thought she saw it sparkle in the sunlight streaming in through her stained-glass window.

The pen was just a quill from a bird; she wasn't even sure what kind. A common unsophisticated writing instrument, very primitive compared to the multicolored felt-tip pens she and her friends liked to use.

Still, maybe the magic was not in the inanimate object itself but in what a person did with it.

"Here's my magic object," she said to Salem. "Thomas Jefferson took a simple quill pen and a plain piece of paper and wrote words that are more powerful than a king's army. Words that would be repeated over and over for centuries by people who valued freedom: 'We hold these truths to be self-evident, that all men are created equal, that they are endowed by their Creator with certain unalienable Rights, that among these are Life, Liberty, and the pursuit of Happiness.' "

"Gosh, Sabrina," Salem said, wiping a tear from his eye with his paw. "That was b-b-beautiful."

Sabrina smiled as she picked up Jefferson's pen. "I hope we still have time to use this!" She glanced at the clock on her desk and gasped. "Salem! I can't believe it! We've only been gone for five minutes, according to this clock."

"That's wonderful!" Salem cried.

"You mean, because we still have time left to transfer the magic to the clock?"

"No," Salem said happily. "Because it means I didn't miss lunch!"

"Salem!" Sabrina said, laughing. "Do you ever think about anything besides filling your tummy?"

"Sure," he replied. "I think a lot about napping.

And about making money. Speaking of which, may I please have my priceless autograph?" He held out his paw.

But Sabrina shook her head as she got to her feet. "Sorry, Salem. It wouldn't be fair to make money off it. Besides, we might need both the autograph and the pen to create the clock."

Now Salem began to bawl.

"Don't cry," she said, patting his head. "At least you got to meet Thomas Jefferson in person."

"But I'll never be able to prove it," he said.

Sabrina zapped up a plate of his favorite seafood to make him feel better. Then, on a hunch, she clicked on the *Woodstock* video.

"Oh, my goodness, it's them!" Salem gasped, nearly choking on a fantail shrimp.

Sabrina smiled. There, near the nighttime stage, hovered several points of light—Tiny Patriots and Tiny Redcoats singing along with Joe Cocker on "I'll Get By with a Little Help from My Friends."

Apparently the dudes had gotten the message.

Something flashed on the screen then, and Sabrina and Salem ducked as something seemed to fly out of the TV.

Sabrina opened her eyes and looked at the object on the floor.

"Mom's peace pendant!" Sabrina squealed. A tiny note was attached to the chain. She picked it up and read the neat, old-fashioned handwriting:

Sabrina dear—

The future is groovy! The boys have called a truce, and we are all getting along just dandy. We are even thinking of starting our own rock band, but we cannot decide on a name. The Yanks like "Paul Revere and the Raiders," but the Brits think that name has already been used and want to call it "George" after George Washington and King George. We shall let you know.

Ah, yes, and here is your beautiful peace pendant back. Each of us bought one of our own. Whenever we wear them, we shall think of you.

Thank you for everything!

> Peace & love,
> Patrick, Harold, and the boys

Sabrina slipped the peace pendant over her head, then picked up Thomas Jefferson's quill pen.

"Okay, Timekeeper! I've got another magical item for the new clock! Where to next?"

Houdini's Keys
By Mark Dubowski

She was standing in the trampled snow, on a New York City street, marveling at the window mannequins. Wasn't that supposed to be Harry Houdini, the famous magician, doing card tricks for a little boy? It looked so real—then it dawned on her that it *was* real—those were real people she was gawking at. They weren't part of a window display. They were in a real restaurant, and she was looking through the front window.

Oh, how embarrassing.

Sabrina Spellman, you are such a tourist, she told herself, feeling awkward and out of place. Oh, well. Rewind, erase, play like it never happened. At least she'd found Harry Houdini.

Here she was in New York in the year 1899. Signs all over town advertised Harry Houdini's act.

It didn't take a rocket scientist to figure out her Clock part was something from his act. Something crucial. *A straitjacket?* She wondered. *His handcuff keys?* Get a souvenir from him and take it back to her bedroom. The Witches' Council needed it for the Great Clock of the Other Realm.

Her problem was to figure out what the magic souvenir was, and how to get it. At least she was doing something, going places, not stuck brain-storming the problem with the Witches' Council, like Hilda and Zelda.

She stepped inside the restaurant, which was warm and delicious with the smell of rye bread, sauerkraut, smoked ham, and sausage. She was in Wolff's Delicatessen, strategically located two blocks from the world-famous Palace Theater, where the sign on the door said, "Come as you are and dine with the Stars."

"Remember your card and watch carefully for the effect," Houdini was saying to the boy at the table. Sabrina went over and watched him shuffle twice then deftly palm the deck and—presto!—it was gone.

The boy and Houdini looked surprised. "And where is the—"

"Jack of diamonds?" Sabrina blurted out, caught up in the trick.

Houdini glanced up.

Way to go, Sabrina, she thought. *You weren't even here when the boy picked the card.* Call it witches' intuition—sometimes she couldn't help herself. Anyway, she'd seen that trick a million times.

"That was what you call a lucky guess," she fudged, and her cheeks reddened, not from cold weather.

Houdini turned back to the boy. "You see? It's magic!" he said, and found the missing card, the jack of diamonds, behind the boy's ear. Then he turned his attention back to the lucky guesser.

"Allow me to introduce myself," he said, offering Sabrina his hand. "I'm Harry Houdini."

"Sabrina Spellman," she replied, and she reached to shake his hand—but found herself holding, instead, Houdini's deck of cards.

"Your turn," he said. "Show us some magic!"

If he only knew he was talking to a real witch, she thought. Council rules said no showing off real magic in front of mortals, but she guessed a card trick would be okay. "Why not?" she said.

Sabrina fanned the deck on the table so the card values showed, turned her back, and said, "Pick a card." Houdini gave the boy a wry look and touched the queen of hearts.

"Done," he said.

Sabrina turned around, shuffled the deck, palmed it, then fanned the cards out on the table again so every card showed—and every card was the queen of hearts.

"Bravo!" Houdini cried. Sabrina was sure he'd

never seen anything like it. Real magic, that is. "You're hired!"

"Hired?" She wasn't looking for a job. She was looking for a key. But she suspected that this might be part of the plan—destiny, beyond her power and control.

"I am in need of an assistant for tonight's show," Houdini explained, with a trace of a Hungarian accent. "Bess has a bad cold." Sabrina remembered the name from a poster she'd seen earlier under the gaslights at the Palace, the first place she'd gone looking for Houdini. The stage manager there had directed her to Wolff's. Bess was Houdini's assistant and his wife.

"You will fill in and give her the night off!" His confidence made the proposal sound like a done deal.

Houdini was already putting on his coat to go. "Coming?"

"Cool!" Sabrina said, totally baffling him. "I mean it's cool outside! And look—it's snowing again." Fat flakes were swirling against the glass.

"The theater is only two blocks from here," he called from the open doorway. "Follow me."

Sabrina turned her collar up and followed him out.

The theater was locked, but that was no problem for Houdini. He had a key. Not the key meant for Sabrina, apparently, because she asked for it and he just said, "I'll get it," and once the stage door was unlocked it went back in his pocket.

"Read that," he told her, pointing to a stack of broadsheets just inside the door. They were advertising flyers contrived to look like sheriff's warrants or reward posters. The copy said:

CHALLENGE.
To the Attention of Mr. Harry Houdini, Esq.
Palace Theater
New York, N.Y.
Dear sir:

We the undersigned directors of the S. & S. Peerless Water Tank Company hereby challenge you to release yourself while handcuffed, locked in a casket, and submerged in one of our tanks such as are used on apartment buildings throughout the boroughs of New York.

S. & S. Peerless Tanks are made of the finest oak. They are installed easily on any roof, are completely watertight, and provide safe, clean, reliable water service for many years beyond those manufactured by any of our competitors.

"Pretty cocky, aren't they?" Sabrina commented.
"Keep reading," Houdini ordered.
The poster went on:

The only condition in the test that we will put you to is this: that you must make the attempt to escape in full view of the audience to prove you have no traps in the stage.

Faithfully yours,

Mssrs. Clancy, Shiflett, and Ostow

S. & S. Peerless Water Tank Company

"Is this for real?" Sabrina exclaimed. "I mean, are they really challenging you?"

"I have to tell you it was my suggestion they make that challenge," Houdini replied. He led her behind a curtain to the stage itself. "I also advised them to print their challenge on handbills and have their people post them throughout the city. It's called show business, Miss Spellman."

They were standing at center stage, looking up at a large wooden barrel on stilts. With the window the Peerless Company had installed to give the audience a view inside, it reminded Sabrina of a beach cottage.

"Does it have a trapdoor?" Sabrina wondered aloud, checking the underside for an escape route.

"No," Houdini said. "It's completely sealed and elevated above the floor, as you can see. But let's have a look at the casket."

He led her to a polished black box with a silk-upholstered interior.

"It's short, but it looks comfortable," Sabrina said.

"Oh, it is," Houdini replied. "I had it made especially for me. I like to be comfortable. And I'm short. Tonight, the chief of police will handcuff me onstage. I'll lie down in the casket, which the Peerless people will lock and lower into their tank of water. Then you'll come in."

Sabrina bit her fingernail. "I hate to disappoint you, Mr. Houdini, but I left my swimsuit at home."

"I don't mean come into the *tank*. I mean come into the act. You simply close the curtain. For ten seconds the audience must not see the tank. Nor must you. *Don't peek!* After ten seconds you will open the curtain again, and voilà! Houdini will be free! Out of the handcuffs, out of the casket, out of the tank."

"That's impossible," Sabrina said. "Especially in ten seconds."

"You're right," Houdini said. "I cannot escape in ten seconds. But I will have almost an entire minute to get out of the handcuffs before they put me in the water. And handcuffs are easy."

He smiled and pulled from the pocket of his jacket a set of keys on a tiny ring. "All the handcuffs in the United States are made by only a few companies, Miss Spellman. Each of these companies makes all of its handcuffs removable with one key. Any set can be opened with the key from another, as long both sets were made by the same company. I have a copy of a key for each brand of cuff, and as I have demonstrated in police departments from

New York to California, there is not a pair of handcuffs made by any manufacturer in this country from which I cannot escape!"

"May I?" Sabrina said, hoping this was destiny calling. If he handed the keys over now, she could probably go home.

He smiled, but the keys went right back into his pocket.

"I get it," Sabrina said. "You're out of the handcuffs before they even put the casket in the water. But you're still locked inside. What do you do about that?"

"Take a close look at the casket," he said. "Remember, I told you I had it made especially for me." He leaned over and opened and shut the lid, opened and shut it again. "It has a lid. People expect that. They don't question it. But they should! They might find out that this casket opens and closes from the end as well!"

With the lid open, Houdini pushed the casket's headboard from inside. A panel dropped away and landed on the floor like a heavy book dropping.

"The trapdoor in the end is held closed with a weight. In the water, this weight anchors the casket on the bottom. When I release it from inside, the head of the casket, now relieved of its anchor, rises to the surface of the water."

"Won't the casket fill up?" Sabrina asked.

"When it's closed, it's watertight," Houdini explained. "And I won't open the end until it has floated all the way to the top. When it breaks the surface, I'll push open the doors and paddle over to the side of the tank."

"Then you can climb out!" Sabrina said, delighted.

"Yes," Houdini said. "And then I will allow the casket to fill with water and sink again as I climb down, and then you open the curtain and—"

"Presto!" Sabrina said. "You'll be free!"

"Exactly," Houdini said with a satisfied smile.

"Almost like real magic," she told him, which was a genuine compliment, coming from Sabrina, an actual witch. Houdini had no idea, but he bowed graciously.

They sat out the rest of the afternoon in the Houdinis' hotel room. Pretty but tired-looking Bess Houdini greeted them in her bathrobe. She was happy to have an understudy.

She gave Sabrina a tour of the Houdini family scrapbook: Houdini in chains, Houdini in handcuffs, Houdini in ropes and straps, Houdini in a dozen other situations from which there appeared to be no escape.

But of course, if you were Houdini, there was always a way out.

"What's this?" Sabrina asked, pointing to a picture of the magician wearing a coat with long sleeves that were wrapped around his middle and tied in back.

"That's a straitjacket," Bess Houdini explained. "They're used in mental hospitals to restrain violent patients so they can't hurt themselves or others. You really have to be Houdini to get out of one, and even for him it's not easy. At a demonstration in Buffalo, Harry struggled for almost an hour before he was able get out."

"Ow," Sabrina said.

"That's right," said Bess. "The jacket had been altered in a way that made it very painful to wear. Harry said some terrible things to the manager after the show, but the man deserved it."

Houdini spent the afternoon working on a book he was writing, one of many in which he revealed the secrets behind his magic tricks. Harry Houdini always advised other magicians not to expose their tricks, as they lost their value when they became too common. But in Houdini's case, letting others know his methods actually magnified his reputation—he was always a step ahead of his last trick with a newer, even more astounding feat.

Bess Houdini helped Sabrina with her costume. She couldn't lend Sabrina something because she, like Harry, was very small. No problem—to Sabrina's regular late–twentieth-century clothing she merely added feathers and a cape, plus a lot of powder and lipstick—makeup, 1899-style.

Sabrina's last job before the show was to pick up her boss's tuxedo from a cleaner across the street from the theater, where people were already lining up.

When Sabrina returned to the hotel with the tux, Houdini dressed, said good night to Bess, and transferred his tiny set of keys to the pocket of the tux. Sabrina watched him put them in the left front pocket of his jacket as usual.

Outside, polar air was gusting across the Hudson River onto Manhattan Island, but Houdini insisted on walking. "Good physical conditioning is the stock-in-trade of the escape artist," he told her. "I started as a trapeze artist, you know." Sabrina was surprised to learn that part of Houdini's training as a magician was to run several miles each day.

They arrived at the theater a half hour before the show in order to give Houdini time with reporters from the New York press. Newspapers had spread Houdini's reputation far beyond the towns where he performed—they had made him famous around the world. But pre-performance interviews were useful in another, less obvious way, too. Reporters made good witnesses. They provided an airtight alibi when detractors accused the master magician of tampering with the props or the stage before the show. Houdini could honestly say he'd been with the press since his arrival.

At last the Broadway precinct police arrived with a new pair of nickel-plated Little Giant brand handcuffs, and Houdini led his entourage to the stage.

The audience welcomed him with a long and affectionate ovation. He'd come a long way from an impoverished childhood to meager wages on the honky-tonk circuit in the Midwest, and now to superstardom, with huge audiences in big-city theaters in New York, California, and Europe.

As usual, the show began with an introduction by the sponsor. A representative of the S. & S. Peerless Water Tank Company repeated the evening's challenge. Houdini, he reminded them, was about to be handcuffed, locked in a casket, and submerged in a water tank. A Peerless Water Tank. This reminder was followed by a seven-minute presentation on the benefits of using Peerless brand tanks. The company man was persuaded to step down at last when Manhattan police captain Morgan Waters came onto the stage wielding handcuffs.

"These handcuffs," he told the crowd, "are of the type used by members of the New York police department to restrain suspects upon their capture or defendants while being transferred from one facility to another."

You put these on the bad guys, in other words, Sabrina thought.

Captain Waters then explained how the handcuffs worked, reassuring the audience that it was impossible for any felon or ruffian to escape them.

"I wish to thank Officer Waters for excluding my name from the categories of felony and ruffianism," Houdini told the audience with a smile, "as I surely intend to escape his handcuffs this very evening!"

Captain Waters was just putting the Little Giants on Houdini's wrists when a man in the audience stood up and stopped the show.

"I dare you, Houdini," he shouted, "to add this ingredient to your magic cauldron!"

It was a reporter for the *New York World*. He climbed to the stage and raised a bundle of cloth over his head. When the house was still, he let the cloth fall out into a shape that the audience recognized immediately as a jacket.

A straitjacket.

"See if you can free yourself from this, Master Houdini!" he cried. To the challenge of the handcuffs, the coffin, and the water-filled tank, he was daring Houdini to add a straitjacket!

What stunned Sabrina was Houdini's reply.

"I accept your challenge!"

Sabrina's thoughts went immediately to Bess Houdini's story of how it had taken Houdini an hour to escape from the jacket in Buffalo. This time Houdini couldn't afford a long struggle. He'd be locked in the small casket. Underwater.

There simply wasn't enough air.

Still, Houdini removed his tuxedo jacket and allowed the reporter to help him into the straitjacket. With the straps pulled tight, and Houdini's arms wrapped mummylike around his rib cage, they added the handcuffs and lowered him into the casket.

Just before the lid was closed Houdini shot a glance at Sabrina.

"Watch carefully for the effect!" he told her and winked.

Slowly but surely they raised the casket above the tank. Inch by inch they lowered it into the water. When it was completely submerged, Sabrina pulled the curtain, as Houdini had instructed. And she prayed.

One. She started the countdown. He had said to wait ten seconds before opening the curtain.

Two. Houdini's tuxedo coat was still on the floor where he'd left it before being put into the strait-jacket.

Three. As Sabrina picked up the tux jacket, she heard something.

Four. Keys! The handcuff keys were still in the left front pocket of his jacket!

Five. Okay. Don't panic. Think! Sabrina told herself.

Six. Panic, panic, panic, panic, panic, panic . . .

Seven. Sabrina slipped behind the curtain and checked the water tank's window. The casket was still on the bottom. Houdini hadn't released the trapdoor weight yet. The casket hadn't floated to the surface. Sabrina gasped and came back around the curtain.

Eight. Think fast! Sabrina knew she wasn't supposed to use magic that might change history, but this was an emergency. She closed her fingers around the handcuff keys from Houdini's tuxedo jacket, shut her eyes, and cast a spell, the words spilling out: "Hocus-pocus, pretty please, give Houdini back his keys!"

Nine. The keys vanished from her hand. *I hope the spell works!*

Ten. Not enough time! She was afraid to pull the curtain back.

Eleven. Afraid to look.

Twelve. Afraid of what she—and Houdini's fans—were about to see.

Thirteen! Maybe there was still time to save him. She yanked on the cord, and the curtain flew open.

The crowd gasped.

Through the window of the S. & S. Peerless Water Tank they saw the casket motionless in the water. And before the tank stood a short man wearing tuxedo trousers and a clean white shirt that was not only perfectly starched and perfectly pressed but also perfectly dry.

The crowd roared its approval.

"You peeked, didn't you?" Houdini said after the show. He was walking Sabrina back to his hotel.

Sabrina's eyebrows shot up. "How could you tell? You were still in the casket."

"I have to admit," he went on, as if he hadn't heard her, "that of all the things I do, I find the straitjacket most challenging. I nearly always underestimate how much time I'll need to escape."

Sabrina smiled. He was being so nonchalant. "You knew all the time, didn't you?" Sabrina said.

"You knew that reporter was going to interrupt the show with that straitjacket challenge. It was a setup!"

"It was my suggestion that he make that challenge," Houdini said. "But as I said, I always underestimate the time. I needed those extra three seconds you gave me. I just assumed you held the curtain for me because you saw that I was a little late getting the trunk to the surface of the water."

Sabrina let out a long breath of air. "That was sort of what you call a lucky guess," she said.

They stopped near Houdini's hotel. It was snowing again.

"One more thing, Sabrina," Houdini said, and from the left front pocket of his tuxedo jacket he withdrew a set of keys—handcuff keys on a tiny ring. "This one"—he removed the key to the Little Giant brand cuffs from which he'd escaped earlier that evening—"is for you."

"Me?" Sabrina said. "But didn't you . . . I mean, don't you . . . need them to escape?"

Harry Houdini smiled. He opened his hand and revealed a second set of keys identical to the set he carried in his jacket pocket. "I always carry a spare set of keys—in my trouser pocket."

Houdini started down the street. Sabrina watched him stroll away.

The snow was falling harder now, and his figure was fading in the storm. He was almost invisible now.

"You know what, Harry Houdini?" Sabrina shouted. "I think you're really magic after all! I mean *really magic!*"

And she could have sworn she heard him say, "You too," just before she popped back into her room.

The Wizard of OR
By Diana G. Gallagher

Sabrina paced her bedroom floor, growing more frantic as each crystal marked the passing seconds in the hourglass. Minutes had passed since the echo of Harry Houdini's voice had faded, and nothing had happened. There had to be *hundreds* of magical moments in thousands of years of history. Justin Time only had to send her to *twelve* of them. So why was it taking him so long to choose the next one?

Salem lounged on the bed, his tail twitching in agitation. "You're making me nervous. Sit down!"

"I can't sit down now!" Sabrina threw up her hands. "I've still got *eight* souvenirs to collect for the new clock, and it's taking the Timekeeper *forever* to send me to the next magical moment!"

"Maybe he needs some help deciding *which* moment." Salem stretched, then called out, "Hey, Timekeep! How about a little trip back to the moment just before I launched my initial assault to take over the world."

"What's magical about that?" Sabrina asked, annoyed.

"You could stop me before the Witches' Council discovers my plan," Salem said. "Then I'd still be a warlock and not a cat. Now, that would be truly magical! In my humble opinion."

"I doubt that anyone could have stopped you, Salem." Sighing, Sabrina sank onto the bed. "And even if I could, helping you retain your warlock status hardly qualifies as a significant magical moment on a cosmic scale."

"That's probably truer than I care to admit." Salem's ears perked forward. "So in the absence of a better idea, why don't we pop over to the fish market? Fish is brain food, right? Maybe a shrimp and lobster kabob will stimulate your gray matter!"

"Nice try, but no thanks." Rising, Sabrina wandered over to her bookcase and scanned the titles. Most of the volumes were classic works of fiction that her dad and mom had given her over the years.

"Please!" Salem begged. "I need a snack to tide me over until my Time's Up Tuna arrives."

"Sorry, Salem. I can't leave until the Timekeeper sends me." Sabrina wondered if her father was working with Aunt Hilda and Aunt Zelda on the sub-sub-subcommittee the Witches' Council had formed to solve the problem with the Great Clock of the Other Realm. Her mortal mother was still working an archaeological dig in South America and didn't have a clue that magic was in peril everywhere. Nobody knew that Sabrina had inadvertently become the only person working on a backup plan to replace, rather than repair, the old clock.

As Sabrina turned away from the bookcase the air shimmered and crackled with a burst of static magic. Her spirits rose when she heard the Timekeeper snap his fingers. *Finally!*

Her hopes were dashed when she was only transported as far as the living room.

Salem was sprawled on the piano. He looked up and blinked. "Hey! Nothing of magical cosmic significance has ever happened in here! Has it?"

"Maybe we should ask him." Sabrina's gaze settled on the young man sitting at an old-fashion wooden desk. He was quite handsome in spite of the white shirt with sleeve garters and vest that tagged him as an antique geek. His pencil hovered over a small notebook as he glanced up, obviously shocked to find himself in the Spellman living room.

"Well, well." Salem cocked his head. "Look who the Timekeeper dragged in."

"Who?" Sabrina shivered as the air crackled again.

"Uh-oh." Salem sat bolt upright on the piano as another Salem ran yowling down the stairs.

"Come back here, Salem!" Aunt Hilda ran after the fleeing cat with a cat carrier. "You're going to the vet and that's final!"

Sabrina recognized the scene. Every year they went through the same ritual when it was time for Salem's annual vaccinations. But why were they witnessing the event instead of reliving it?

Eyes wide, the strange man slowly stood up and scribbled something in his notebook.

"But I hate getting shots!" The second Salem cowered helplessly in the corner as Hilda pointed and transferred him into the carrier. Then the air crackled again and they both vanished.

Salem shuddered. "I hope this isn't a repeating time disruption loop. I'd really rather not watch this particular scenario over and over again."

"That cat talks!" The man gasped.

"Hi, there!" Sabrina smiled at him. "By any chance are you someone important?"

"Uh, no. No, I'm not. I run a small weekly newspaper called the *Aberdeen Saturday Pioneer,*" the man said as Aunt Vesta popped in, wearing an elegant white evening gown and a diamond tiara. She held a sparkling magic wand in her hand. The man's eyes bulged. "I don't think I'm in South Dakota anymore."

Another Sabrina, dressed in jeans, wandered in and flopped down on the couch.

"Sabrina! Why aren't you dressed for the Storybook Witch Gala?" Aunt Vesta asked.

The second Sabrina pouted. "Because Aunt Hilda and Aunt Zelda, the wicked witches of Westbridge, grounded me!"

"Well, we'll just see about that!" Eyes flashing, Vesta waved her magic wand. Sparkling red shoes appeared on Sabrina's feet, but she was still wearing her jeans. Vesta scowled at the wand. "What's wrong with this thing?"

"Nothing." Aunt Zelda wandered in wearing the traditional black costume of most fairy-tale witches. "Sabrina can't go—"

The man made another note when they all popped out.

"Do you have any idea what's going on here, Salem?" Sabrina asked.

"It's just a wild guess, but we seem to have hit a pocket of time fluctuations where events from the past replay and overlap with what's happening now." Salem's eyes narrowed thoughtfully. "Things could get a little weird."

"A little weird?" Sabrina rolled her eyes, then turned her attention back to the unfamiliar man. "What happened just before you arrived?"

"Uh, well, let's see. . . . Harry Swanson ran into the office to report that he saw a huge tornado touch down by Emma Coleman's farm. I started to write down the information and then—I was here." The man frowned as he scanned the living room. "Wherever *here* is. This doesn't look like 1890."

"That was more than a hundred years ago—"

Sabrina held up her finger. "Never mind. I'll send you back from whence you came, okay?"

"No!" Salem shouted in alarm. "He could end up lost forever in time and space if you try to use magic!"

"Oh, right." Sabrina winced. Magic, like time, was running amok throughout the Mortal Realm and the Other Realm. Even the simplest spells were not working properly.

"Are you saying I can't go home?" the man asked.

"Not just yet, Mr.—"

"Everyone calls me Frank, though my name is actually—" He jumped as the living room suddenly filled with dozens and dozens of golden orange poppies. Aunt Hilda and Aunt Zelda were both asleep in the midst of them.

"Oh, boy!" A lot of strange things had happened in the Spellman house since Sabrina moved in with her aunts, but Cousin Dorma's poppy revenge after she awakened the old goat was one of the worst! "Come on, Frank! We have to get out of here."

"Why?" Clutching his pencil and notebook, Frank cautiously edged around his desk.

"Because, uh, this many poppies can make people sleep forever."

Actually, poppies could make *witches* sleep forever, but Sabrina figured Frank already had enough unbelievable stuff to process.

"Really? I don't feel sleepy." Frank jotted down a

note. "Although I must be asleep because I'm having a very strange dream."

"There ya go!" Sabrina grabbed his hand as the scene shifted forward a few minutes.

Instead of being asleep on the floor, Aunt Hilda was dancing. "I finally got past the doorman at Studio 54!"

Aunt Zelda was lying on the back of the couch swimming the English Channel. "I can see Calais!"

"Hey! Wait a minute!" Sabrina thought back, puzzled. "Where am I? I mean, where's the me that should be trying to get rid of the poppies?"

"An interesting question," Salem waded through the orange flowers to join Frank and Sabrina by the stairs.

"Do you have an interesting answer?" Frank asked expectantly, his pencil poised over the notebook.

"Actually, I do have a theory." Salem nodded. "I think we've stumbled into a time meld where the past becomes part of the present. Like an interactive temporal zone."

Sabrina yawned as another fluctuation rippled through the room. Val, Harvey, and Libby walked into the poppy-filled living room from the kitchen where they had spent all night studying for the Brain Busters competition.

"Sabrina?" Val asked hesitantly. "Are you all right?"

"No, I'm not." Sabrina snapped without meaning

to. She wasn't punchy from lack of sleep this time. *Time!* She had a much bigger problem.

Val cringed slightly, intimidated by the sharpness in Sabrina's tone. "Gosh, Sabrina. I'm sorry."

"Don't be." Sabrina patted Val's shoulder. "It's not your fault that magic as we know it is about to end, and instead of looking for a souvenir from a magical moment in history for the new clock, I'm stuck in a time warp!"

"Poor thing," Harvey said to Val. "Sabrina's so exhausted her imagination's gone berserk. I know my brain's turned to mush from all that cramming."

"Brains won't stand in *your* way, Harvey." Libby smiled with barbed sweetness. "I wouldn't worry about it."

"You are so heartless, Libby," Sabrina said.

"Yes, but at least I'm not a freak like you."

"Excuse me." Val timidly raised her hand. "If we don't get going, we'll be late for the Brain Busters contest. Mr. Kraft will be furious, and I hate it when he yells."

"Mr. Kraft is the least of our problems at the moment, Val!" Sabrina almost lost her balance when a yellow slide walk formed under the group. Salem leaped into her arms as the walk lurched forward and whisked everyone to the stairs.

"This wasn't in the script!" Salem dug his claws into Sabrina's sweater as the yellow walk turned into a yellow escalator that carried them to the second floor. On the landing it promptly changed back into a slide walk and stopped in front of the linen closet.

"If it's okay with everyone, I think I'll get off here." Val ran into an invisible barrier when she tried to step off the yellow path. "Then again, maybe not."

Lightning flashed and thunder boomed in the linen closet.

Frank jumped. "What was that?"

"Special effects!" Sabrina grinned inanely. "My aunts have, uh, a flair for the dramatic."

"It's not going to rain in here, is it?" Harvey held his hand out to check for drizzle.

"I really hate this house," Libby said.

"At the moment, I'm not terribly fond of it either." Sabrina braced herself as the closet door flew open.

"Drat!" Drell stared out. With his frizzy dark hair, frantic eyes, rumpled white shirt, and black cape, he looked totally panicked.

"Drell! What are you doing here?" Sabrina asked cautiously.

"I don't know!" The chief warlock threw up his hands in exasperation. "I was on my way to a Witches' Council briefing on the millennium emergency, but the transit system brought me here instead!"

Sabrina panicked when Drell's nervous gaze flicked to the mortals, who shrank back from his imposing presence. Although the rules, including those pertaining to mortals exposed to the Other Realm, had been suspended during the crisis, Sabrina decided to play it safe. Things were bad enough without having her friends and Libby turned into insects on a technicality.

"You know, Drell"—Sabrina eyed him levelly, hoping he'd pick up on her intent—"I don't care if you *pretend* you're a wizard with magic powers, but I really wish you wouldn't play in our linen closet."

Frank leaned over and whispered in Sabrina's ear. "He thinks he's a wizard?"

"Delusions of grandeur," Sabrina whispered back, "but he's harmless."

"Harmless!" Salem stiffened in Sabrina's arms. "What realm have you been living in?"

"Quiet, Salem. I'm just making sure we're covered in case of unexpected repercussions when the clock crisis is over." Of course, Sabrina realized, if the clock wasn't fixed by midnight, magical backlash wouldn't be a problem. Further discussion was cut short as the slide walk zipped them all into the closet.

"I've got a really bad feeling about this!" Val grabbed Sabrina's arm when the door slammed closed. Everyone flinched when the closet repeated its thunder-and-lightning routine.

Acutely aware that real time was passing, Sabrina tensed. She couldn't afford to take a side trip to the Other Realm while her window of opportunity to secure another magical souvenir diminished. She was not, however, being given a choice. She was also not terribly surprised when the door opened and it quickly became apparent that Roland was responsible!

The annoying little troll greeted her with open arms and a grin. "Sabrina! Welcome!"

"I don't think so." Sabrina hit the closet return button, but nothing happened. "What's wrong with this thing?"

"Apparently it goes where it wants, when it wants," Drell huffed.

"Great." Furious, Sabrina stepped out of the closet. Dozens of trolls, winged fairies, leprechauns, and wood nymphs were gathered in a village square decorated with black lanterns and streamers. Several yellow slide walks wound between quaint thatched cottages and converged in the central plaza.

"Why didn't you tell me your cousin Roland lived in your linen closet, Sabrina?" Harvey asked accusingly.

"Because he doesn't. He, uh, lives . . . over the rainbow! He slid into school on a rainbow last Saint Patrick's Day, remember?"

"Oh, right." Harvey nodded. "I knew there had to be a logical explanation."

Frank blinked. "That's logical?"

"It is for Harvey," Libby said. "The rest of us are obviously the victims of mass hysteria induced by lack of sleep and exposure to poppies."

"So we're hallucinating? That's a relief!" Val smiled uncertainly. "I think."

Roland stomped up to Harvey and poked him in the knee. "I didn't invite you, farm boy! The invitation was for Sabrina."

"Invitation to what, Roland?" Sabrina demanded indignantly. "I don't like being shanghaied, especially when I have important things to do!"

"I'm having an end-of-magic party!" Roland beamed. "Kind of a last fling before all us magical people cease to exist."

"A party?" Salem jumped out of Sabrina's arms. "Where's the shrimp dip?"

Roland scowled at the cat. "We don't serve *shrimp* at gatherings of little people."

"That figures." Salem sighed. "How about tuna? Cheese? Any kind of munchies will do."

"Rainbow, munchies . . ." Frank flipped to the next page in his notebook and scribbled more notes.

"You're celebrating?" Sabrina glared at Roland, aghast. "Why aren't you doing something to help?"

"Because he's a troll." Drell sneered. "And trolls don't do anything without an ulterior motive."

"Continued existence would motivate me. In fact, it has!" Sabrina whirled and motioned Drell aside. She couldn't tell him *exactly* what she was doing, but she could hint. "While you and my aunts and the others are working on a plan to fix the old clock, I'm working on an alternate plan."

Drell frowned. "I don't remember authorizing a backup plan."

"You didn't, but it can't hurt to have one, can it?" Sabrina didn't give him a chance to respond. "Of course not! So you've got to send me back to the mortal world so I can get on with it! I'm running out of time!"

"Aren't we all?" Drell's massive shoulders sagged. "Sorry, Sabrina, but what little magic I have left is too unpredictable. I can't afford to waste a spell on your commendable but probably hopeless scheme, whatever it is. Things are not going too well in the OR at the moment."

"But . . . but what if I'm right and you're wrong?" Sabrina quailed under Drell's incredulous scrutiny. She had stepped over the line of acceptable audacity, and she quickly took two steps back. "Okay, so that's not likely, but what if?"

Drell raised his hand to silence her, then squinted thoughtfully. "Actually, I might be able to help you, but you've got to do something for me first."

"Name it." Sabrina winced, wondering if he was going to ask her for something impossible—like persuading Aunt Hilda to grovel at his feet or removing Salem's sarcastic streak. Time would really end before either of those things happened.

"Excellent! If you get the hands of the Great Clock back from Belinda, I'll send you and your entourage back to the mortal world." Drell frowned at his finger. "At least I'll try."

"Fair enough. Now, who's Belinda and how come she's got the clock hands?" Sabrina didn't want to appear suspicious, but there had to be a catch.

Drell's dark eyebrows bristled. "Belinda is a nasty old witch who had her powers revoked decades ago because she refused to stop dabbling in black-market spell ingredients. She stole the clock hands because she wants all magic to end."

"She can't do magic, so she doesn't want anyone else to have powers?"

"That pretty much sums it up." Drell pointed to a slide walk that meandered out of the troll town past a cornfield. "That road will take you most of the way. You can't miss Belinda's hovel. It looks as vile as it smells."

Although Sabrina didn't want to waste time wandering around the Other Realm, it was her only option if she wanted Drell's help getting home. "Let's go, guys! We're gonna take a little hike!"

"On an empty stomach?" Salem gasped. "Roland isn't serving anything but veggies!"

Libby stubbornly planted her hands on her hips. "I'll just wait here until the hallucination ends and all this goes away."

"I hate to admit it, Sabrina," Val said apologetically, "but I have to side with Libby on this one."

"Looks like you're outvoted, Sabrina." Roland gleefully rubbed his hands together. "Guess you're staying to party after all."

"Wrong, Roland." Sabrina held up her finger. *"This* is the only vote that counts." As the pouting troll stalked off, Sabrina closed her eyes, crossed the fingers on her other hand, and chanted:

Magic, hear my desperate plea.
Send them to that road for me.

She pointed and warily opened one eye. Everyone was still standing by the entrance to the linen closet. Either the spell had fizzled entirely, or it had been delayed.

"Oh, no!" Roland screeched and slapped his palms to his face. "Your closet killed my gladiolas!"

A cluster of brilliant red flowers and green leaves stuck out from under the linen closet door. They suddenly turned brown and withered into dust.

Sabrina frowned. There was something vaguely familiar about everything that had happened since Frank popped into her living room, but she wasn't sure why.

Everyone suddenly executed an about-face and began skipping toward the yellow slide walk.

"What's happening?" Val squealed.

"I don't know, but nobody pulls my strings and gets away with it!" Libby linked arms with Val and Harvey, an act of camaraderie that was obviously not her idea.

"In case you haven't noticed, Libby, somebody's

getting away with it." Harvey skipped twice on his left leg so he was in step with the two girls.

Although she wasn't under the influence of the spell, Sabrina skipped up to Frank with Salem scampering at her heels. Skipping was a twist she hadn't anticipated, but at least the spell had everyone headed in the right direction.

"I think I know what's happening," Frank said softly.

"You do?" Sabrina winced.

Frank nodded. "I think that tornado hit the newspaper office and knocked me out cold." Before he could continue, everyone skipped aboard the slide walk, and Sabrina's spell disengaged. The conveyor immediately lurched forward.

"And we're off!" Harvey shouted as the slide walk quickly gained speed. Several cornfields zoomed by in a golden blur.

"What? No dining car?" Disgusted, Salem flopped down on his stomach and rested his chin on his paws.

Sabrina moved over to Frank, who had sat down to catch his breath and enjoy the ride. Considering that he had popped forward a century in time and hadn't had Val's, Harvey's, and Libby's experiences with Spellman weirdness, the young man was taking the bizarre excursion rather well. "What were you saying about being knocked out?"

"Oh, yes." Frank leaned closer. "This must be a

subconscious dream message like the ones that psychiatrist Sigmund Freud is studying."

"A message?" Sabrina asked, her curiosity piqued. "About what?"

"I'm not sure, but I suspect it has something to do with how I've spent my life so far. I've managed a chain of theaters, written and produced a play, run a store, and worked on the paper, but—" Frank shrugged and sighed. "Well, I haven't found any of those endeavors very satisfying."

"What do you want to do?" Sabrina suddenly had the uneasy feeling that maybe Frank was a magical moment that had come to her instead of her going to him. If so, she had squandered most of her time by ignoring him!

Frank shifted uncomfortably. "I'm a little embarrassed to say. The few people I've told think it's silly."

"You have to do what's right for you, Frank, not what other people think you should do." Sabrina prodded him for more information. "What's your last name?"

"Oh, ewwww!" Libby clamped her fingers over her nose as the slide walk ground to a stop at the edge of an eerie forest.

Val turned green and keeled over.

Harvey caught her before she hit the walk. "She must be really stink-sensitive."

" 'Vile' doesn't quite describe that odor, does it?" Salem gagged. "Smells like something a dog would love to roll in."

Sabrina's stomach churned. The average putrid swamp smelled better than the stench wafting through the leafless dead trees. Cousin Zsa Zsa's Pure Ambition products were pleasantly aromatic by comparison. Belinda couldn't be too far away.

"We're here! Let's get this over with." Sabrina jumped off the slide walk. Nobody followed her.

"Get what over with?" Libby glared at Sabrina. "I'm not going anywhere near the source of that awful smell."

"But I might need help getting the clock hands back from Belinda!" Sabrina pleaded.

"This is just some horrible illusion. Why should I help you do anything?" Libby asked obstinately.

"Because you won't snap out of this, uh, hallucination if you don't, that's why," Sabrina countered.

Val swayed unsteadily as her head cleared. She gazed into the dark, gloomy forest and flinched. "I'd rather not, but if we have to . . ."

"That's the spirit, Val." Frank smiled and tapped his notebook with his pencil. "Lead on, Sabrina. I'm eager to see what happens next."

"So am I," Harvey said. "If this is just an illusion, nothing really bad can happen, right?"

"You had to ask." Salem groaned.

Filled with trepidation, Sabrina headed down an overgrown path through the trees. She assumed Drell had asked her to retrieve the clock hands because he didn't want to deal with the awful stench, but what if there was another reason? Although Belinda's magic powers had been revoked, the old witch might have an edge if Sabrina's own magic failed. And her finger had been malfunctioning with disturbing regularity.

Sabrina also wanted to find out more about Frank, but she wouldn't be able to concentrate on him until she had accomplished Drell's mission and was breathing fresh air again—back in Westbridge.

"That's far enough!" a gruff voice called out. "Scram! Get off my property! You're trespassing!"

Through the gloom, Sabrina saw an old cottage with dangling, broken shutters, decayed siding, and a rotting roof. An old woman with oily, tangled hair stood by the front door brandishing a broom.

"Are you Belinda?" The sickening stench intensified as Sabrina moved forward.

"None of your business! Go away!"

"Gladly!" Libby turned to retreat.

"Not just yet." Frank grabbed Libby's arm and hauled her back.

"I think I'm gonna be sick." Val covered her mouth.

Harvey gingerly stepped back.

"We'll leave as soon as you give me the clock hands you stole," Sabrina announced boldly.

"Why don't you just come on over here and get them, missy?" The old witch leaned on the broom. Her skin and clothes were covered with grime, and her teeth were black.

Sabrina saw the large clock hands on the ground

in front of Belinda and hesitated. They certainly *looked* like the hands of the Great Clock, but the stink was overpowering and she was afraid she'd pass out if she got too close. "How long has it been since you've had a bath?"

"Just before my powers were revoked I banned water from my domain. Stinking is my first line of defense!" Belinda cackled hysterically. "Drell won't even come near me!"

No kidding! Sabrina raised her finger to conjure a no-smell spell, then thought better of it. The way magic was going berserk, the spell might eliminate her nose altogether! She held her nostrils closed with her thumb and forefinger and strode forward.

"Then there's my second line of defense!" Belinda laughed. "Nobody wants to tangle with a magic forest full of cranky trees!"

A magic forest? Sabrina yelped as a branch reached down and grabbed her hair. The ugly trees weren't quite as dead as they appeared!

"Hey! Let go!" Libby's jacket snagged on a gnarled tree branch. When she tried to yank it free, the twisted twig tightened its hold.

"Uh-oh!" Val's eyes widened as the trees lining the path to the cottage door began to close in on them.

Harvey jumped when a root squirmed out of the ground and twined itself around his ankle. Frank stuck his pencil behind his ear and grabbed the root to stop it from dragging Harvey into the grotesque woods.

A large log rolled toward Salem. He leaped up and sank his claws into the bark, then couldn't extract them. "Sabrina! Do something!"

"What? Ow!" Sabrina winced as the tree pulled several long blond hairs out of her scalp by the roots. She didn't have a clue why the forest was so hostile, but Belinda was cranky because she had lost her powers. The old hag seemed to take great pride in her disgusting body odor and appearance!

Inspired, Sabrina raised her finger. Since the old witch had had her powers revoked for practicing mal-magic, any witch in good standing could reverse Belinda's spells! Sabrina couldn't be sure her own magic would work, but that was a risk she had to take.

Stinking witch who has no power,
I think it's time you took a shower!

Sabrina pointed. Within seconds thunder rumbled overhead and a cloudburst dumped sheets of rain on the cottage, Belinda, and the surrounding trees. The trees immediately let go of their captives and raised their branches toward the sky.

No wonder they were so cranky! Sabrina thought. The trees had slowly been dying of thirst in Belinda's drought.

Belinda screamed and tried to duck into the shelter of her cottage, but the door was stuck closed. Flapping her arms and squealing, she turned in crazed circles, but she couldn't escape the water pouring from the sky.

Sabrina dashed forward, grabbed the clock hands, and ran back to the group.

"Hey!" Val grinned as water streamed down her face. "The rain is making the smell go away!"

"But the way that old crone is acting, you'd think she was going to melt!" Libby sneered.

Melt? A witch? Sabrina stared as Frank made a notation, then stuffed the notebook in his shirt to protect it from the rain. How could she have been so dense? *Frank?* "Are you L. Frank—"

The group popped en masse back to the linen closet in Roland's village.

"You got them!" Drell strode out of the closet and took the clock hands from Sabrina's arms.

"Uh, yeah." Sabrina tore her gaze away from Frank. "So can we go home now?"

"I hope so. Maintenance is pretty sure they fixed the closet problem." Smiling tightly, Drell herded everyone into the closet. He stayed outside. "Just hit the Return button. It was low on pixie dust."

"You're not coming, Drell?" Sabrina frowned.

"No. I might have to make a few detours, but I can pop myself back to clock headquarters from here. I don't have time for any side trips."

"Neither do we!" Sabrina protested.

Drell punched the Door Close button. "Bye!"

"But—" Sabrina stuck her foot between the door

and the jamb, then noticed Roland running toward her with his chubby little arms open wide.

"Come back, Sabrina! Come back! I want to spend my last hours with you . . ."

"We're out of here!" She removed her foot and pressed the Return button. As soon as the lightning flash and thunder boom faded away, she cautiously opened the door. "Home!"

"Cats and children first!" Salem sprang through the door and ran into Sabrina's bedroom.

When everyone else had exited, Sabrina closed the linen closet door and sagged against it.

"I don't know about the rest of you, but I'm leaving!" Libby paused at the head of the stairs. "I really hate your house, Sabrina."

"So I can't expect you to visit again any time soon, right?" Sabrina asked hopefully.

As Libby opened her mouth to respond, the air rippled and she vanished along with Harvey and Val.

"Frank!" Sabrina's head snapped around. "Oh, good. You're still here!"

"Yes, but I'm ready to wake up now."

"No! I haven't"—the air shimmered, instantly transporting Sabrina and Frank to his desk in the living room—"finished, yet!" On the verge of panic, Sabrina blurted out the question she had been trying to ask since they left Belinda's. "You're L. Frank Baum, aren't you?"

"Yes." Frank frowned. "But I don't remember telling you my whole name."

"I'm a good guesser." Sabrina laughed nervously. "You really want to write stories for children, don't you?"

Frank stared at her. "Yes, but writing children's books doesn't pay very well. I have responsibilities and a family to support."

"But maybe that's what your dream message was all about. Fulfilling your dream to be a writer! A *rich* and *famous* writer." He didn't look convinced, and Sabrina feared that her chance to influence his magical moment would be lost forever. "I mean, look at all the great material you just . . . uh, dreamed up! Add a plot and some really strange characters, and what a book that could be, huh?"

Frank grinned as he walked back to his chair and sat down. "I was giving that some thought. In fact, I've already thought of a title: *The Wonderful Wizard of OR.*"

"*Oz,*" Sabrina said. "Call it *The Wonderful Wizard of Oz.* Trust me."

"Oz." Nodding, Frank leaned back with his hands behind his head and his feet on the desk. "It *would* make a great book, wouldn't it?"

"Yes. Absolutely." Sabrina exhaled with relief, then suddenly remembered that she needed a souvenir for the new clock. "Can I have your pencil? Please!"

"Sure!" Frank pulled the pencil from behind his ear and tossed it into Sabrina's outstretched hand.

And then he was gone.

And Sabrina was back in her bedroom.

Clutching the pencil, she glanced at the hour-glass. More granules had fallen through. A *lot* more. She wearily sank onto the bed beside Salem. This adventure had used up too much of her time. But on the brighter side, she had another souvenir for the new clock.

Now if she could just get the rest before the hour-glass crystals ran out, she still had a chance to save magic and all the magical beings everywhere.

Even Roland.

Rain Likely, Chance of Lava
By Mark Dubowski

They met at night on the trail, halfway up the gorge. Sabrina had climbed up from the river, following the moon, and the others had climbed down, following her sound. They found each other where the cliffs rose out of the trees in a solid gray wall.

"Hi there," she said, watching their spears, and the words came out in a language the Timekeeper had given her for this trip, to the year 12,000 B.C., to find a rock with "fire within." That was all she knew about why she was there.

Hilda, Zelda, the Timekeeper, and the Witches' Council seemed far away. She felt buried deep in time.

"This way," was all one of the cave dwellers said.

They walked up a zigzag staircase of rocks stacked inside a rock chimney all the way up to a massive ledge of smooth, dark stone overhanging rubble and bald trees bleached as white as bone. Others came out of caves in the rock wall along the ledge to see her, including a girl about her age, who came and led her away. The girl took Sabrina to a circle of stones around a bed of hot coals and gave her something to eat. She was hungry, so the food tasted good, but she didn't know what it was. She started to ask, then changed her question.

"Who are you?" she said. It came out in grunts and murmurs.

"Roxanne," the other girl said.

"I'm Sabrina." Exhausted, she fell asleep.

"That was funny last night," Roxanne said. They were sitting cross-legged on an outcrop of stone on a boulder-strewn hillside, watching the sunset colors behind a black stack of rock that was the chimney of a volcano. "You said you were from far away."

"I am," Sabrina said. She'd been there a whole day now, without a clue about the thing she was there to find.

"But you said far away in *time*," Roxanne said.

Sabrina was ready to tell her. She needed help. What difference would it make? "I meant it, Roxanne," she said. "I know it sounds sort of crazy, but stay with me. When I said far away, I really meant timewise, too. I . . . I'm from another time."

Overhead a wide-winged bird cried. A cool wind

swept up from deep in the gorge where the river ran.

Roxanne smiled and said, "I know! I know exactly what you mean. I feel the same way."

"No," Sabrina said. The other girl hadn't understood. "I mean—"

"My elders don't understand. It's like they're living in the past." Roxanne went on.

Sabrina shook her head and started to explain, but Roxanne was on a roll.

"It's like they're in the Ice Age or something, you know? If we have a problem or something, I'm like, okay, let's deal with it, you know? And they're like—"

"Never mind," Sabrina said with a sigh.

"Yeah, exactly!"

The Timekeeper had given Sabrina the ability to speak Roxanne's Stone Age language, but that didn't mean she could get her point across.

Earlier that day she had mentioned her pet cat, Salem, leaving out the fact that he was back in Westbridge, in modern times. To everyone in Roxanne's tribe, cats meant only big and dangerous saber-toothed tigers.

"But all cats aren't bad," she had told them, and she had used the end of a burnt stick to make a drawing on the wall of their cave, a stick figure of Salem and a stick figure of herself. Starting with his size, she meant to show them that her cat was nothing like a saber-toothed tiger.

Unfortunately all they got from her lecture was the idea to create their own cave drawings. Now the cave walls were covered with stick-figure drawings of heroic battles they'd had with saber-tooths.

"If you want to know who's *really* in a time warp, it's Ogen," the other girl went on. She combed her hair back with a carved bone, letting it fall onto the woven grass poncho she wore over a leather undergarment. "He is totally bronto."

Saurus, Sabrina thought, filling in the rest of the word. Ogen was a shaman—the tribe's doctor and judge and after-dinner speaker. *In another time,* Sabrina thought, *he would have made a pretty good sumo wrestler as well.*

"I would really like to talk to him," Sabrina said. Of all the people in the tribe, Ogen seemed most likely to know where she could find the object the council had sent her to retrieve.

"With Ogen, you mainly listen," Roxanne said. "Come on. It's about time for supper."

Because that day had already passed, its effect on Sabrina was nil. Still, it worried her. Theoretically, she could be stuck there practically forever.

They climbed down from the rocks and followed the steep trail to the caves below. As they went deeper into the gorge, the sky above narrowed to a band of blue-black between the cliff walls. There was thunder in the distance, but the sky over the camp was still starry and hung with a sickle moon.

Finally the trail brought them around the boulders in front of Ogen's cave and then lower, to the ledge where the women were cooking over red coals in the fire ring.

Sabrina had noticed how respectfully they tended the fire and how, over the day, they continually fed it with deadwood. Then at night, before sleeping, they covered it with stones from a border around the fire to keep the embers live until morning. Sabrina wondered if one of the stones from the fire ring was what the council wanted—circled around the fire the rocks had a "fire within." *But,* she thought, *if you took any rock alone, it encircled nothing and had nothing to distinguish it from the others.*

"Does it ever go out?" Sabrina asked. "The fire, I mean."

"Why?" the other girl said.

Sabrina gave her reason for asking: "I was a Brownie. They tested us a lot on fire safety."

But Roxanne didn't mean *why ask.* She meant *why put it out.* "Fire *means* safety," Roxanne said, clearly not understanding why anyone would let a fire go out. It kept them warm, and it kept the saber-tooths away.

"I guess you're right. We're camping, but it's different from Brownies," Sabrina said. "Back then, a big campfire meant we were about to have S'mores."

"S'mores?"

Sabrina winced. She kept forgetting how much explaining it took to answer a simple Stone Age question. To tell Roxanne about S'mores, she would have to explain graham crackers, chocolate bars, and marshmallows, none of which had been invented yet.

"Food," she said at last.

"You're right," Roxanne said with a smile, "It's time to eat." And they joined the rest of the tribe at the fire ring.

When the meal was over, Ogen stepped into the firelight and told a story about an adventure in which he took a secret trail to the hot center of the volcano. From its heart, he claimed, he had captured fire. The same fire around which they were sitting that night. At the end, everybody clapped.

"That's the same story as last night," Sabrina whispered.

"It's the same story every night," Roxanne whispered back. "Ever since he and Slag went to the volcano."

"Slag?" In the story Ogen went alone.

"Two went. Slag is the one who went into the volcano to get the fire. Ogen brought the fire home."

Sabrina looked around at the faces in the firelight. "Which one is he?"

"Who?"

"Slag."

"Slag is the one who went inside the volcano."

"I know, I know," Sabrina said, squirming, "but

where is he now?" She tilted her head a little and waggled it at the others around the fire.

Roxanne finally understood. "He's not here. He's still in the volcano."

Sabrina grimaced and looked over her shoulder at the chimney of rock that loomed over the gorge. *Fire within,* she thought. Then she turned back to Roxanne.

"Slag's not in the story, though. I wonder why Ogen dropped him."

"If the fire goes out," Roxanne explained, "Ogen will have to go to the volcano again. Someone will have to go with him." She tossed a chip of wood from the ground onto the coals, and it blackened around the edges and then flared. "It'll be better for the one who is chosen not to remember Slag."

"No wonder you guys keep the fire going," Sabrina said. At home in Westbridge, there was a cardboard tube of matches on the hearth in the living room. Sabrina wished she had it now, to give to the tribe.

The moon rose and polished the leaves around the camp with pale light. The fire went down to red embers, and the tribesmen banked it with stones and retired to the caves, where they slept on the skins of animals they had hunted or otherwise outlived, according to the way their world was.

During the night the earth trembled.

When Sabrina woke up, the tribespeople were already moving out of the caves into the moonlight.

She rolled out of the blankets and went outside, where rocks were coming loose from the gorge walls and falling into the trees. She watched a piece break off one of the natural stone chimneys on the other side of the chasm, saw it crash through the branches and raise a plume of water as it plunged into the river.

Some of the others were already on their way up the trail toward Ogen's cave to see it. Sabrina and Roxanne followed them to a high place where the chimney of the volcano was black against the stars. Light shone through a crack on the shoulder of the mountain where lava spilled from a break in the rock caused by the tremor. Sabrina could see the tribespeople were unworried by small eruptions.

Reassured, they left the cliffs, except for Ogen, who dutifully stayed to praise the mountain for lasting through the earthquake.

Back at the camp, while the others went into the caves for the night, Roxanne showed Sabrina how to bank the fire again, putting back the stones that had rolled off during the tremor and covering the coals for the night.

"You can do it," she told Sabrina, leaving some of the work for her and going back into the cave.

A pair of eyes focused on Sabrina from under the fern fronds that hung over a boulder at the edge of the camp—cat eyes. Sabrina dropped the rock she'd been holding and ran to the spot.

"What are you doing here?" she whispered. It

was Salem, and she was glad to see him. He was clean and well-groomed, and he reminded her of home.

"The Timekeeper sent me to find out what's taking you so long," he told her. "You're way overdue."

Sabrina brushed ash from the fire circle off her hands. "I'd be out of here in a minute if I could find the right rock," she told him.

"You're in the Stone Age. Just grab one and go."

"No, no, no. It's got to have 'fire within,' " she said. "Whatever that means."

"He's not making it easy, is he?"

Sabrina leaned against the trunk of a cottonwood. "The Timekeeper? No, he's not. I've been wondering about the rocks around the fire circle, but it takes a bunch of them to make a 'fire within.' Then there's the volcano. But I don't think he wants me to bring back a volcano."

"Not if you're flying, anyway. Then you're restricted to items that will fit into the overhead luggage compartment or under the seat in front of you," Salem said.

"Be serious. I'm tired of camping."

"What about taking back just a piece of the volcano?"

"Maybe. But it's kind of dangerous up there. When we have more time, remind me to tell you about a guy named Slag. There's a secret trail, but the only one who knows it is Ogen, the shaman—"

"Speaking of . . ." Salem interrupted.

"No, a shaman is . . ." Sabrina started to explain, but Salem was gone. She turned and saw Ogen, back from the overlook to the volcano, watching her now.

"I thought I heard something," Sabrina said weakly, then hurried off toward the caves. "I have to bank the fire!" She was making excuses, and she knew it probably showed.

The storm had moved closer, and cloud lightning flashed over the camp and the fire circle. From the opening of the cave she watched Ogen look at the place where Salem had hidden, then go away.

It rained hard during the night. Runoff washed down the rock walls of the gorge and flooded the river against its banks, and the canyon rang with the sound of rushing water long afterward.

Roxanne saved the bad news for morning. "The fire went out," she told Sabrina, shaking her blankets.

Sabrina hoped it was a dream and the shaking only an earthquake.

"I didn't do it," Sabrina said, half asleep and already worried about Ogen. Roxanne had left her to bank the fire, and she couldn't remember if she had finished before Salem appeared and before Ogen had scared her away.

"Ogen has a saying," Roxanne assured her. "Accidents happen."

"He said that? About the fire?"

"No. About Slag."

"Slag. I remember him. Good old Slag. He's the one who went into the volcano, isn't he? Still there, I hear tell."

"It's a tough job, but somebody's got to do it," Roxanne told her—another one of Ogen's sayings.

Ogen's men came to Sabrina's cave and brought her before him and the tribe. Ogen gave a speech about the storm and the need to rekindle the fire. *As stories go,* Sabrina thought, *it's a nice change from the old How I Won the War–style yarn he'd been telling,* but it had a bad ending: this time he'd picked Sabrina to go with him to the volcano.

Sabrina thought about the Brownies and that she might show them how to rub sticks together to start a fire, but the camp and everything around it was soaked. And she'd never been able to get that to work anyway. She wondered if Salem had managed to stay dry.

"The elders say it is a great honor to accompany Ogen in the fire quest," Roxanne told her as the tribe followed Ogen and Sabrina up the trail. "Is that bogus or what?"

It was customary for the entire tribe to go along for the first part of the journey, carrying spears. Sabrina had never seen them look like an army before.

"The spears are purely ceremonial," Roxanne told her. "Unless you suddenly change your mind about volunteering. I'll miss you, Sabrina."

When they neared the place where Sabrina and Ogen would go on alone, Sabrina brightened. It was still far below the volcano. "Don't worry," she whispered to Roxanne. "As soon as Ogen and I are alone, I'm going to make a break for it." She was ready to go back to her own time. The council could buy a new clock; they could have her allowance for the next five hundred years if that's what it took.

"The trail goes through saber-tooth country," Roxanne pointed out. "The volcano will be less painful."

Sabrina didn't notice that the others had fallen behind until she and Ogen were alone on a trail that wound between tall rocks, making it impossible to run. If she made that choice, Ogen's long spear was still fitted with a stone point.

Sabrina tried talking, but Ogen wouldn't answer, and then finally he sent her out in front of him so he wouldn't have to listen, either. They reached the summit at noon.

"It's hot up here!" Sabrina commented, but the heat wasn't the result of the weather or the time of day. Heat from the throat of the volcano changed the air at the top to steam. A current of air from the gorge swept it off the mountain into the form of a long cloud that hung over the valley below.

"Stay." Ogen left her on a high bare rock while he made the first offering to the mountain, a handful of ash from the ruined fire at the camp. When the pieces hit the lava pool below, they twinkled and burned again.

"It's got to be about a bajillion degrees down there," someone whispered.

"Salem!" Sabrina gasped. "I'm sure glad to see you. Which way to the twenty-first century?"

"I'd love to help," he told her apologetically.

"That sounds like a cop-out."

"Mitigating circumstances. This is saber-tooth country, you know."

"So?"

"I have to survive, Sabrina. The council that turned me into a *cat* has the ability to change me into cat *food* at any time. I've been good, and they've kept me nice and safe from Mr. Sabre-tooth."

"I shouldn't have worried about you," Sabrina said. "Just remember that if I don't get out of this, neither do you. The clock needs that rock."

"What's the plan here? With fat boy, I mean."

"Ogen gives me the spear and lowers me by the ankles into the crater. After a few minutes he pulls me up, and I hand the spear to him like a lighted match. Theoretically."

"There's a flaw?"

"I happen to know what happened to his last helper," Sabrina replied.

"And that would be . . ." Salem asked.

"He's still in the volcano."

"Not good."

"Exactly. Because that's just where I'll be, unless you or the Timekeeper gives me a helping hand. Roxanne doesn't know anything, and negotiating with Ogen is like trying to sell Hilda a broom—it's never going to happen."

"Again, I'd love to help. But there is that saber-tooth to think about."

Ogen ended his chant at the rim of the crater. It was time to light the match. "He doesn't seem worried or afraid of tigers," Sabrina said.

"You have to keep in mind that the spear he is carrying has a nice sharp flint point," Salem said. "That's all I can say." The he scatted over the side of the boulder just as Ogen reappeared. The shaman climbed onto the rock and explained very briefly what he had to do; the only part Roxanne had left out was the part where he lashed the spear to Sabrina's arm.

"In case you drop it," Ogen lied.

In case I drop dead, Sabrina thought.

They clambered off the rock and went to the rim. The air was like a steam bath, and everything was shadowy except the red-orange pool in the crater.

Sabrina prepared to watch her entire life flash before her eyes.

Ogen removed the flint point from his spear and pocketed it.

"Prepare to—" the shaman started to say, but Sabrina held up a finger.

"Wait a minute," she said. "I've got an idea."

* * *

"I knew you could do it," Salem purred.

"Thanks to you. Thanks to that clue you gave me when we were on the volcano."

They were on their way back to the twenty-first century; in Sabrina's hand was a narrow sharp-edged triangular stone.

"I wouldn't mention that clue to the Timekeeper. He probably thinks it's important for you to figure these things out for yourself," Salem said.

"I did figure it out," Sabrina said. "You told me Ogen's flint spearhead kept him safe from saber-toothed tigers. Using it to make a spark and showing him how to turn that into fire was my idea."

"I'm sure he was impressed."

"Of course. He set me free." Sabrina smiled with relief.

"The easier to take credit for the discovery, my dear."

"For history's sake, it's better to leave me out of the story," Sabrina said. "I was only passing through the Stone Age. And we both know the tribespeople would have discovered it themselves, eventually."

"It's so much more convenient than going to the volcano or waiting for lightning to strike," Salem said. "And you won't be forgotten, Sabrina."

She took one last look around. "Roxanne will remember, you mean."

"Others too," Salem said. "Our pictures are on the wall of the cave, remember?"

"I forgot about that!" Sabrina said.

"Archaeologists will eventually discover the site."

"They'll freak," Sabrina worried. "Domestic cats didn't exist during the Stone Age."

"Not to worry," Salem said. "I took the liberty of adding a pair of large canine teeth to my portrait. They'll know me for what I am."

"A saber-tooth?"

"A Saber*hagen*. King of the jungle! Conquerer! Feared by man and beast! Regal, majestic, and sovereign! Divine ruler!"

"Catch . . ." Sabrina said, tossing him the precious flint. Salem caught it in his jaws.

Poof! Before he could say another word they were back in Sabrina's bedroom.

Cupid's Arrow
By Nancy Krulik

Sabrina shivered and pulled her jacket tightly around her as she attempted to figure out where and when Justin's magic had carried her this time.

She knew she was in a van parked outside her house. Okay, so she hadn't gone far. And it was cold, so it obviously had to be winter. But *which* winter?

Harvey sat beside Sabrina, shifting uncomfortably in the front seat of his father's exterminator van. "Sorry about the van, Sabrina," he apologized as he fiddled with the radio knobs. "My car isn't working right, so I had to borrow my dad's. I hope you don't mind." Harvey pulled a small gift box from his coat pocket. "Anyhow, I bought this for you. I hope you like it. Happy Valentine's Day."

Sabrina took the small velvet box from Harvey's

hands and looked at it curiously. *Valentine's Day? Which Valentine's Day?* she wondered.

The DJ on the radio answered that question for her. "Today is the first Valentine's Day of the new millennium," he announced. "And here's an oldie but a goodie going out from Willard to Zelda. We really had to dig into the vault for this one!" The DJ began to play an old Doris Day tune.

Valentine's Day 2000. Justin had sent Sabrina into the future. Still, compared with all the crazy places and times she'd visited today, spending next Valentine's Day with Harvey was a real treat.

Sabrina fumbled with the ribbon on the box. She was dying to know what Harvey was going to get her for Valentine's Day. But deep in her heart of hearts, she knew it wouldn't really be fair to Harvey if she opened the box now. When the real Valentine's Day came along, she would have ruined Harvey's surprise. *That is, assuming this Valentine's Day is completely unchangeable,* she thought as her curiosity got the better of her. *And what if this gift is the piece of the clock I need?* She began untying the ribbon.

But as Sabrina looked at Harvey's sweet face, she knew she couldn't take a chance of hurting him on the real Valentine's Day. Besides, the probability of the piece she needed being handed to her as a gift just seemed too slight. Sabrina knew she had to work to get the items she needed.

"Harvey, I can't open this. Not now," Sabrina said

slowly as she reluctantly handed the small box back to him.

"Why not?" Harvey asked her. "It's Valentine's Day, and you're my Valentine." Harvey took the box and looked into Sabrina's eyes. "Unless you're not my Valentine anymore . . . ?"

Sabrina sighed. Harvey was so insecure. "Of course I am," she reassured him. "It's just that, I, um . . ." Sabrina's brain was racing. She had to make up something, and fast! "It's just that I didn't get *you* anything yet. And I don't want to open your present until you can open mine."

Harvey smiled with relief. "It's okay Sabrina. I don't need anything. I just like being here with you. Come on, open this."

Ordinarily, a comment like that would have made Sabrina incredibly happy, but tonight she had other things on her mind. "No, no, no, Harvey," she told him. "I want to wait until I can afford a present for you. I've been saving for it, and I should have enough cash soon. So hold on to that gift."

Harvey put the little box back in his pocket. Sabrina looked at him for a moment. *Harvey is so cute!* Sabrina would have given just about anything to sit here in the car with him for hours, just staring at the moonlight. But she didn't have time for that now. She had to get inside and try to find some more items that might be needed to build a new Great Clock—before the sand in the hourglass ran out! She gave Harvey a quick peck on the cheek and opened the car door. "I had a great time. Thanks!" she said as she got out of the car.

"Happy Valentine's Day," Harvey mumbled with confusion as he watched Sabrina run toward her front door.

Sabrina was feeling confident as she opened the door to her house. She had once again successfully avoided hurting Harvey's feelings, and she knew that, come Valentine's Day, Harvey would have something special for her—even though they were going to be driving a van with a picture of a dead termite on its side.

She walked into the living room and was greeted by the sound of one hundred hands clapping vigorously.

"Thank you, thank you," Sabrina said, taking a deep bow. Then she looked at the hands. They seemed pretty strange—especially since they weren't attached to bodies. They were just hands, clapping all on their own. How weird was that?

"Salem? What's going on here?" Sabrina asked as the cat padded his way down the stairs.

"Don't ask me. Lots of odd things have been going on today. And this time you and your aunts can't blame me for them."

Salem was interrupted by dance music coming from the kitchen. When Sabrina and Salem entered the room, they discovered a swing band playing on a stage surrounded by dancers who were doing the lindy.

"It don't mean a thing, if you ain't got that swing!" a vocalist sang out.

Sabrina was just getting into the rhythm when the band and the dancers disappeared.

"Boy, weird things happen when magic goes out of whack," Sabrina told Salem. "But I do love a good swing band!"

Salem rolled his eyes. "Can we get back to the problem at hand?" he urged Sabrina. "That sand is sifting faster and faster through the hourglass. And not only am I concerned about my future—or lack of one—but the more I see sand, the more I need to use my litter box, if you get my drift."

"Oops. Sorry," Sabrina apologized. "Okay, so what does the clock need? Hey! Speaking of swing, how about a pendulum?"

"Now you're cooking!" Salem said.

Sabrina opened the fridge. "Nothing here looks like a pendulum," Sabrina said. Her stomach grumbled. "Boy, am I hungry," she added.

"Let's take this again," Salem told Sabrina. "You need a pendulum for a clock. It's Valentine's Day, and—"

"I got it!" Sabrina interrupted him. "Chocolate. Valentine's Day and chocolate go together. The clock's pendulum is made of chocolate."

Salem shook his head and looked at her with dismay. "Which means it would melt and get covered with flies. I don't think so," he said.

Sabrina had to agree, which put her back at square one. "I wish I had some kind of clock expert who could help me with this," she moaned.

"Or a Valentine's Day expert," Salem suggested.

"Like Cupid," Sabrina agreed. "Hey! Why don't I just ask Cupid for advice? I could invite him for tea and see what ideas he has!"

Sabrina grabbed a pencil and a piece of paper. She quickly scribbled out an invitation for Cupid. Then she folded the paper three times and popped it into the toaster. But the paper didn't move. The Other Realm postal service had been temporarily disrupted, due to the trouble with the Great Clock.

"Terrific! Now what am I supposed to do?" Sabrina moaned.

Just then a letter popped up out of the toaster. Sabrina quickly tore open the envelope. "This letter is from three months ago," Sabrina said, checking the OR postmark. "And it's not even addressed to us. This clock emergency is sure making the post office unreliable."

"I couldn't tell the difference from the usual service," Salem sniffed.

"Very funny," Sabrina told her cat. "I'll try mailing my letter again. Maybe it will reach Cupid. It can't hurt to try."

This time the letter disappeared into the toaster. Sabrina waited and waited until finally a reply popped up out of the toaster. It was marked "Do Not Bend: This Heart is Fragile," but the heart-shaped red envelope was folded and torn in several places.

"It's from Cupid," Sabrina told Salem as she read the note. "He'll be here in a few minutes. I'd better get the tea ready."

By the time Cupid arrived, Sabrina had managed to pop a tea bag into a mug of boiling water and put a few Oreos on a plate. It wasn't high tea at Buckingham Palace, but it would have to do.

"Could you make it coffee instead?" Cupid asked Sabrina as he popped into the kitchen. He plopped onto a kitchen chair and wiped his middle-aged brow. "I've been up all night trying to get couples together, and I'm too old to be pulling all-nighters. Besides, it's impossible to get people to meet face-to-face these days. It's all e-mails and faxes, and you wouldn't believe the things people say over the telephone. It's no surprise that so many marriages end in divorce—when people actually go so far as to get married. I'm telling you, the romance business is not what it used to be."

"That's a shame," Sabrina replied, commiserating with Cupid. She picked up the plate of Oreos and waved them under his nose. "Cookie?"

"No, thanks," Cupid said. He patted his stomach. "Got to watch my weight. The diaper's getting tighter and tighter these days."

Sabrina shook her head. She'd known Cupid for a few years now, and she'd never gotten used to the sight of a middle-aged man running around in a diaper carrying a bow and arrows. But there he was, right in her kitchen. "I suppose you're wondering why I asked you to come over."

"For tea, of course," Cupid answered.

"Well, that was part of it," Sabrina told Cupid as she handed him a mug of coffee, "but I also want to ask a favor of you."

Cupid looked suspicious. "Look, if you and your boyfriend Henry—"

"Harvey," Sabrina corrected him.

"Harvey," Cupid repeated, "are having problems, you'll have to solve them yourselves."

Sabrina shook her head. "No. It's not Harvey and me. You've heard about the trouble with the Great Clock of the Other Realm, haven't you?"

Cupid nodded but didn't say anything.

"Well, I'm trying to solve the problem by building a new clock. I need something to serve as the pendulum of the clock. I think it must have something to do with Valentine's Day," Sabrina explained.

Cupid wiped his mouth with a napkin, stood up, and turned to leave. "Well, I don't have anything that can help you," he said. "I travel light. All I have with me are a few diaper pins and my arrows."

The arrows! An arrow looked like a pendulum—sort of. "I'll need one of your arrows," Sabrina said quickly.

Cupid shook his head. "Forget it," he told Sabrina. "I'm not going to help you build a new clock."

Sabrina stood up and stared Cupid straight in the eye. "If you don't give me the arrow, the Great Clock will wind down. We'll all turn into mortals. All of our powers will be gone."

Cupid shrugged. "That's fine with me," he declared. "I'd rather be mortal. I don't want to be responsible for people falling in love anymore. Love only seems to cause misery. Nobody knows that better than you, Sabrina. Look at your family. Your parents are divorced, your aunt Hilda is desperately seeking anyone, and the only man I could come up with for your aunt Zelda is Mr. Kraft."

Sabrina couldn't argue with Cupid. When it came to love, her family did not have a great track record. But that didn't mean that *everyone* did poorly in love, did it?

"Love is a beautiful thing," Sabrina insisted. "It makes people's lives richer. Even if the love affair doesn't work out, the memory is still sweet. Don't you get it? Love is the reason we're all here."

"Not today it isn't. Today everyone's here to make it big in the stock market or to come up with something that's new and improved, even though the old one worked just fine," Cupid argued.

Sabrina was frustrated. How was she supposed to get an arrow if Cupid was going to be so cynical? If only she could get some famous lovers together so that they could tell him how important love was!

"That's it! I'll throw a Valentine's Day party!" Sabrina said suddenly.

"Today's not really Valentine's Day," Cupid told her.

"Well, technically maybe not," Sabrina agreed. "But because of the problems with the Great Clock, I just celebrated *next* Valentine's Day with Harvey. So I guess it could be Valentine's Day again any minute now!" She ran up to her room and started pulling books from the shelves.

"What are you doing now?" Salem asked Sabrina. "This is no time to work on your book report. A lot of witches are depending on you to fix this clock. *I'm depending on you.* I don't want to be scarfing down canned cat food from a bowl for the rest of my life."

"Relax, Salem. I've just run into a little glitch in getting that arrow from Cupid. But I'm going to summon up a few of his closest friends, and they can tell him how wonderful their lives were, thanks to his power," Sabrina explained to the cat.

"Like who?" Salem asked.

"Like Romeo and Juliet," Sabrina said, picking up a literature book from her English class.

"That's not a good choice," Salem said.

"Why not?" Sabrina asked.

"You obviously didn't finish reading the play," Salem told Sabrina. "And besides the fact that they didn't exactly live happily ever after, Romeo and Juliet weren't real people."

"So?" Sabrina countered. "Shakespeare had to get his inspiration for them somewhere. And my guess is that he was inspired by Cupid. Same goes for Margaret Mitchell's Rhett Butler and Scarlett O'Hara from *Gone With the Wind.*"

"Can't you come up with any *real* couples?" Salem asked.

Sabrina pulled out her history book. "Sure, here's a good one," she said as she turned to the section on ancient Egypt. "Cleopatra and—"

"No. Not Cleo!" Salem begged. "Please don't invite her to your party."

"Why not?" Sabrina asked. "She was one of the great lovers of all time."

Salem buried his head in his hands. "I wouldn't know," he said with a sour voice. "The one time I made a date with her, she stood me up—for Julius Caesar. I never want to see her again!"

"Well then, how about I invite her and Marc Antony instead of Caesar? That would serve Caesar right," Sabrina said, trying to console the cat.

"I guess," Salem agreed finally. "I just hope she doesn't make fun of me."

Sabrina stroked Salem's dark fur. "She probably won't even recognize you," Sabrina assured him. "You were walking on two feet the last time you and Cleopatra met."

Sabrina stared at the books for a long while. Ordinarily, pulling people from books was a simple trick. Any baby witch could do it. But Sabrina's powers were severely hampered today. The Witches' Council had forbidden any extracurricular witchcraft, in order to preserve energy. And while Sabrina knew that getting her guests to her house was a necessity, she could see how a Valentine's Day party might be misconstrued as a recreational activity.

Sabrina crossed the fingers on her left hand for luck. Then she waved her right forefinger at the pile of books on her desk.

I need couples from long ago,
Folks like Juliet and Romeo.
Rhett and Scarlett would be neat.
Cleo and Marc again must meet!

Ping! Sabrina heard a sound that told her something magical had happened. But when she looked around her room, she could find none of the people she had summoned.

"I guess the council's decree got in my way," she moaned to Salem. "I'm going downstairs to try one more time to persuade Cupid to give me an arrow."

As Sabrina walked slowly down the steps, she heard people speaking in the living room.

"I declare, I have never seen a plantation like this," said a woman with a soft southern accent.

"Frankly, my dear, neither have I," a man's deep voice replied.

" 'Tis danger in the air, I fear. Perhaps your father's knight is near," a young man announced.

"Fear not, my love. 'Tis a sign from above," a girl responded. "Now we are together once more. Do not think of things like war."

Sabrina was so excited that she took the rest of the steps two at a time. Her guests had arrived!

"Hello, everyone," Sabrina greeted Rhett, Scarlett, Romeo, and Juliet. "Hey, where are Cleopatra and Marc Antony?"

"Over here, my dear," Cleopatra called from the couch. "A queen is always resting."

"You *are* quite ar-resting my love," Marc Antony told Cleopatra as he knelt by her side.

"Oh, brother," Salem moaned quietly.

Sabrina put her finger to her lips to silence Salem. She did not want her talking cat to frighten any of her guests. "Will you all excuse me?" she asked them. "I need to talk to someone in the kitchen."

Sabrina walked into the kitchen and found Cupid still sipping his tea. "There are some people here to see you," she told Cupid.

"I told you I'm not into pairing people off anymore."

"Oh, you won't have to do that," Sabrina assured him. "These people are pretty much paired."

Cupid stood up and adjusted his oversize diaper. "Oh, all right," he said with a sigh, as he followed Sabrina into the living room.

Sabrina pointed to the happy couples. "Surprise!" she shouted to Cupid. "Here are some people for whom love was the most important thing in their entire lives."

Even Cupid had to agree that Sabrina's party was one big happy love-in. Romeo and Juliet were dancing a romantic waltz in the corner, obviously remembering the night they first met at the costume ball. Rhett and Scarlett were sitting on the steps laughing as they recalled the time Rhett had brought Scarlett a new hat from France—and she'd put it on backward. Marc Antony was feeding grapes to Cleopatra, and the queen was happily petting Salem, unaware that the black cat had once been her suitor.

"Do you see how much joy you brought to these people?" Sabrina asked Cupid. "With everything that happened in their lives, they have held on to these joyous memories for centuries."

Cupid nodded and Sabrina breathed a sigh of relief. She figured that any minute now he would turn the arrow over to her. But before she could suggest that, the doorbell rang.

"My, what interesting chimes they be. Who could be calling now for thee?" Romeo asked Sabrina.

Sabrina ran to the door and peeked out. *Oh, no!* It was Harvey. How was she going to explain this to him? Sabrina slowly opened the door and walked out onto the porch.

"Are you ready for school?" Harvey asked Sabrina.

"School?" Sabrina asked without thinking.

"Yeah. We're going to be late."

Sabrina squinted into the sunlight. She couldn't tell Harvey that it had been night just a few minutes ago. After all, he didn't know that Justin's spell was bouncing Sabrina back and forth from one time period to another and from night to day.

Sabrina put her hand to her mouth and began coughing wildly. "I'm . . . uh . . . going to go to school a little late today," she said between fake coughs. "I'm not feeling too great, so I thought I would take it slowly."

Harvey nodded. "Okay," he told her. "Do you want me to take your paper to first-period English class for you?" Harvey reached past Sabrina's shoulder and pushed the door open. He nearly knocked over Sabrina's guests, all of whom had gathered by the door to cavesdrop on her conversation.

"Hey, who are all these people?" Harvey asked Sabrina.

"These people?" Sabrina repeated nervously. "They're all members of a traveling theater troupe. They're staying with us. You know my aunts. They are always willing to help out people in the arts."

"Cool," Harvey said as he looked over the cast of characters. He pointed to Cupid. "Who are you supposed to be?"

"I'm Cupid, of course."

Harvey frowned. "I thought Cupid was a baby."

"We all have to grow up sometime, Herbie," Cupid replied indignantly.

"That's *Harvey*," Sabrina corrected him.

Just then, Romeo jumped out in front of the group and brandished his sword at Harvey. "Sir, thou dost dare to stare at my lady fair? I challenge thee to a duel!"

Harvey grinned. "Hey, that's pretty good," he told Romeo.

Sabrina gulped. "Harvey, I think that's your signal to get out of here," she told him. "He's not kidding. He really wants to fight you."

Harvey looked at Sabrina. "Don't you think he's taking his role a little too seriously?"

"You know Method actors," Sabrina said. "They really *become* their characters. Now run!"

Harvey got a good look at Romeo's sharp sword and decided to take Sabrina's advice. He took off down the street. Sabrina slammed the door shut and blocked Romeo from going after Harvey.

"Look, he's gone," Sabrina told Romeo. "No harm done. Let's all sit down now."

Romeo stared angrily at the closed door but said nothing. Finally, Cleopatra broke the silence. "What is this school the young man spoke of? I have never seen such a place."

"Nor have I," Juliet remarked.

"It's a place where girls and guys go to learn," Sabrina told the crowd. "Harvey and I go to Westbridge High School."

"You learn alongside boys?" Scarlett O'Hara asked incredulously. "How unseemly. And yet how fun!"

"I wish to see this high school," Cleopatra told Sabrina. "You will take us there."

Sabrina shook her head. "I don't think that's a good idea," she said nervously.

"I was not asking you," Cleopatra replied. "That was an order from your queen. You will do as I say, or you will meet an untimely demise."

Sabrina sighed. Then she picked up her aunt Zelda's car keys from the shelf. "Fine, Your Majesty," she agreed unwillingly. "Your chariot awaits."

Sabrina's guests were fascinated by her aunt's car, which Sabrina turned into a minivan to accommodate Scarlett's dress. By the time they arrived at school, the lovers had mastered the art of opening and shutting the automatic windows, turning the radio on full blast, and running the windshield wipers at top speed. Rhett Butler even attempted to grab the wheel from Sabrina and drive on his own, but she stopped him before he could cause a major accident.

Sabrina parked the car and led Cupid and the lovers through a back entrance of the school. She hoped to show them around quickly, while everyone was in class. That way, they'd be out of sight.

"This is the nurse's office," Sabrina said quickly as they passed a small room with the door shut.

"Over there is the library, and down there is the cafeteria. Okay, you've seen the school. Now let's go home."

Sabrina tried to rush her guests through the deserted hallway to another exit, but her path was suddenly blocked by Mr. Kraft.

"Where do you think you're going, Miss Spellman?" he demanded. "Who are all these people, and why don't they have hall passes?"

Sabrina started to explain that they were members of a visiting theater troupe, but before she could get the words out, Cleopatra smiled alluringly at Mr. Kraft and asked, "Who might this gentleman be, Sabrina?"

"Mr. Kraft," Sabrina replied. Then she whispered in Cleo's ear, "He's the vice-principal. Leave him alone, or we could all wind up in big trouble."

"So you're the one charge," Cleo said as she sidled up beside Mr. Kraft. "I thought I sensed something powerful about you."

Mr. Kraft blushed bright red. He was obviously pleased with the attention.

Marc Antony was not pleased at all. He obviously hated the way Cleo was flirting. To get back at her, he opened the door to the nearest classroom. There he found Mrs. Quick teaching in the front of the room. He grabbed the startled teacher around her waist and planted a big kiss on her lips. Mrs. Quick was taken by surprise—but it was a surprise she apparently liked.

"Oh, no!" Sabrina exclaimed. "Marc, get out of there—right now!" But Marc Antony did not budge. He stayed in the classroom, flirting with Mrs. Quick.

Before Sabrina could turn around and ask Cupid for help, she noticed that the other lovers had disappeared. They were loose in the school, and Sabrina had no idea where or with whom they might wind up. She had to find them, and fast!

Sabrina peeked into the nurse's office. No one was there, except the nurse. She was busy filing.

"Sorry," Sabrina said as she turned and walked toward the cafeteria.

The minute Sabrina entered the cafeteria, she knew one of her guests had caused some problems. The girls were all standing on one side of the room looking extremely angry. Sabrina soon learned that they had every right to be annoyed. Their boyfriends had rejected them—so they could be near Scarlett O'Hara.

Scarlett had planted herself in the middle of the cafeteria. She was surrounded by teenage guys. She smiled flirtatiously with each and every boy, slowly closing her eyelashes over her bright green eyes and then looking straight at them.

"Oh, my, you boys are all so chivalrous. This reminds me of that barbecue they had at the Wilkes's house. All the boys there were chivalrous, too," she said in her syrupy southern drawl.

"Can I get you a plate of mystery meat?" one boy asked Scarlett.

"Oh, no, Scarlett, please let me get it," begged another.

"No, you promised I could," a third boy butted in.

Before long, the three boys were fighting over which one could bring Scarlett her lunch.

Sabrina walked over to Scarlett and tried to ease her out of the cafeteria. "Let's go," Sabrina urged, "before this gets completely out of hand."

But Scarlett wouldn't budge. "Fiddle-dee-dee," she declared. "I'm having too much fun to leave."

"I knew this would happen the minute I left you alone!" Rhett Butler shouted as he barged into the cafeteria. "Scarlett, you cannot be trusted. This is the final straw. There is nothing left between us."

Scarlett turned and stared at Rhett. "Frankly, my dear, this time *I* don't give a—"

"Okay, that's enough," Sabrina interrupted her. "Rhett and Scarlett, you two go out to the car. You can play with the windows until I get the others together."

Sabrina pushed Rhett and Scarlett out of the cafeteria. Cupid met them in the hall. "You see what I mean?" he asked Sabrina sadly. "Love causes nothing but sorrow."

"But that's not true," Sabrina insisted. Before she could explain why love was wonderful, she heard crying coming from the janitor's closet.

Sabrina walked over and opened the closet door. There she discovered Juliet, weeping among the mops.

"My love hath judged me unfairly," she told Sabrina. "I have been faithful through eternity."

Sabrina smiled kindly at Juliet. "I know you have. And Romeo will figure that out—as soon as we find him." Sabrina was especially interested in finding Romeo—and not just for Juliet's sake. She was worried about Harvey. She hoped Romeo had not tracked him down and challenged him to yet another duel.

As it turned out, Sabrina had no reason to worry about that. Romeo had other things on his mind. He was busy flirting with Libby.

"Hi, freak," Libby greeted Sabrina. "This handsome hunk says he's a friend of yours. But I can't believe a loser like you could even know a guy like this. Look at him. He's a better Romeo than Leonardo DiCaprio was."

Sabrina rolled her eyes.

"Romeo, do my eyes deceive me?" Juliet sobbed. "Hast thou committed an impropriety?"

"No more than thou hast, my sweet, when Harvey's eyes thine own did meet," Romeo responded.

"Ooh, I just love the way you talk," Libby giggled.

Just then Marc Antony and Cleopatra stormed down the hall side by side. Mr. Kraft followed close behind them.

"What could you possibly see in him?" Marc bellowed. "He's such a nothing."

"He's not a nothing. He's a powerful leader," Cleo responded. "He runs this entire kingdom. He told me so himself."

Mr. Kraft looked sheepishly at Sabrina. "That's not exactly what I said," he told her. "I just told Cleo that I was in charge of things at the school."

Sabrina shook her head at Mr. Kraft.

"Please don't tell your aunt Zelda about this!" Mr. Kraft pleaded with Sabrina as he trailed after the Egyptian queen.

Cupid had seen enough. He turned and plodded sadly toward the exit. Sabrina ran after him. "Cupid! Wait!" she cried out. "I really need that arrow. I'm sure if I look hard enough, I can find a couple who are happily in love. Give me another chance."

Before Cupid could answer, Harvey called to Sabrina as he came rushing down the hall. "Sabrina, you made it! How are you feeling? How's your cough?"

"My what?" Sabrina asked without thinking. Then she remembered the excuse she had given Harvey for not going to school with him. "Oh, it's a little better." She coughed again, just to make her illness seem real.

"There stands the scoundrel!" Romeo shouted from the end of the hallway.

Sabrina began pushing Harvey toward the door.

"You'd better get out of here," she told him. "That Romeo is crazy. He even likes Libby."

"I'm not going anywhere, Sabrina," Harvey insisted as he took a small package out of his jacket pocket. "I bought you these extra-strength cough drops. I want to make sure you're all right."

Sabrina took the box and popped one of the cherry-flavored squares into her mouth. "See? I'm fine," she said. "Now get out of here!"

Cupid smiled at Harvey and Sabrina and handed her an arrow. "I guess I was wrong," he admitted to Sabrina.

"You were?" Sabrina asked.

Cupid nodded. "Some people are obviously truly in love and meant to be together. I see that now."

"Which couple proved that?" Sabrina asked incredulously as she stared at the feuding characters down the hall.

"None of them," Cupid said. "It was you and Harvey. You two have shown me that love can exist in this day and age. The way you care about each other's health and welfare is what love is all about. Now go home and find what you need to build that clock. There are people out there who need me."

Sabrina smiled. "You got it," she assured Cupid. Then she gave Harvey a peck on the cheek and said, "I think Cupid's right. I should go home—and nurse this cold. I'll call you later. Thanks for the cough drops."

"No problem," Harvey said with a smile as he

walked off to class. Cupid followed close behind him, then simply disappeared.

Now that she had the arrow, Sabrina didn't need the feuding lovers. So she pointed her finger at Scarlett, Rhett, Cleo, Marc, Romeo, and Juliet.

You six are no longer needed here.
You've caused us all much trouble, I fear.
So with the silence of a mime,
Return to your own place and time.

With that, all of the lovers disappeared. *Or did they?*

"Wh-wh-what happened to Romeo?" Libby shouted as she pointed to the clock on the wall.

Sabrina looked up to find Romeo trapped inside the big clock in the school hallway. His arms were pointed to the numbers. He looked like some sort of Renaissance-era Mickey Mouse clock.

"Sabrina, isn't it time for you to go back to class? . . . *Aah!*" Mr. Kraft shouted as he looked at his watch. Sabrina came running over and peered over his shoulder. A tiny Cleopatra was caught behind the plastic of the watch, which Mr. Kraft had gotten free by sending in five cereal box tops. It was definitely *not* a watch fit for a queen.

From the shouts she heard bellowing through the halls, Sabrina could tell that other students and teachers had discovered Rhett, Scarlett, Juliet, and Marc Antony in other clocks throughout the school.

The lovers were all trapped in their own time, all right—their own time*pieces!* Sabrina's spell had gone wrong. Quickly she tried to make things right.

Take back your feuds and angry looks.
In short, you guys, hit the books!

And with that, Sabrina's guests disappeared. The clocks and watches were all back to normal, but Libby and Mr. Kraft were more than a little confused. Sabrina just looked at them and smiled. "Weird dream, huh?" she asked. Then she ran out the door, clutching Cupid's arrow to her side.

As Sabrina got into her aunt's car, she felt very confident. She had another part of the clock now, and Cupid's arrow would ensure that love would endure throughout time. Best of all, she only had a few more pieces to go.

"I think I'm beginning to take control of the situation," she murmured.

Ping.

"Or maybe not," she said as she landed with a thud on her bedroom floor.

The Play's the Thing
By Brad Strickland

Sabrina could no longer tell if the Spellman house was the Spellman house. The living room was a grotto full of foot-tall pink mushrooms, and through an opening in the rock walls she could see a long-necked orange-striped dinosaur grazing on some ferns. The staircase had vanished, and in its place were two teleportation booths from a couple of centuries in the future. She stepped into the lower booth and out of the upper one.

Her room, thank goodness, was still her room. And in it, Justin Time sat tilted back in a chair with his feet propped up on her bed, munching on a sandwich. "Hi," he mumbled. "Hilda and Zelda are still with the Witches' Council, so I'm holding down the fort. Ready for your next trip?"

Sabrina rolled her eyes. "I'm exhausted! And I never know what time it is!"

"Does anybody really know what time it is?" Justin asked.

Salem strolled in. "Ask me if I really care," he said. He sniffed suspiciously. "What are you eating?"

Justin held up his sandwich and made a face. "Tuna, but it's terrible."

Sabrina said, "Ew! That's cat food!"

With a shrug, Justin replied, "Oh, well, for cat food it's not all that bad." And he took another bite. "You're doing pretty well so far, Sabrina. In fact, I can even tell you what you need to look for next. It's something that has held a lot of magic in its time, so a good part of the enchantment must have rubbed off."

"Hey, buddy, that's *my* tuna you're eating," complained Salem.

Sabrina ignored the irate cat. "What am I looking for?"

"A cauldron," Justin Time said. He held up the remnants of his sandwich. "Want the rest?"

Salem sniffed. "It's got people spit on it!"

"What cauldron?" Sabrina demanded, wanting to shake both of them.

"The cauldron of the Lancashire Witches," Justin said.

Sabrina wasn't sure she had heard correctly. "The what?"

"I know all about that!" Salem exclaimed.

"If you don't want the rest, I'll finish it," Justin said, popping the last bite of cat-food sandwich into his mouth.

"Come on!" Sabrina yelled. "Will you *please* tell me who or what the Lancashire Witches are, and how I can find their cauldron?"

"I can tell you," said Salem. "The Lancashire Witches lived in England in the sixteenth and seventeenth centuries. They were a terrific group! They were the most cooperative witches ever. I'd say their cauldron probably has gobs of good magic clinging to it."

"Time's getting very short," Justin added helpfully, rising from his chair. "Ready to go?"

"Okay, okay," Sabrina said. "Get me there!"

Salem ran to her feet. "Get *us* there!"

"What?" Sabrina said. "No way!"

"Big way!" the cat told her. "You don't know anything about the Lancashire Witches, and I know everything! I even used to date one of them! So I'm coming along as your guide. Let's get moving, Sabrina. I don't want to end my days as a common ordinary house cat! Come on, come on, we're wasting time!"

"Here you go," Justin said, and he snapped his fingers.

Sabrina went spinning back through time, back through space, and into pitch darkness. . . .

* * *

"Where are we?" she grumbled, feeling springy earth beneath her feet. The air smelled like ferns and oak leaves, and it was clammy and damp. Sabrina took a step in the darkness and—*whack!*—a wet branch slapped her across the face. "Yuck!"

"We're in a forest," came Salem's voice from near her feet. "Probably the one near Pendle Hill. That's where the coven used to meet. It's near Manchester."

"Well, I can't see a thing," Sabrina said, trying to untangle a persistent brier from her hair. "Ouch! Take a look around."

"Me?" Salem asked.

"Ouch," Sabrina said, finally disentangling the briar. "Yes, you. Cats can see in the dark, can't they?"

"Oh, let's stereotype the cat, shall we? Let me take a look," returned Salem sarcastically. "Oh, yes, indeedy. Very nice scenery, I must say. I can see the dark woods and the dark ground and the dark trees and the . . . you know what? To this cat, *everything* looks dark."

"Oh, give it up," Sabrina told him. "You asked to come along, remember? I didn't exactly invite—hmm." She sniffed. "I smell smoke."

She heard Salem take a deep snuffle. "So can I! And where there's smoke on a late, dark night, there's a fire. And where there's a fire, you might just find a cauldron! Come on—it's over this way."

Sabrina took a step and bumped into a tree. "Wait a minute, Salem! Which way?"

"This way," said Salem from somewhere ahead and to her left. She followed as best she could, tripping over a root every five or six steps. Then through the twisted black trunks of trees all around, she saw a warm reddish glow. Soon she was near enough to hear a woman's voice:

"When shall we thirteen meet again, in thunder, lightning, or in rain?"

"Rain?" asked a squeaky voice. "Alice, don't you dare call a meeting in the rain! I can't do anything with me hair when it's damp, and you knows it!"

"Anne, I was just trying for a bit of style," the first woman said with a sigh. "All right, all right, when can we get together again, weather permitting?"

After a pause, another woman—from the sound of her voice, Sabrina guessed she was younger than the others—said, "I can't meet next Saturday, 'cause my cousin's getting married and I'm the maid of honor."

"Monday's out for me," another one said. "Wash day, you know, and what with the new baby there's no end to the didies and washcloths."

"I can't make it Tuesday," said another voice. "I have a prior engagement in York."

"Me either," added a fifth. "Relatives visitin' from out of town."

Salem whispered, "Here we are! You go on. I'll, uh, sort of guard the rear."

"Salem?" Sabrina whispered, but trying to find a black cat in the dark was like trying to find one specific needle in a needle factory. Sabrina moved carefully through the ferns and undergrowth toward the fire, listening as the witches tried to set a new meeting date.

"Well, if everyone's tied up all next week, how about a week from Wednesday?" asked the first one.

"No good," said a sixth woman. "That's the day I'm to take the curse off Squire Robinson's cattle, and you know how many cattle he has. It's going to be an all-nighter, if I knows my witchcraft."

"That Thursday's good for me, though," someone else said. Murmurs of agreement arose, and by the time Sabrina stepped into the circle of ruddy firelight, the thirteen witches gathered around the campfire had all marked their calendars.

"Hello, Sabrina dear," said the tallest of the group, a handsome woman in middle age. "You've come for the cauldron, I expect."

"Huh?" Sabrina said.

"Because we're witches, of course," said a plump white-haired woman who looked a bit like a grandmother and a bit like a wrinkled apple. "My name is Alice, by the way. Oops, sorry, I've been reading the future all night long, and I'm still a few seconds ahead of everyone else. First you should ask the question."

"Uh, how did you know I came for the cauldron?" Sabrina asked.

"There you are," Alice replied with a smile. The smile faded as she turned to a thin, red-faced, embarrassed-looking young woman, probably not much older than Sabrina. "Jannet, you might want to explain the situation."

"Uh," Jannet said, turning even redder as she blushed. "Uh, I sort of, uh, lent the cauldron to someone and, uh, and—"

"And we never got it back," sniffed a portly dark-haired witch. "And see what we have to make do with now!"

Sabrina saw that they had all gathered around a sort of cauldron—if you could call a badly riveted iron bucket hanging over the red embers of a campfire a cauldron. "I sort of really need your real one," she said.

A red-haired witch patted her shoulder. "Of course you do. It's the Great Clock again, isn't it? I'm old enough to remember the YIK problem."

"Y *one* k," corrected Sabrina automatically.

"That wasn't what *we* called it," the redhead said. "We just said, 'The Great Clock's going to stop! Oh, dear! Yik, yik, yik!' " She paused thoughtfully. "Sounds a bit foolish when I tell about it now."

"Hey! How did you solve the YIK problem?"

"Sorry, dearie," she replied. "We responded before the deadline and Father Time took care of it all."

"Where's dear Salem?" the first witch asked. "I know he's with you, but where's he hiding?"

"I don't know," Sabrina said, looking around.

The head witch made a tutting sound. "As if I didn't have the foresight to know he's been changed into a cat!" She raised her voice and said, "I didn't mean to hurt anyone's *felines!*" With a wink at Sabrina, she said, "My name is Anne, dear. Anne with an *e.* Jannet, you were going to tell us about the cauldron."

"Uh," the youngest witch said. "Uh, the cauldron's probably in London. You see, some strolling players came through town, and they needed some props for their play, so . . . well, I lent the cauldron to one of them—a handsome young man, you know—and after the play, well, I sort of forgot about it, and they went back to London."

"Of course you have to," the grandmotherly Alice said, giving Sabrina a friendly, encouraging pat.

"I have to go to London, then," Sabrina said. Then she shook her head, confused. Alice was a few seconds ahead of her again.

"We'll send you, of course," the older witch told her kindly. *"Our* magic is still working properly. Get ready, dear."

"How will I get there?" Sabrina asked. Then she pressed her hands to her head. "Wait a minute. Please stop answering my questions before I ask them. It's making me crazy!"

Alice smiled apologetically. "I'm sorry, dear. I'm

almost completely back to the present now, anyway. Of course you will."

"All right," Sabrina said. "But I'll have to find Salem first."

"I'm here," said a small voice. Salem crept out from under a fern. "Hi, Annie," he muttered. "Long time no see."

"Well, you're not bad looking, for a cat," Anne said, winking at Sabrina. "All right, dear, pick him up and we'll send you straight to London. Jannet, who's she looking for?"

"The King's Men," Jannet said. "A London acting troupe. Their theater is in Southbank."

"We'll get you there about ten o'clock tomorrow morning," Anne said. "So everyone will be awake and you can get right down to business. Here you go!"

They began to chant:

"Our cauldron's gone, and that's a fact,
Where directors direct and actors act!
In London Town the stage is set—
Here goes Sabrina with her pet!"

Sabrina suddenly yelled, "Wait, wait! What year is this?"

The fading voice of Anne called back, "It's the third of June 1605! Good lu-u-u-u-uck!"

Salem grumbled, "Pet! Ha!"

And then bright sunlight stabbed Sabrina's

eyes, making her wince. She blinked until she could see again. "Great," she said to Salem. "I'm practically back where I started! Okay, let's see what we can do." She was standing on a roughly cobbled surface in a narrow alleyway between two buildings. In the distance she could see a river rushing past. The Thames, she supposed, since the city around her had to be London. When she ventured out of the alley, she found herself on a busy street filled with horses, wagons, and crowds of pedestrians. Dust rose everywhere, and the street smelled strongly of horses and the reminders they dropped. Wrinkling her nose, Sabrina stopped a friendly looking man and said, "Excuse me, could you tell me where to find the King's Men?"

"Eh, poppet?" the man said in surprise. "Why, what would'st thou? Prithee, maid, ye be not a Londoner, or an' ye do, thy speech rings strange!"

"Oh," Sabrina said. She bit her lip. Usually her magic automatically caused her to speak appropriately. *Guess I'm on my own now,* she thought. Aloud, she said, "Uh, prithee would'st thou tell me, sir, whereabout mayhap I might find the King's Men?"

"Marry," the man said with a laugh that lit up his broad red face, "have they not the whole Globe for a playhouse? Good day, wench!" He strolled off into the crowd.

"Might I suggest a little translation spell?"

Salem whispered in a voice hardly louder than a purr.

"Let's hope it works," Sabrina said through clenched teeth. "You know how unreliable my magic's getting." She thought a moment and then said,

No foreigner me. It's imperative!
Let me speak and understand like a native!

She heard the faint sound of bells tinkling, and then she tried again, stopping a woman this time.

"Excuse me," she said. "I'm new in town, and I'd like to know where I could see the King's Men."

The woman smiled. "I could tell from your outlandish dress that you're not from here," she said. "The King's Men act in the Globe Theater, dear. It's down the street and on your left. I think they plan to act a comedy today."

"Thanks!" Sabrina said. She plunged into the crowd, ducking and weaving—and occasionally sidestepping horse reminders—as she made her way toward the theater. To Salem, she whispered, "The Globe Theater, 1605. That means William Shakespeare, doesn't it?"

"You got it," Salem said. "What a hack! Stole every plot he ever used. If you ask me—"

"Shh!" Sabrina cautioned. "You should remember what they did to talking cats and witches in 1605! It involved stakes and bonfires, you know." Ahead of her she saw the theater, three stories high. Its plaster-and-lath walls were circular, and over the main doorway a signboard hung. It had no words on it, but a picture of Atlas holding up the globe showed clearly enough what it was.

Thinking she was in luck for a change, Sabrina made her way to the entrance and started through an arched, tunnel-like passage. A very large man stepped in front of her. "Hold it, lass," he said. "Theater's closed right now. No show this morning. Come back at two."

"I need to see Master Shakespeare," Sabrina said.

"Not a chance. He's busy," the man said. He was tall, with curly black hair and a rough, battered face. Sabrina didn't think he would be easily fooled.

From behind him, a balding, anxious-looking man said, "Heneage? Actors, I hope?"

"Nay, Master Will," the tall man said, turning to look over his shoulder. "Just a passing country wench, come too early for the show."

"Master William Shakespeare!" Sabrina called out. "May I have a word with you?"

"I've no time," Shakespeare said. He was wearing brown tights and a white shirt, the cuffs stained with black ink. He looked both exhausted and wild-eyed. "I've got to recast a major part for *A Midsummer Night's Dream*." He pulled at his long fringe of brown hair and lifted his eyes to the heavens. "Why, oh, why, did everyone keep telling the child to break a leg? Now see what's happened!"

"Uh, the actor broke a leg?" Sabrina guessed.

"Backed right off the stage and *crack!* Won't be able to act again for weeks! Now I'm without a Helena for my play! Where are my actors for auditions? Ordinarily, they crawl from the very woodwork, but today not a one so far! We've got four hours before the play starts! Come and see me in three or four days, young lady. I'm just too busy right now!" He turned and was gone.

The tall man loomed over Sabrina. "You heard Master Will. Three or four days," he rumbled.

"But that won't do," Sabrina said. "I don't *have* three or four days. I'm not even sure if I have *one!*"

Clearly, however, getting past the big man wasn't an option. Sabrina turned away, thinking furiously. Maybe the Globe had a back entrance. Maybe she could sneak in.

A walk around the walls told her that wasn't possible. "Man, the fire inspector should close this place down! The only entrance is the front door, and that's guarded. What am I going to do now?" she asked Salem.

"Hey, don't ask me," Salem said. "I didn't know this was going to turn into a wild-cauldron chase." He thought for a moment or two, and then he added, "Too bad you couldn't simply audition for the part of Helena. If they're having tryouts, that would get you inside."

"Brilliant!" Sabrina said. She looked around and ducked into another alley. When she was sure she was out of sight, she said, "Okay, let's hope I've got enough magic left for this, and that it behaves itself! Um, let me see." She chanted:

The script is ready, the play's the thing,
So let me get right in the swing!
Scenery, costumes, setting, stage!
Make me an actor of the Elizabethan age!

"No!" yelped Salem, but he was too late.

After a woozy moment of transformation, Sabrina said, "I feel funny." Her voice sounded odd, deeper than normal. She walked toward the street, passed a window, stopped, did a double take, and looked hard at her reflection in the glass. "No wonder I feel funny! I'm a boy!" she yelled.

"I tried to stop you," Salem said. "In the Elizabethan age, all the actresses were boys. Uh, I mean, all the women's parts were played by boys. And by the way, King James is on the throne now, so—"

"I'm kind of cute," Sabrina said, turning her head this way and that. She had short, curly brown hair and was wearing a velvet doublet over an open-collared white silk shirt, fawn-colored tights, and silver-buckled shoes. "Good build, too. I could sort of go for me. I mean, I'm no Harvey, but I'm pretty cute in a kind of English way." She smiled at her reflection. "And my teeth are good, too!" She'd been a boy once before, when she drank "Boy Brew," but this was different. She didn't know how boys of this time acted.

"Well, congratulations on your accomplishment," Salem said. "Remember, though, this spell may go blooey on you any second, or it may not last for long. And what if time runs out and you get stuck here in 1605 as a mortal boy?"

"I wouldn't like that so much," Sabrina admitted, uneasily aware again of how quickly time was passing. "Okay, let's do it!" She picked Salem up and carried him back to the entrance to the Globe. The tall man stepped in front of them, scratched himself, and asked, "What's your business, lad?"

"Uh, auditions," Sabrina said. She scratched herself. "I was in a pub nearby and I heard about them."

The tall man spat. "Yeah?"

Sabrina spat. "Right, right. I heard Master Will Shakespeare is looking for someone to play Helena. I'm your girl. Uh, guy. Uh, actor."

"Right you are. In you go," the guard said. "First door on your right, all the way around, into the tiring-house. They'll give you a script. Break a—"

"Don't say it!" Sabrina warned.

The guard grinned, looked sheepish, and scratched his head. "Uh, yeah. That's how we got into this mess, innit? Right."

Sabrina hurried through the door and found herself in the lowest of three tiers of seats. To her left, she saw the theater yard. Three men sat there on stools, and on stage a tall, pimply young man was singing in a high tenor voice. "He won't get the part," Sabrina whispered. "Too many zits!"

She found the second door, opened it, and stepped into a small room with a table and a chair in which a young man sat frowning at a piece of paper. A short, chubby man with spiky gray hair saw her, bustled over, and said, "Trying out for Helena, are you? Name, please?"

"Sa— uh, Samuel Spellman," Sabrina said quickly.

"Experience?"

"Oh, you know. Here and there. Village plays. That sort of thing," Sabrina said with a weak smile.

"Um-hmm," the man murmured. "Amateur acting it is." He handed her a sheet of paper. "Memorize this speech. You'll be asked to show your talent in any way you choose—song, dance, whatever. Then you'll have to deliver this monologue. You'll go on after Giles here."

Giles, a stocky young man with messy black hair, grinned weakly. "I've got butterflies in me stomach," he said in a high, piping voice.

Sabrina nodded weakly and found a quiet corner where she could study the script. When she was sure no one except Salem could hear her, she whispered, "Okay, I got us inside the theater. Now how do I find the cauldron?"

"It's gotta be backstage here somewhere," Salem said. "This room is called the tiring-house."

"Why's it called that?"

Salem glared. "I don't know. Maybe because the actors get so exhausted putting on and taking off their costumes? Clothes and props and things are stored backstage. Maybe I could sneak away and find the prop room."

"I can't do this!" said Giles suddenly, standing up. His eyes were terrified and wide. "I'm going back to the printer's, I am. Being an apprentice may be dull, but going on stage is downright scary!" He darted out.

"Scratch Master Giles," the gray-haired man said grimly. "All right, Master Samuel, you're on. Break a—"

"Don't say it," Sabrina groaned.

She walked hesitantly onto the stage. The theater had no roof, and the late-morning sunlight streamed in. In front of the stage, the theater yard had been covered with fresh straw. Three wooden stools stood there, a few feet away. Will Shakespeare sat on the middle one, his head in his hands, looking absolutely miserable. The man on his right did not look up from the big book in front of him. He dipped a quill pen into an inkwell balanced on his knee, held it over the book, and said, "Name, please?"

"Sa-Samuel Spellman," Sabrina told him, and he scribbled in the book.

"What's with the cat?" asked the man on Shakespeare's left, and Shakespeare's head came up sharply.

"It's, uh, a dummy," Sabrina said, trying to think fast. She laughed in an embarrassed way. "That's my talent that I'm going to show you. I'm a ventriloquist. I make the cat talk."

"I'll get you for this," Salem growled under his breath.

"I see," the first man said, looking up from his book. "Do you need any props?"

"Just a chair," Sabrina said. She stepped back as the gray-haired man brought one from backstage. To Salem, she whispered, "Act like a puppet! This is our only chance!"

"As if anyone would be fooled by a real cat pretending to be a puppet," huffed Salem. But he clenched his teeth and added, "Okay, okay, I'll play along. I know a lot of jokes."

"Not your corny old jokes," Sabrina groaned.

Salem had gone limp. "It's the seventeenth century! They'll be new jokes! Trust me! We'll knock 'em in the aisles! We're on," Salem whispered.

Sabrina sat in the chair. She put her hand behind Salem, as if she were operating a ventriloquist's dummy. He straightened up and stiffly turned his head from left to right. Sabrina thought he made a pretty convincing dummy. She cleared her throat and said, "Hi, folks. We're Sam and Salem. Hey, we just got into London this morning. How do you like London, Salem?"

Moving his head in a jerky way, staring at nothing with glassy eyes, Salem said, "Huh! You're such a cheapskate! You booked us into the chintziest inn in town!"

"What's wrong with the inn?" Sabrina asked.

"What's wrong with it!" Salem exclaimed. "Why, the room's so small, I have to go outside to change my mind! The ceiling's so low, all the mice are humpbacked!"

"You're grumpy today, Salem," Sabrina said. "What's the matter? Did you get up on the wrong side of the bed?"

"That bed is so narrow it only *has* one side!" Salem snapped.

Sabrina felt her smile freezing on her face. Nobody was laughing. She said, "Well, don't you think—"

"Ah, yes," Shakespeare called from the pit. "Very, uh, very, yes. Good ventriloquism, your lips hardly moved, but I presume you got your material from a joke book? A very *old* joke book?"

Sabrina shrugged.

The three men whispered together for a few moments, and then Shakespeare said, "Sam, where have you acted before, exactly?"

"Here and there," Sabrina said. "I played Sleeping Beauty when I was eight years old. And I've been in other plays." Sensing she was losing him, she added desperately, "I've done lots of dinner theater."

Shakespeare gave her a long blank look. "Dinner theater?"

They didn't have dinner theater back then, she realized. She said, "Uh, I mean, I've acted for my dinner. A lot."

"Acted for your dinner," Shakespeare repeated wearily. "I see. Well, Sam, I'd advise you to get another act if you plan to stay in London. That ventriloquist bit might be all right for the provinces, but this is a sophisticated London audience we're talking about. And you'll certainly need a more realistic-looking dummy."

Keeping her forced smile in place, Sabrina kept a tight hold on Salem, who was growling. "Thank you, Master Will."

"You're welcome. Now, have you memorized the speech?"

"No," Sabrina admitted.

Shakespeare sighed, picked up a bound script, and walked to the apron of the stage. "A cold reading, then. Helena's speech on this page, if you please."

Sabrina stood up and turned to put Salem on the chair. "Take a nap," she whispered. "You're a puppet, remember."

Salem glowered at her, but he went limp.

Sabrina took the book from Shakespeare, read through the speech once, and found that it had stuck in her memory. *Must be the spell,* she thought. *It's made me a good actor.* Feeling a surge of confidence, Sabrina laid the book down and stepped to center stage. Trying to imitate her own natural voice, she began to speak: "How happy some o'er other some can be! / Through Athens I am thought as fair as she. / But what of that? Demetrius thinks not so; / He will not know what all but he do know."

Sabrina kept an eye on Shakespeare as she recited the rest of the speech. She saw him sit up straight, his eyes wide. The playwright waved his hands, an excited expression on his face. "Stop, stop! You've acted this role before, haven't you?"

"No," Sabrina said, surprised.

"You mean to tell me you just glanced at the page and memorized it?" Shakespeare demanded. "Just like that?"

"I've, uh, always been a quick study," Sabrina told him.

"Do you know any other speeches?" Shakespeare asked suspiciously.

For perhaps the first time in her life, Sabrina thanked her lucky stars for English class, where she had been forced to memorize a Shakespearean speech. "Sure," she said. "In fact, I saw a play that your troupe acted in Manchester not long ago, and I can remember a speech from it. How's this?" Striking a dramatic pose, she began to recite Lady Macbeth's lines: "The Thane of Fife had a wife: where is she now?"

Shakespeare listened to the speech and murmured the next cue line: "The Gentlewoman answers: 'She has spoke what she should not, I am sure of that: heaven knows what she has known.'"

Sabrina picked up the cue, pretending to scrub her hands: "Here's the smell of the blood still: all the perfumes of Arabia will not sweeten this little hand. Oh, oh, oh!"

Shakespeare clapped his hands. "Well done, well done, Master Samuel!"

"Thank you," Sabrina said, taking a bow. "That's a speech from *Mac*—"

"Stop!" yelled all three men at once.

Shakespeare mopped his bald head with a handkerchief. "Don't say it!"

"Uh, okay," Sabrina said, confused.

"Gentlemen, we have our Helena!" roared Will Shakespeare.

The man who had handed him the script said, "Will, the costume won't fit him."

"We'll find another costume!" Shakespeare said. "He's here and he can memorize the script. We go on in three and a half hours!"

"After all," Sabrina added helpfully, "the play's the thing, isn't it?"

"Yes, exactly," said Shakespeare, smiling. "The play's the thing. One of my better lines. Come lad, and I'll find you a costume and give you the script!"

Will led Sabrina backstage, where they rooted out a blond wig and a rather pretty lavender dress with a black velvet bodice. "I'll, uh, change after I read through the script," Sabrina said, putting the limp form of the "puppet" Salem down in a corner. "Now, about my pay—"

"Standard salary," Will Shakespeare said. "After three years' apprenticeship, you get a percentage of the house. Until then—"

"I don't want any money. I just want one of your props," Sabrina told him.

"A prop?" Shakespeare asked blankly.

"Yes. A cauldron your troupe picked up in Manchester. I think you used it for *Mac-*"

"Don't say that title!" Shakespeare ordered. "Lad, we call it the Scottish play. 'Tis a bad bit of work, I fear, and each time we play it, it brings naught but ill luck. Even to say its true title aright inside a theater is to doom the performance of that day. Look ye, here's the script. I have a thousand details to attend to. Be ready, for we go on at two."

As soon as she was alone, Sabrina changed into the dress. "Something feels funny," she muttered. "People are starting to sound Shakespearean again."

Salem raised his head, saw that the coast was clear, and sat up. "Your spells are wearing off," he said. "Time's running out."

"You'd better see if you can find that cauldron," Sabrina said, buttoning her bodice. It was a tight fit. No doubt about it—she was a girl again. She picked up the script and realized with a flood of panic that her super memory was seeping away, too. She flipped pages, desperately trying to cram all of Helena's speeches into her head before the spell went completely.

At one-thirty, Will Shakespeare, dressed as Egeus, the father in the comedy, stopped to ask her how things were going.

"Not so hot," she had to admit. "I've got all the speeches by heart down to the last few pages, but I'm, uh, tired. I'm not sure I can get these one, two, three—these last five speeches."

"Make shift, lad, make shift!" Shakespeare said urgently.

"I have an idea," Sabrina said. "Could you bring me, like, some ink and a quill and some paper? A *big* quill and some *large* paper?"

"Of course," Shakespeare said. "But wherefore?"

"To make cue cards," Sabrina said.

"Cue cards?" Shakespeare looked at her as if one of them had gone completely nuts, and he wasn't sure which.

But the paper and quill came, and Sabrina hastily printed out the speeches. "Now," she said, "if someone out in the crowd could hold these up just at the right time, I'll read them."

"Marry, you have hit a device of wondrous use!" Shakespeare exclaimed. "The top box nearest stage right is not sold. I shall have Master Dickon hold the cards for thee. E'en with a broken leg, he can do that!"

Just past two o'clock, Sabrina stepped on stage

with a sick feeling of failure in the pit of her stomach. Hundreds of people stood in the theater yard, craning their necks to see her. More hundreds sat on benches in the three tiers of galleries all around the stage. And her first line had gone right out of her head!

But then the boy playing Hermia came to her and said, "Godspeed, fair Helena! Whither away?"

And to her surprise, Sabrina heard herself come right back with Helena's line: "Call you me fair? That fair again unsay!"

It was almost as if the theater had its own magic. From that moment on, Sabrina coasted through. Even toward the end of the play, after Puck and the fairies had mixed all the lovers up and then unmixed them, she could read the cue cards without any problem. Finally, Puck made his curtain speech—"If we shadows have offended, think but this and all is mended"—and the actors took their bows.

Sabrina rushed backstage. Salem waited for her there. "Found it," he whispered. "It's this way!"

Grabbing her real clothes, Sabrina followed him upstairs to a small, dark room. She hastily took off the wig and changed from the Helena costume. "Where is it?" she asked.

"Under here!" Salem dived into a low shelf, and Sabrina stooped. She saw the iron cauldron, grabbed it, and hauled it out, grunting. It was small but heavy.

"Finally!" she said.

From behind her, a mild voice said, "Lad, they'll dock my pay if thou steal'st it."

Sabrina turned. Will Shakespeare stood in the doorway, hands on hips. "Uh, hi," she said.

Shakespeare shook his head as he peered into the dark room. "Much thanks for saving the play, Samuel. I see thou hast changed thy garments. Pray do not forget to leave the wig as well. But art thou indeed so enamored of that rusty pot that thou would'st risk the clink? For stealing is a crime, thou know'st."

"Uh, look," Sabrina said. "I'll level with you. I know the reason that *Mac*— No, I won't say it! I know the Scottish play is jinxed. It so happens that this cauldron once belonged to some *real* witches. It, uh, it hath no nonstick coating, so much magic hath stuck to it. Here, I'll show thee. Where hideth mine cat puppet?" She reached onto the shelf again and plucked out the slack form of Salem. "Behold, a puppet." She put him into the cauldron. "And now . . . a living cat!"

Salem poked his head out. "Hi!" he said.

Shakespeare laughed. "Well, well, mayhap 'tis worth the price of a cauldron to see such a trick. Take it, lad, take it for thy pay, and let me give thee a word of advice. Go back to the provinces, my boy. If thou wishest to be a player, wait until thy voice hath changed, then try again. Thou hast some talent, but truly none would take thee for a real girl."

"What!" Sabrina yelled. Then she took a deep breath. "Uh, I mean, thanks. Gotta go! All's well that ends well, I guess, huh?"

Shakespeare blinked. "All's well that ends well," he muttered. "All's well that ends ... Where's my quill? Paper! I need paper and ink! Now!"

And Sabrina, carrying Salem in one hand and the cauldron in the other, left him to his playwriting.

To Tell the Tooth
By Nancy Krulik

Ping!

Sabrina felt a small jolt as she suddenly popped into her third period history class. She wasn't really all that surprised to wind up back at school. By now she was used to the fact that much of her magic was out of her control.

She looked around the dreary classroom and sighed miserably. For some reason her history class was suddenly being taught by Mr. Kraft, the vice-principal, instead of by her usual history teacher. That was *not* a good sign. Having Mr. Kraft around usually meant trouble for Sabrina. And if there was one thing she did not need today, it was another calamity.

But trouble *was* in the air. Mr. Kraft smiled diabolically, picked up a pile of papers, and passed them around the room. "Surprise! It's time for a pop quiz. You will have thirty minutes to finish this exam," Mr. Kraft told the class. "There will be no hall passes, no talking, no looking at your neighbor's paper. You may begin."

Great! A test during vacation! With a sigh Sabrina looked down at the paper in front of her. None of the questions seemed at all familiar. It was as though she had forgotten everything she'd ever learned about history. This was like some sort of weird dream. No, not a dream. A nightmare!

"Calm down, Sabrina," she whispered to herself. "Just take these questions one at a time."

Sabrina focused on the paper in front of her and read the first question: "Patrick Henry once proclaimed, 'Give me liberty or give me _____.'"

Sabrina's stomach rumbled. She had been so busy working on fixing the Great Clock that she hadn't taken time to eat. Now the only thing she could concentrate on was food. Without thinking, Sabrina scribbled three words in the blank: "a ham sandwich." She was pretty sure that wasn't what Patrick Henry had said, but at least she'd put something down.

It was obvious to Sabrina that taking a history test during winter vacation, when school wasn't even open, had something to do with the Great Clock. Sabrina wasn't sure if Justin Time had sent her into the past or the future, but she did know there must be an object here that she could use to build the clock. The problem was, every time she lifted her eyes from her paper to look for that object, Mr. Kraft glared at her. And she couldn't get up to look around the school; Mr. Kraft had clearly said that no hall passes would be given out.

By the time Mr. Kraft announced, "Pencils down," Sabrina knew she had failed the test—big time! She stood wearily and looked around the classroom for something she could use for the clock.

"Boy, that was a rough test," Harvey said as he swung his backpack over his shoulder and stepped up next to Sabrina. "I hope I got enough answers right to get at least a C. How'd you do Sabrina?"

"That test was definitely one for the history books," Sabrina joked weakly. "Anyway, I'm glad it's over."

"Are you heading to the cafeteria?" Harvey asked her.

Sabrina knew she should look around for items to use on the Great Clock, but, hey, even a witch on a mission had to eat. She nodded at Harvey and walked down the hall beside him. But just as she reached the cafeteria door . . .

Ping!

"Surprise!" Mr. Kraft announced to the class. "It's time for a pop quiz. You will have thirty minutes to finish this exam. There will be no hall passes, no talking, no looking at your neighbor's paper. You may begin."

Oh, no! History class is repeating itself! Sabrina buried her head in her hands and looked down at the quiz paper in front of her. There it was, the same question about Patrick Henry. And she still could not recall the answer.

"Why is this happening to me? I can't remember a thing!" Sabrina moaned quietly as she picked up her pencil. "Who cares about history anyway?"

Mr. Kraft walked by. "If history is forgotten, it will repeat itself, Sabrina," he remarked.

Sabrina jumped up out of her seat. "That's it!" she exclaimed as she ran for the door.

"Sabrina Spellman, where are you going?" Mr. Kraft demanded.

"Sorry, Mr. Kraft. I can't stay," Sabrina told him. "I have to go find a piece of history!"

Sabrina would have liked to pop home using her powers, but the way magic was going lately, there was no telling where she might wind up if she tried that. So, instead, she ran all the way home.

By the time Sabrina reached her bedroom, she was out of breath, hot and sweaty. She plopped down on her bed next to Salem, who promptly jumped out of the way.

"Ooooh," the cat moaned. "Take a shower!"

"I have an idea about another item we need for the Great Clock! I need a piece of history."

Salem moaned again. "Well, that narrows it down to about two billion years," he said sarcastically.

"Then I'd better get started," Sabrina replied. She glanced at the hourglass that sat beside her on the desk. The sand was almost half gone now. There was no time to waste. Sabrina began going through her history textbook page by page, looking for something that might work.

"Do you have any idea what you're looking for?" Salem asked her. "I sure hope so, because it's not like something is just going to jump up and bite you."

Sabrina ignored her cat and kept reading. There was no time to argue.

Salem was also aware that time was slipping by. "You'd better hurry up," he urged Sabrina. "Otherwise everything you've become accustomed to in your life will disappear in an instant!"

Ping! Sabrina felt Justin's time-travel magic setting in again. When she opened her eyes, she found herself beside a blue lake in a beautiful tropical garden. There were palm trees everywhere. Sabrina took a deep breath. The air was so pure, it practically hurt her lungs. And there wasn't another person in sight.

"Where am I?" Sabrina asked out loud. *"When* am I?"

Just then she heard a loud rustling coming from behind a row of palm trees. She turned around to see the biggest lizard she had ever seen. It had to be as tall as an apartment building, with a huge green tail as long as a limousine.

Wait a minute! That's no lizard. That's a dinosaur!

Sabrina tried hard not to panic. After all, she remembered that not all dinosaurs were carnivores that ate meat. Some were plant-eating herbivores. The huge dinosaur opened its mouth and let out a roar that shook the treetops. Squinting in the sun, Sabrina saw a mouth full of huge sharp teeth.

That dinosaur is no herbivore!

"*Justin!* Get me out of here!" Sabrina screamed desperately.

The dinosaur bent down, opened its mouth even wider and—

Ping!

Sabrina found herself safely back in her room.

"That's it!" Sabrina breathlessly told Salem. "I need a dinosaur tooth!"

Salem looked at her with a quizzical expression—or as close as he could get with his small, furry face. "Why?" he asked.

"I need to place something in the clock that will preserve history. A dinosaur tooth would do that, and it would also be a reminder that things can disappear forever," Sabrina explained.

"Good thinking," Salem replied. "Now, genius, where are you going to get your hands on a dinosaur tooth?"

Sabrina sighed. She wasn't going back to the time of the dinosaurs again, that was for sure. She could try popping into the Natural History Museum in Boston, but with magic so unpredictable, there was no telling where she might wind up.

"Oh, this is just great," Sabrina sighed. "I figure out a piece of this puzzle, but I can't get my hands on it. I mean, who do I know who would just happen to have a dinosaur tooth lying around?"

Sabrina was so upset that she started biting her nails, as she had often done in stressful situations ever since she was a child. She remembered her mother telling her when she was a little girl that if she kept biting her nails she would wear down her teeth until there was nothing left to leave for the Tooth Fairy.

The Tooth Fairy!

Sabrina opened her desk drawer and began dumping papers all over the floor.

"Have you lost your mind, Sabrina?" Salem asked her.

"No, just my tooth," Sabrina answered.

"You lost those years ago."

"I saved one baby tooth," Sabrina explained. "When I was about eight, I wanted to see if the Tooth Fairy would leave some money under my pillow even if I didn't leave her a tooth."

"Did she?" Salem asked. No matter what the situation, Salem was always interested in stories about money.

Sabrina shook her head. "Nope. My mother told me that was because the Tooth Fairy doesn't *give* children money. She *trades* money for their teeth." She pulled a small brown envelope from the desk drawer and peeked inside. "Here it is."

Sabrina took the small white tooth out of the envelope and placed it under her pillow. Sure enough, within seconds a rush of wind came through Sabrina's window. The wind carried with it a small woman with bright red hair. She wore a white lace dress and tiny silk slippers. On her back were two large delicate wings. She looked at Sabrina through tired bloodshot eyes.

"Aren't you a little old for this?" she asked Sabrina. "I only trade for baby teeth, you know."

Sabrina reached under her pillow and pulled out her tooth. "This is a baby tooth. It's been a few years since it fell out."

The fairy took the tooth from Sabrina and examined it. "Looks like the real thing," she proclaimed and handed Sabrina a crisp new dollar bill.

"Wow! I only used to get a quarter," Sabrina exclaimed.

"Inflation," the Tooth Fairy explained simply.

"But I don't want any money for the tooth," Sabrina told the Tooth Fairy. "I want to trade this tooth for one that's older and bigger. I need a dinosaur tooth. Do you happen to have any?"

The Tooth Fairy nodded. "Of course I do. But I don't trade teeth for teeth. I only trade teeth for money. However, if you really want the tooth, we could make a deal."

"I'll give you anything!" Sabrina vowed.

"How about trading lives for a while?" the Tooth Fairy asked Sabrina.

Sabrina looked curiously at the Tooth Fairy. "What do you mean?"

"Look, I haven't had a night off in centuries," the Tooth Fairy said. "I've never seen even one of the top-ten prime-time TV shows! For once, I'd like to sit back, eat a pint of Häagen-Dazs, and channel-surf while someone else does the flying."

"What do I have to do?" Sabrina asked her. "Is it hard work?"

"It's not brain surgery or anything. You just put on the wings and trade the teeth for cash." The Tooth Fairy pulled a list out of her pocket and opened it up. The list reached all the way to the floor. "Here are the names of kids who lost teeth today. If you go to all of their houses, I'll give you a dinosaur tooth."

Sabrina gulped. That was a long list! How was she ever going to visit all of those kids?

The Tooth Fairy laughed at Sabrina's shocked expression. "Hey, this is nothing. I've only got the northern corridor tonight. You should see what happens when I work a double shift. Relax. It goes pretty quickly once you get the hang of it."

Sabrina took the list from the Tooth Fairy's hand and read it over. There were plenty of names but no addresses. "How do I know which houses to go to?" she asked.

The Tooth Fairy slipped off her wings and placed them on Sabrina's back. "These babies are attracted to teeth like magnets to a refrigerator," she said. Then she removed her pearly white necklace and placed it around Sabrina's neck. "You'll need this, too. Can't be a Tooth Fairy without it."

Sabrina looked down at the necklace. It was a collection of baby teeth. "Yuck!" Sabrina exclaimed. "These things have been in people's mouths."

The Tooth Fairy had no sympathy. She simply handed Sabrina a white leather pouch filled with brand-new dollar bills. "Better get going. You have a lot of teeth to trade for. Those Gummi Bears are keeping me really busy," she said.

Sabrina's back ached under the weight of the wings. They looked as light as a feather, but they felt like iron. Still, the wings had to be more reliable than Sabrina's magic was lately. She tentatively climbed up on the windowsill and prepared to fly off on her tooth mission.

"Hey, where do you guys keep the boob tube?" the Tooth Fairy asked as Sabrina took off.

"It's in the living room," Sabrina called out as she flapped her wings and headed for the first house on the Tooth Fairy's list.

Sabrina's first stop took her way up to the coast of Maine and straight into the bedroom of Katie Lewis. Sabrina flew in through Katie's bedroom window and stared at the sleeping girl. She looked so sweet in her little plaid nightgown with a teddy bear wrapped in her arms. Gently, Sabrina slid her hand under Katie's pillow, removed a small white eyetooth, and placed a crisp new dollar bill in its place.

That was easy, Sabrina thought as she placed the tooth in her pocket and walked back toward the window. *I'll have that dinosaur tooth in no time!*

"Hey! Get out of my room. Help! Burglar!"

Sabrina was shocked by the loudness of the high-pitched shouts. She turned around to find Katie sitting straight up in bed, screaming at the top of her lungs. This was not good. If Sabrina got caught in Katie's room, someone might think she really was a burglar. And with her magic as unreliable as it was, she might not get out of the room in time to avoid a jail sentence. Sabrina ran over to the bed and tried to quiet Katie.

"Shhh," Sabrina urged the frightened six-year-old. "I'm not a burglar. I'm the Tooth Fairy. See, I've got the wings and the necklace and everything. Check under your pillow. I already left you a dollar."

Katie slipped her hand under the pillow. Sure enough, she pulled a dollar out.

"See?" Sabrina said as she walked back toward the window. "Told ya. Now I'm in kind of a hurry so—"

But before Sabrina could reach the window ledge, Katie opened her mouth to scream once more.

"What's wrong now?" Sabrina asked, rushing back to the girl. "Why are you afraid of the Tooth Fairy? Everyone loves the Tooth Fairy."

Katie shook her head emphatically. "You're not the Tooth Fairy," she said.

Uh-oh. Sabrina hadn't counted on the kids knowing what the Tooth Fairy really looked like. "Sure I am," she replied nervously.

"You can't be," Katie insisted.

"Why not?"

"Because there's no such thing. When my teeth fall out, it's my mommy who puts the money under my pillow."

Sabrina looked surprised. "Who told you that?"

"My big cousin Jesse," Katie said proudly. "He's fourteen, and he knows everything!"

Sabrina sighed. There was nothing like an older cousin to ruin a child's imagination. Sabrina was furious. Children were supposed to believe in the Tooth Fairy. It was one of the most magical parts of childhood.

"Okay, I'll level with you," Sabrina told Katie finally. "I'm not the Tooth Fairy."

Katie opened her mouth wide once again. But before the girl could scream, Sabrina added, "I'm a friend of hers. I'm just doing her a favor tonight. The Tooth Fairy really does exist!"

Katie laughed. "Oh, sure. And I'll bet Santa Claus and the Sandman are real people, too."

Sabrina was sad. She couldn't believe a little girl

like Katie could be so cynical. She had to do something to make this child believe again. But what could she do? Sabrina knew better than to disturb anyone in the Other Realm—they were all busy trying to solve the Great Clock problem—but this was a real emergency. Sabrina had no choice. She shut her eyes, put her fingertips to her forehead, and concentrated. No matter how weak her magic was, she just had to get this message out to the OR. Quickly she chanted a spell:

*Santa, leave the trains, dolls, and elves
    behind.
I need you here to change Katie's mind.
And, Sandman, let the dreamers be.
It's important for you to be here with me.*

Sabrina opened her eyes and waited. And waited. And *waited*. But nothing happened.

Katie looked at Sabrina and shrugged. "Told you so."

Sabrina sighed. There was nothing more she could do. She walked to the window and prepared to fly off. But before she could flap her wings, she was greeted by a gust of polar air.

"Ho-ho-ho!" Santa Claus shouted as his sled whisked in through the open window. "Sorry it took so long for me to get here, but Rudolph has a cold, and his red nose kept flashing on and off. It's hard for me to navigate the sled when that happens. Plus,

I'm a little tired from last week. So what can I do for you Sabrina?"

Sabrina smiled. "I think you've already done it," she said, pointing to Katie. The little girl was staring open-mouthed at Santa Claus.

"Do you know who you are?" Katie babbled nervously, pointing to Santa.

Santa smiled. "Ho-ho-ho!" he laughed. "I believe I do. And I know who *you* are, too, Katie. I know when you are sleeping; I know when you're awake. I also know if you've been naughty or nice. And if you want that pony next year, you'd better start cleaning your room."

Katie gulped and hastily threw an old chocolate bar wrapper in the wastebasket.

"Enough of this excitement. It's bedtime," the Sandman announced as he jumped into the room. He straightened his long white nightgown, adjusted his white stocking cap, and pulled out a handful of magic sleeping sand.

"Boy, I'd better close that window tomorrow night," Katie whispered Sabrina. "Anyone can get in here."

Sabrina shook her head. "Not anyone," she assured Katie. "Just folks with magic."

The Sandman's magic sand reminded Sabrina that time was passing quickly. The sand in that hourglass was rapidly shifting toward the bottom. If Sabrina didn't get moving, she'd never gather all of the items she needed for the Great Clock of the Other

Realm. And if time ran out, no one would have any magic, not even Santa! Sabrina would hate for mean kids like Katie's older cousin Jesse to be right about there not being any magic left in the world.

"I think you're in good hands," Sabrina told Katie. "Santa and the Sandman can answer any questions you might have. I've got more houses to visit. See ya!"

And with that, Sabrina jumped out into the night sky. Suddenly she felt a hard tug on her wings. *That magnetic pull the Tooth Fairy told me about sure is strong,* Sabrina thought.

Sabrina headed to houses all over New Hampshire, Vermont, Rhode Island, Massachusetts, and Connecticut, and she managed to get in and out of every one without waking a single child. By the time she left the Carp twins' room, Sabrina was feeling extremely confident. This Tooth Fairy thing was kind of fun.

Sabrina felt another sudden tug on her wings. She turned southward and began flying toward New York City. She was off to visit Ronald Towers.

When Sabrina arrived at Ronald's apartment, she was careful not to rest on the windowsill in Ronald's room. A small sign in the window said that the apartment was protected against break-ins. The wings allowed her to pass through the glass without breaking it. But even so, after Katie's screaming, Sabrina took care to be extra quiet.

Ronald's room was dark except for a night-light that burned in the corner of the room. Sabrina smiled. She remembered being little enough to be afraid of monsters in the dark, and asking her parents for a night-light. Of course, she now knew that some of those night monsters were really nice guys. It was the monsters like Libby, who hung out in high schools during the day, that were really to be feared.

Sabrina tiptoed over to Ronald's bed and gently tried to slip the tooth out from under his pillow. Ronald immediately sat up in bed and flashed a bright yellow light in her eyes. He grabbed Sabrina's hand to keep her from touching his tooth. "Wait!" he ordered Sabrina. "You're not just *taking* that tooth!"

"Don't worry. I'm the Tooth Fairy, not a thief," Sabrina assured Ronald.

"I know who you are," Ronald said. "What I want to know is how badly do you want this tooth?"

"What are you talking about?" she asked.

"I've read all about you Tooth Fairies. I know that trading is your game. It's your job to collect *all* the teeth that fall out of kids' mouths—of which this is one." He held up a yellowed baby tooth with a cavity in it. "I also know you give every kid a dollar for his tooth."

"That's right," Sabrina told him. She waved a crispy dollar bill in the air. "And here's yours. So if you'll just hand over that tooth, I'll give you your cash and be on my way."

"I'll want a lot more than one little dollar," Ronald demanded. "This isn't just any old tooth. It was hard work losing this sucker. You wouldn't believe what I had to go through! Terry Burns punched it out."

"Is Terry Burns a tough guy?" Sabrina asked.

"Really tough. Terry is the toughest kid in school," Ronald assured her. "And worse yet, Terry is a *girl*. Do you have any idea how humiliating that was?" Sabrina thought it was really cool that the toughest kid at Ronald's school was a girl. But she couldn't let him know how she felt. Time was running out, and Sabrina really needed Ronald's tooth.

"What do you want for the tooth?" Sabrina asked Ronald finally.

"About ten bucks would do it," Ronald told her.

Sabrina could feel the color rising in her cheeks. This kid was really getting on her nerves. But Sabrina held on to her sweet-fairy persona. "I only have enough money for each child to receive one dollar," she explained as patiently as possible.

Ronald walked over to his desk and pulled out a brown ledger book. He opened to a fresh page and pulled out a black pen. "That's okay," Ronald told Sabrina. "I'm sure we can work something out. You can give me one dollar now and pay me the rest in weekly installments—with interest, of course."

"Are you out of your mind?" Sabrina demanded, all of her fairylike cool disappearing. "I'm not giving you ten bucks."

Ronald didn't even break a sweat. "Then I'm not giving you this tooth," he said calmly. "And I know you need it. Otherwise, you haven't done your job. And you know what happens to fairies who don't do their jobs, don't you?"

"What?" Sabrina asked him.

Ronald smiled and slid his finger across his neck like a dagger. "Does the term 'pink slip' mean anything to you? Fairies who don't *do* their jobs *lose* their jobs. Now if you'll just sign this contract . . ."

Sabrina looked from the window to Ronald's desk. The kid was right. She did need his tooth. Otherwise the Tooth Fairy would not give her the dinosaur tooth she needed for the new Great Clock. And the Tooth Fairy would expect her back soon. There was no time to argue with Ronald. Sabrina really had no choice.

"Okay, Ronald, have it your way," she said slowly.

"You mean you'll sign the contract?" Ronald asked triumphantly. He held his pen out to Sabrina.

Sabrina shook her head and walked toward the window. "No, you get to keep your tooth," Sabrina said. "Your price is too steep for me. See ya!" She spread her wings as wide as they would go.

Ronald jumped up from his desk. A single tear fell from his eye and ran down the right side of his face.

Sabrina couldn't believe it. "The Ronald" was crying.

"But you can't leave without trading," Ronald wept. "Can you?"

Sabrina nodded. "Of course I can," she assured him. "It's in my union contract."

Ronald pouted. "I've always hated unions," he told Sabrina. "Okay. Sometimes a guy has to take the best offer he can get." Ronald handed the tooth to Sabrina.

Sabrina reached into her pouch and pulled out a dollar bill. "Here you go," she said as she examined the boy's partially rotted molar. "But do yourself a favor, Ronald. Brush your teeth a little better. And floss. Remember, you don't get any money when you lose your permanent teeth."

She waited for Ronald to crawl back under the covers. Then Sabrina flew out the window with a grace that would have impressed even Superman. She really had this flying-with-wings thing down to a science. She also seemed to be becoming a real businesswoman. "I guess bluffing is the real art of the deal." Sabrina laughed to herself as she flew off to her final stop, across the river in New Jersey.

Sabrina's last visit was on a quiet tree-lined street. All of the houses looked exactly alike. They were all white ranch-style homes with green shutters, perfectly manicured lawns, and two cars in the driveway. Sabrina hoped that her wings didn't fly her into the wrong house by mistake.

Sabrina finally landed on a windowsill of the

third house on her right. She peeked inside and saw a ten-year-old boy sleeping soundly in his bed. Sabrina looked at her list. *This must be Jason Smith,* she thought to herself as she hopped off the sill and into the room.

Sabrina stepped gingerly toward the bed. It wasn't easy. Jason's room practically qualified as a national disaster area. Socks hung from the lamps, a pile of smelly T-shirts took up most of the floor, and Jason's jeans were rolled up in a ball at the foot of his bed. And speaking of balls, Jason had a huge collection of them. Sabrina almost had to fly to avoid tripping over Jason's tennis ball, baseball, softball, soccer ball, and basketball. "Ow!" Sabrina moaned as quietly as possible, she stubbed her toe on a submarine built entirely of Legos, which was hidden beneath a pair of gym shorts.

When she finally made it to the bed, she reached under Jason's pillow and gingerly felt around until she found the small hard tooth he had placed there. She gripped the tooth between her fingertips and began to slide it out from under the pillow.

Zap!

Sabrina felt a sharp shock fly through her fingers and down through her body.

"Ouch!" she shouted as she yanked her hand out from under the pillow. Then she covered her mouth. She didn't want to wake Jason.

Once again she slipped her fingers underneath the pillow and reached for the tooth.

Zap! Sabrina bit her sleeve to muffle her scream. The shock was even stronger this time. Something was going wrong. And it hurt—badly! This mission was getting dangerous. Sabrina didn't wait around to find out what would happen next. Great Clock or no Great Clock, she was getting out of there!

When Sabrina returned home, she found the Tooth Fairy sitting in the living room with a big bowl of popcorn in her lap, watching TV. She was staring blankly at the screen. Her bloodshot eyes didn't seem to be registering anything. Every now and then she would change the channel and eat another kernel of popcorn.

"Hello, I'm back!" Sabrina announced. "I just flew in from New Jersey, and boy are my wings tired!"

The Tooth Fairy used the remote to switch channels once again. "Did you get all the teeth?" she asked without ever looking away from the TV.

"Well," Sabrina began sheepishly, "not exactly. I—"

The Tooth Fairy sat up and clicked off the TV. "What do you mean, not exactly?" she demanded. "That was our deal. You collect the kids' teeth and I give you the dinosaur tooth."

"I tried," Sabrina insisted, "but at the last house I had trouble getting the tooth out from under the pillow. I kept getting zapped."

The Tooth Fairy grabbed the list of names from Sabrina's hand. "Let me see that. Who lives at the last house?" The Tooth Fairy looked at the name and shook her head.

"What's wrong?" Sabrina asked her.

"That kid never learns," the Tooth Fairy said. "Jason Smith has been pulling this stunt for the past six months. He buys teeth from the kids in his class for eighty-five cents apiece."

"Why would they sell their teeth to him at that price when you would give them a dollar?"

"He usually gets to the kids who lose a tooth at lunchtime by biting into an apple or something. They sell him their teeth so they can buy an extra snack. Then he puts some other kid's tooth under his pillow and expects me to give him a dollar. It never works. But you've got to give the kid credit for sticking with it."

"So it wasn't even his tooth?" Sabrina asked.

"Nope. That's why you got zapped. It's a little warning sign for Tooth Fairies. We never trade for teeth that don't come from their rightful owner. That tooth was beneath Jason's pillow under false pretenses."

"If Jason's tooth was a phony, then I guess I'm finished," Sabrina said. She peeled off her wings and necklace and gave them back to the Tooth Fairy. Then she returned the white pouch and handed over a pocketful of teeth.

Sabrina waited impatiently as the Tooth Fairy added the new teeth to her necklace, tied the pouch around her waist, and attached the wings to her back. Finally she reached down behind the couch, picked up an enormous petrified tooth, and handed it to Sabrina. Sabrina felt her legs buckle under the weight of the giant bicuspid.

"There ya go, kiddo," the Tooth Fairy said as she put the remote back on top of the TV and headed for the door. "Thanks for the night off."

"You're welcome," Sabrina called out as she watched the Tooth Fairy fly away. Then she walked up the stairs to her room.

"What do you think you're doing?" Salem asked as he padded into the room and discovered Sabrina lying on her bed. "Wake up! You have a clock to work on, young lady!"

"I'll just take a little catnap, I promise," Sabrina assured Salem as she closed her eyes. "You should know about those. Just five minutes. I only need a little rest."

But a catnap was not in Sabrina's future—or was it her past?

Ping! Once again she heard an all-too-familiar high-pitched sound.

"Here we go again," Sabrina said, as Justin's time-travel magic took over.

Spellbound
By Mel Odom

Hollywood, 1944

"**Y**ou're here about the job, right?"

Sabrina gazed around the small office in which she had materialized. Only moments ago she'd been in her bedroom in Westbridge, trying to nap before starting the next part of her search for new clock parts. She didn't have a clue as to why she was suddenly here, except that this was somehow related to the Y2K madness that was affecting magic.

Wherever *here* was, and *if* the Timekeeper's spell had worked properly, one of the items she needed to build the new clock was nearby. All she had to do was find that item.

The job offer sounded like maybe the right place to start looking. "Yes," she replied, having no idea what job the man was talking about. Her magic was kind of on the blink at the moment and not always dependable, but so far the spells the Timekeeper had woven to help her look for things had worked pretty well.

The office was neat and orderly. The tall man in the wrinkled dark green suit looked exhausted as he slid into the straight-backed chair behind the desk in front of her. He pushed aside piles of documents and reached for an old-fashioned phone with a rotary dial. From the way he was dressed and the fact that a manual typewriter sat to the right of the desk, Sabrina guessed that she was nowhere near her own time. She glanced down at the dress she wore to confirm that fact: a light blue A-line number with puffy sleeves. *Definite ugh.*

At least it did appear she was still in America at the moment. She breathed a sigh of relief. *Home is a much easier neighborhood to search in.* After some of the things she'd been through, she was ready for some familiarity.

"I have to warn you, the job may already be filled," the man said as he lifted the phone and dialed. "A lot of people in this town want to work with Mr. Hitchcock."

"Hickok?" Sabrina repeated. "The actor? Um, yes . . . of course. . . ."

She glanced around the office again, searching desperately for reference. The movie posters lining the walls of the office were unfamiliar to her. She easily recognized Vivien Leigh in *Gone With the Wind,* though. She and Valerie had watched the movie a couple of times with Aunt Hilda. And Rhett and Scarlett had just put in an appearance at her non–Valentine's Day party.

The man stared up at Sabrina as if he was looking at an alien. "Jack Burnett, Hollywood Temp Services," he automatically told the person at the other end of the line. "Hold the phone." He covered the mouthpiece with one hand and pinned Sabrina with his gaze. "You don't know who Alfred *Hitchcock* is?"

Sabrina thought furiously. *What movie is he working on? Please don't tell me. I have to grab one of the birds from* The Birds! "Of course I do. I . . . uh, just didn't know the job was for *him.*"

Burnett rolled his eyes, clearly unhappy.

Before the man could say anything, Sabrina caught sight of the movie poster behind him. The poster showed a red-haired woman desperately clutching a dark-haired man who held an open straight razor behind her back. The image sent a shiver through Sabrina at the same time it fascinated her. The people in the poster looked familiar. At least the woman did.

The bottom half of the poster was covered with print: "David O. Selznick presents Ingrid Bergman and Norman Thompsen in Alfred Hitchcock's *Spellbound.*"

Burnett didn't seem impressed by Sabrina's casualness toward working with the legendary director.

She leaned toward him, desperate to get the job.

Something had led her there. "Hitchcock was—*is* a director," she repeated, remembering the man now because he was one of Hilda's favorites. Sabrina hadn't seen many of Hitchcock's movies, but she remembered being creeped out by *The Birds*. Salem had insisted on commenting on the menu during the tense parts of the movie until Hilda had chased him out of the Spellman living room. "I only said actor because . . . he always does cameos in his movies!" she finished triumphantly.

Burnett leaned back slightly in the straight-backed chair.

Knowing the man wasn't totally convinced, Sabrina said, "I really, really need this job." She said it with the kind of desperation that indicated tears were sure to follow.

Burnett looked even more uncomfortable as he backed away even more. "Sure, miss, take it easy. I don't want any waterworks in the office. It's bad for business." He uncovered the phone. "Hey, Bobby, you still need a script girl for *Spellbound,* right? Yeah, well, I got a girl here who'd be perfect for the job." He gave Sabrina a wink.

Sabrina glanced back at the poster on the wall behind Burnett. The straight razor seemed to gleam in the man's fist as he desperately held on to the woman embracing him.

Burnett finished his call and cradled the phone. "Okay, the job's all yours."

Looking at the poster, Sabrina suddenly didn't

feel so happy. She remembered that *Psycho* was another Hitchcock film, and it had scared her nearly as badly as *The Birds*.

Burnett scribbled briefly on a notepad. "You know Hitchcock is kind of"—he hesitated, his pencil coming to a rest—"eccentric."

"Yes." Sabrina nodded. *I could have told that from the man's movies.*

"I just thought I should mention it." Burnett glanced up at her as he tore the top sheet off the pad and passed it over to her. "In case you'd forgotten."

"Thanks." Sabrina took the sheet and quickly looked at it. The hastily scribbled note said only "Selznick Studios."

"You'll find a cab outside," Burnett told her. "Any one of the drivers will know where the sound stage is."

"Hitchcock's new film? Yeah, I heard some stuff about it." The cabbie sped through the studio lots, one hand on the wheel, the other gesturing as he spoke. He was a big, broad man with a fierce mustache. He narrowly avoided a group of Martians and dwarf cowboys.

Sabrina sat in the back seat of the cab and hung on to the strap as she watched the last of the Martians jump out of the way, swirling a glitter-streaked red cape. The Martian's mottled green features knotted up into a grimace as he screamed at the cabbie. Two of the dwarf gunmen clawed their pistols from their holsters and fired blanks at the cab. She wondered if the Martians and the cowboys were some of the time-shift anachronisms that appeared occasionally, but the cabbie didn't seem surprised to see them.

"The film's some kind of psycho thriller," the cabbie said, ignoring everything that had nearly happened. "See, Ingrid Bergman plays this hoity-toity psychiatrist, right? She's all ice—you know the kind, always right about everything, kinda living in her own world." He swerved again, barely skating by a finned rocket ship being pulled along on a small cart.

How could you tell if something weird was going on in Hollywood? Sabrina wondered. *Weirdness sells.* In every alley she glanced down, another movie was being filmed. She spotted gangsters with tommy guns, more aliens, guys in military uniforms, cowboys and Indians, and Spartan soldiers carrying spears. "A psychiatrist," she repeated, trying to keep the conversation going. *Maybe I should have just asked for directions.*

"And Norman Thompsen, he plays this guy that might be a murderer," the cabbie went on. "He shows up at the sanitarium pretending to be this psychologist guy. Only he ain't. He's a guy supposed to have lost his memory, but he thinks maybe he murdered the doctor he's pretending to be."

"A murderer?" Sabrina remembered the straight

razor clasped in the man's fist. "He kills Ingrid Bergman?"

The cabbie shrugged, then made a hard right turn down another street, passing a film crew shooting a fight in a cowboy bar. She thought she recognized Will Smith as one of the cowboys, but he looked totally lost, peering over his small lensed glasses at a director who was yelling at him.

On what looked like a downtown main street the cab came uncomfortably close to one of the tall cranes with a camera and cameraman mounted on it. Two masked men firing pistols dashed from the entrance to the Fourth National Bank, gunning down policemen. Sabrina ducked below the window, just in case the robbery in progress was actually real. That was definitely a problem in Hollywood.

"Nobody knows if Thompsen's character kills Ingrid," the cabbie said. "I talked to Thompsen about it last week." The cabbie looked over his shoulder at Sabrina while driving, making her nervous. "He don't know either, because Hitchcock's changing the script. It's gonna be anybody's guess." He placed his finger against his nose. "But I'll tell you what, that Thompsen, he's sweet on Ingrid. Hollywood papers and reporters haven't picked up on that yet, but I know."

Sabrina let out a small "eep" as the cabbie turned left and nearly took out a railway car sitting in front of a painted desert. Luckily, no one seemed to be around.

"You know Hitchcock, though," the cabbie said. "The guy likes surprises. He's not going to tell it all before he's ready. Ingrid goes kind of soft on Thompsen's character in the movie, but outside the picture there's no way she's interested in him the way he is in her. All this romantic folderol, I tell you, can be a real pain for an actor and an actress. They don't know where the make-believe world begins and the real world ends."

"Look out!" Sabrina yelled as a caped figure in a red-and-blue outfit dropped out of the sky and landed on the street in front of them.

The cabbie didn't even touch the brake. Incredibly, the caped man grinned and ran toward the cab. Sabrina pointed at the man, intending to move him to the side out of harm's way with her witchcraft.

Magic, work in a hurry,
Magic, work in a rush.
Move that man
Before he's turned to mush!

But her magic didn't respond; it felt like congealed oatmeal in her stomach. *Is it already too late? Has the Great Clock stopped? Am I trapped here?* She thought about her mom and Harvey, her aunts and her dad, and Salem. She might never see them again.

She was sure it was too late to save the caped man, but incredibly he leaped up, touched one booted foot to the front of the speeding cab, and pushed hard.

Glancing behind her, Sabrina saw the man somersault over the cab, his cape trailing behind him, then land on his feet like a cat. A big grin spread across the young man's face as he turned toward the departing cab.

"Stuntmen." The cabbie stuck his arm out the window and casually waved. "You gotta love 'em because they make movies worth seeing. And Terry Smith, the guy who doubles for Galaxy Man, he's one of the best in Tinseltown. Cocky guy, though. Almost gave one of the new drivers a heart attack last week."

The stuntman waved back, then dashed into a nearby alley.

The cab screeched to a stop at the curb. "Here we are, little lady."

Sabrina glanced out at the studio lot. A placard with David O. Selznick's name on it hung on the outside wall of a large warehouse.

"Hitchcock and his film crew are shooting interiors today," the cabbie said, "so you'll find them inside." He hopped out and opened Sabrina's door.

She stepped out of the cab and paid him from the small pocketbook that had come with the dress. She couldn't believe how cheap the taxi fare was, but she was definitely glad the pocketbook had come with money.

The cabby climbed back into his vehicle and shot

Sabrina a look of regret. "If you're here about a part, little lady, Hitchcock's already got his cast. Ain't even any bit parts left that I've heard about."

"I'm not an actress," Sabrina told him. "I'm going to be a script girl."

The cabbie gave her a kindly smile. "You should try for a part while you're out here. You got that look, little lady. Pretty as you are, you belong in pictures." Without another word, he tossed her a wave and drove away.

Sabrina watched him go, feeling good about herself. Then she recalled the millennium problems affecting the Other Realm. Remembering the straight razor on the movie poster send a cold chill down her back.

"Have you done this kind of work before?"

Sabrina stared at the action taking place in the soundstage. Camera-equipped dollies rolled quietly back and forth on tracks as Alfred Hitchcock directed the movements of the actors and actresses. The large warehouse the movie set was in appeared cavernous, filled with dark shadows that shifted constantly. In comparison, the stage area looked tiny.

Moviemaking is so cool, Sabrina thought. She wondered how Aunt Hilda would have felt about being on the soundstage during filming. Of course, she had probably already seen a movie being made. Sabrina had been kind of lost on the Selznick lot at first, but she'd gotten directions from carpenters to the main set.

"Not in a long time," Sabrina answered.

Bobby Dawson glanced at her. "You don't look old enough to do this job *now.*"

Sabrina tore her attention away from the set. Even though she only knew part of the story from whispered conversations around her, she'd been drawn into the mood and atmosphere of the scene. Ingrid Bergman, dressed in a robe, had just wandered into the sanitarium's library because she couldn't sleep. However, Norman Thompsen's character was already there, sleeping in a chair.

Sabrina wondered if this was where the straight razor came in. She hoped not—she wasn't ready for that. "I'm old enough."

Dawson didn't look convinced, but he also didn't look much older than Sabrina. He was tall and lean. His close-cropped hair still managed to look unruly, and his dimples kind of reminded her of Harvey. That made her sad and anxious. If the millennium problem didn't get solved, next year wouldn't exist and she and Harvey would have absolutely no future together.

"Do you know what you're supposed to do?" Dawson asked.

"The scripts." *That has to be a safe answer, right?*

On the set, Ingrid Bergman noticed Norman Thompsen for the first time. She'd just taken a book down from a shelf. She'd also noticed that the note she'd gotten from Thompsen's character earlier in the film didn't have the same signature as the one in the book the sanitarium doctor was supposed to have signed. Hitchcock had rolled film on her reaction to the discovery a half-dozen times.

"Right," Dawson said. "You'll be distributing the scripts. Hitchcock keeps them locked up tight. He doesn't like the Hollywood reporters to know anything until he's ready to tell them. Any time you handle the scripts, you're going to have to sign for them, then have whomever you deliver them to sign for them also. Got it?"

"Got it." Sabrina answered automatically, watching as the actress walked toward Thompsen who was shaking off sleep.

"This is important," Dawson said with a trace of irritation. "This is a Hitchcock film. A lot of people out here believe he's going to be a real success in the business."

Remembering what Aunt Hilda had said about the director, Sabrina nodded. "He is." The sudden look on Dawson's face told her maybe she'd said too much. Before she could modify her certainty, a woman's scream echoed through the soundstage.

On the stage, the actress tripped and almost fell. She flung out a hand and grabbed the back of a chair, narrowly recovering her balance. Even as she stood up, though, a wall of library shelves fell toward her.

Sabrina pointed, afraid that the massive weight of the shelves and the books would crush the actress. She spoke quickly, her mind searching frantically for words.

Shelves filled with books
Return to where you were at.
Don't fall.
Don't crush Ingrid flat.

Sabrina saw the magic sparkle briefly, immediately lost in the harsh lights illuminating the soundstage. A vaudeville hook formed in the air and reached out for the actress like a master of ceremonies yanking a bad act off the stage. Well, her spell hadn't kept the shelves from falling, but Sabrina was happy that the actress had been saved by her efforts.

But then, jolted by Sabrina's magic, the woman fell again. The shelves and books slammed into the floor. Hollow booms echoed around the soundstage, interrupted by worried voices asking the actress if she was okay and demanding to know what had happened.

"Now what?" Dawson exclaimed angrily. He started toward the soundstage. Sabrina trailed after him, hoping no one had seen her use her magic.

Norman Thompsen reached Ingrid Bergman before the other actors and stagehands did. Gently he helped her to her feet.

271

Sabrina tiptoed behind Dawson, barely able to see over the man's shoulder.

"Are you all right?" Thompsen asked. He was blond and wide-shouldered, his hair swept back and his jaw thrust out like the matinee idols of the forties. He held on to the actress's arm possessively.

"I'm fine," Miss Bergman said shakily, staring down at the scattered books and shelves covering the floor. "They just barely missed me." She looked up at Thompsen in confusion. "How did you get over here in time to pull me out of the way?"

Thompsen shook his head. "I didn't."

"But someone yanked me back. I felt it." The actress looked at the people around her. "Someone saved my life."

Sabrina held her breath, hoping everyone ignored what the actress was saying and stayed satisfied that she was all right.

Without warning, a door at the left side of the soundstage suddenly burst open. An actor dressed as a space pilot darted across the soundstage, shooting shock troopers with his laser gun. He dived to the floor and rolled, pantomiming several more shots.

At the end of the sequence, the actor got up and squinted into the bright lights, grinning good-naturedly. "Hey, George, you think we got it on that take? I don't know about this blue-screen stuff." He put a hand over his eyes and stared out at the cameras. "George? Where is everybody?"

"Hey, Buck Rogers," one of the stagehands yelled, "you're on the wrong soundstage."

"Sorry." The actor looked confused. He gave them a salute with his space gun, then walked back toward the left side of the stage and disappeared.

Sabrina let out a tense breath. The actor's appearance was only a reminder of how little time remained to fix everything before magic vanished forever.

"Miss Bergman." Alfred Hitchcock was shorter than Sabrina, so rotund he was almost oval shaped, and balding. He wore a black suit despite the fact that the stagehands and actors were casually dressed. "Are you all right?" His words were breathy and very British.

The actress brushed herself off. "I appear to be." Sabrina noticed that the woman's hands were shaking.

"My dear, do you know what happened?" the director asked, looking around the stage.

Thompsen glanced at the director angrily. "Those bookshelves nearly fell on her." He regretfully let go of the actress's arm as she stepped away from him.

Sabrina could see the bright glints in the actor's eyes and knew immediately that Thompsen cared very much for his costar. That look made her miss Harvey even more at that moment.

"I'm fine," the actress said quietly. "It's all right."

"It's not all right," Thompsen growled. He leveled a finger at the short director, standing taller to emphasize the difference in their height. "You're running a disaster area here, not filming a movie. Someone's going to get hurt."

Hitchcock's eyes narrowed and hardened. "Don't be a boor, Mr. Thompsen. This set measures up to the most rigorous security standards." The director glanced at the tall man beside him. "Mr. Gellman, if you please."

Gellman touched his baseball cap in a salute and stepped up onto the set.

"That's the fifth time Miss Bergman has nearly been seriously hurt since we began filming this movie," Thompsen said.

The fifth time? Sabrina looked at Hitchcock for answers. *That's four times too many.* The image of the straight razor on the movie poster flashed through her mind again.

The director shifted his gaze to the actress. "I assure you, Miss Bergman, everything that can be done to ensure your safety is being done. We have the very best security Mr. Selznick can provide."

"Yeah," Thompsen exploded. "Maybe Selznick's very best isn't good enough." He stood in front of the actress as if to protect her from the director.

Sabrina watched, growing more confused by the moment. She was just here long enough to grab something to take back to build her millennium clock. She didn't want to be involved in any of this. She tried to remember if she'd ever seen *Spellbound* during one of Aunt Hilda's old-movie marathons. Something nagged at her, lurking in the back of her mind like the memory of a bad first date. Something wasn't right.

"It wasn't an accident," Gellman declared, his loud voice carrying because of the soundstage's acoustics.

Sabrina glanced at the man, knowing he'd become the object of everyone's attention.

The security chief held up a thin black cord. "Someone set up a trip wire," he informed them. "It was placed just inside the door." He pointed behind the toppled bookshelves. "Those shelves were tampered with, too. Someone tilted them forward on wooden shims so they'd fall easily. It didn't take much to yank it all over—just Miss Bergman stepping on the cord."

"Oh, wow," Sabrina said, totally getting into the moment. Since nothing had actually happened to Ingrid Bergman, Sabrina turned her attention to the mystery. She felt certain what was going on here was all tied in somehow to the problem she was trying to solve back in the Other Realm. But what was she supposed to do about it?

"You see?" Thompsen demanded. "Someone is trying to stop production on this film."

"That," the director said, speaking clearly and with conviction, "is not going to happen." He glanced at the security chief. "Mr. Gellman, I expect you to investigate this matter forthwith and find some resolution."

The man didn't appear happy with the assignment. He twirled the black cord. "Can I call in the police?"

Hitchcock sneered. "Don't be ridiculous. I don't want amateurs anywhere around my sets."

"The police have more training in this kind of investigation than I do. They have more men, more tools."

"However, they are less gifted in the excuse department than you are, Mr. Gellman." The director stared the security chief down.

Gellman lowered his eyes and let out a long breath.

Sabrina felt sorry for the man. Mr. Kraft had nothing on the British director. She thought maybe she'd rather take a detention slip from the school vice-principal than deal with Alfred Hitchcock.

"Miss Bergman," the director said, "I'll grant you the space of a half hour to compose yourself before we reshoot this scene. We'll be set up by then. Please report back. If you need any more time, do let me know." He inclined his head slightly. "And do know that I am very grateful that nothing of ill consequence has happened to you." Without another word, the director turned and walked away.

"Boy," Thompsen snarled, "he's a piece of work. What a cold fish." He glanced at the actress and touched her shoulder.

Sabrina couldn't help seeing the concern in the actor's eyes. She remembered how she felt when

Harvey looked at her that way. It really felt good, except that the actress wasn't interested in Thompsen. That was too bad, because Sabrina thought they made a really cute couple. And Norman Thompsen didn't seem to have a clue.

"I'll be all right." The actress blinked and held her hand to her head. "And don't judge Mr. Hitchcock so harshly. He's actually soft-hearted."

"Soft in the head maybe," Thompsen muttered. "Let me walk you to your bungalow."

"I'll be fine." The actress waved away his offer and took off by herself.

Thompsen watched her for a moment, then walked away.

Sabrina felt even worse for Thompsen. It was evident the man was worried about his costar.

"Spellman." Dawson's voice cut into her thoughts. "Let's get to work. Hitchcock doesn't rewrite his writers, but he does ask them for rewrites under his direction. We've got pages to get out for this afternoon. Let's go. Chop-chop."

Sabrina sighed and trudged through the warehouse behind Dawson. Life in Tinseltown wasn't all glamour.

I hope I won't be here long, or I'm going to starve or end up washing dishes for my meals. Sabrina explored the contents of the purse she'd ended up with on her latest journey. *Or maybe the script girl will get paid sooner than later.* The pocketbook contained half a pack of Wrigley's Doublemint gum, a small box of tissues, and fourteen dollars and change.

She stood outside the studio lot, in line with the stagehands at the lunch wagon. Bobby Dawson had ordered his lunch in, and the stars of the movie were served meals inside their private trailers.

A large woman in a yellow-and-black flannel shirt with the sleeves hacked off barked orders to two small boys. They made sandwiches as she called them out, selecting meats, cheeses, and condiments, then wrapping the finished product in wax paper. They added a handful of potato chips, which left greasy spots on the brown paper bags, then doled out coffee or bottled soft drinks.

"Stay away from the roast beef," one of the carpenters told Gellman in a loud whisper that Sabrina overheard. "I heard from Jonesy this morning that it made a couple guys shooting Flynn's new picture sick as dogs."

Gellman nodded, but he seemed to be lost in thought.

Sabrina stepped up beside the security chief. "This morning was exciting, wasn't it?"

He looked down at her, his eyebrows knitting together under his baseball cap. "Do I know you?"

Sabrina introduced herself and stuck out her hand.

"So you're the script girl, huh?"

Sabrina nodded. The line to the lunch coach

moved surprisingly slowly for such a limited menu. She wondered if Hollywood had a version of the Slicery.

"Have you got stars in your eyes?" Gellman asked. "Are you here to check out the stuff dreams are made of?"

Sabrina shrugged. "Is there another reason to come out here?"

"Nope. Not if you like movies. Still, my best advice is go back to wherever you came from. This place chews people up and spits them out."

"You don't sound as if you like it much."

The security chief shook his head. "Not much."

"So why stay?"

A sad laugh rumbled out of Gellman. "Have you taken a look at that Pacific Ocean out there? You can't go any farther west."

"I guess not."

"The stars they got out here," Gellman said, "the guys and dolls you see up on that big silver screen, and you think how gorgeous they are and what stand-up Joes they are . . . well, they aren't what they seem to be. That's only pretend, like everything else out here."

Gellman sounded as bitter as week-old llama tongue, Sabrina thought, remembering some of Aunt Zelda's experiments on her laptop. She guessed that the security chief didn't much care for his job. "This morning's accident wasn't pretend."

"Don't get caught up in the Hollywood machine," he said. "You don't know if that accident was faked or not."

"Why would it be?" Sabrina asked.

"Sensationalism," he replied. "Every time a star gets his name in the trades, and especially in the main news section, it's money in the bank. The production studios know that too."

"Mr. Hitchcock doesn't want the newspapers to know about this movie," Sabrina said.

Gellman shook his head and snorted with forced laughter. "You *are* green, aren't you?"

Sabrina felt her cheeks flame. If she hadn't been sure that the movie and its cast and crew were somehow linked to whatever she was supposed to take from this time period, she'd have left. *Okay, I'd leave if my magic were working right. When you don't have magic, there's always wishful thinking.*

"Listen," the security chief went on, "I'm sorry if I offended you. I didn't mean to. But what happened this morning will be all over this burg by tonight."

"You sound as if you think the studio might have had something to do with the accident." Sabrina took another step forward as the line moved.

"One thing I am sure of: a trip wire was involved, so it wasn't an accident."

"What about the other four times?" Sabrina asked. Her mind whirled as she tried to figure out what was going on and what her part in it was.

Gellman's eyes narrowed. "You seem to know a lot for someone who just got here."

Sabrina thought quickly. "Bobby Dawson mentioned the other accidents while we were getting the script changes ready for this afternoon."

"Dawson's got a big mouth."

Sabrina didn't have anything to say to that.

Gellman led the way nearer the lunch coach. "The first three incidents could have been accidents. And none of them seemed aimed at anyone in particular. The fourth time, though, Norman Thompsen started hollering that someone was out to get Miss Bergman."

"Like today."

"Yeah."

"He seems very protective of her."

"The guy's got a real case for her," the security chief agreed. "Just before we started filming, Thompsen lost his mother. Evidently he was really close to her. His attention's stopping just short of embarrassing Miss Bergman."

"So what are you going to do?" Sabrina asked.

"Me?" Gellman nodded to the lunch wagon woman and gave his order. "I'm going to look for whoever's pulling pranks on the set. In the meantime, I'm going to hope nobody gets hurt." He got his brown bag and coffee after only a short wait.

When she got to the window, Sabrina ordered a ham and cheese sandwich, chips, and strawberry soda. She was really hungry and was surprised at how good the sandwich tasted when she unwrapped it from the crinkly wax paper.

She ate outside and dreaded reentering the building. Why did everything have to be so confusing? And why had the movie poster shown that straight razor? She wondered if Hilda, Zelda, Vesta, and the other Witches' Council members had found a solution to the clock problem. She hoped so, because her own progress was going so slowly.

Farther down the street she saw a man dressed in a swamp-creature outfit talking to a futuristic astronaut. Both of them were getting frustrated. The astronaut was very demanding.

Evidently at his wit's end, the swamp creature tore off his oversize fish head and yelled at the astronaut. In response, the astronaut took off his helmet. A cloud of gray gas escaped into the air. A dozen antennae wobbled into view, jutting from a face the color of lime Jell-O and shaped like a pyramid. Some of the antennae had eyes.

The swamp monster screamed in horror. Before he could move, the astronaut shot him with a purple beam that froze the man in midscream. The astronaut shook his head, touched a brooch on his chest, and immediately disappeared in a rush of glittering particles. Even before Sabrina had time to wonder where the astronaut had been from, the guy in the swamp-monster suit finished screaming. People looked at him but kept walking.

Too weird, Sabrina thought. *Time really needs to*

get back to normal. While she was taking a swig of strawberry soda, she glimpsed a shadowy figure in a trench coat standing at the other end of the soundstage. She turned to get a better look, but the shadowy figure disappeared in the alley.

The big eye stared back at Sabrina from the canvas. It looked weathered and old, as if it had seen terrible things, maybe even before time started to go wacky. The artist had built the paint up, giving the eye depth. She knew she wasn't going to forget it any time too soon.

"What are you doing here, child?" a deep, imperious voice demanded from behind her.

Taken by surprise, Sabrina whirled around.

A narrow, angular man stood in the doorway. He wore a black gown that hung down to his ankles and was splotched with paint. A black beret was cocked jauntily on his head, a tassel hanging down one side of his wild hair. The ends of his mustache were waxed and carefully upturned. His hawklike gaze transfixed her.

"I was sent to find Mr. Dali," Sabrina explained, feeling nervous when she sensed the man's agitation. "I was told he'd be here."

The man put his hands on his hips with lots of attitude. "Dali stands before you. He is waiting to hear what you have to say, and he doesn't like having his time wasted."

Sabrina stood humbled by the reproach. "Mr.

Hitchcock wants to talk to you about the set design for the dream sequence."

Dali entered the room grandly, acting as if he owned all that he surveyed. Judging from the canvases taking up space all around the large room, Sabrina figured that might be true.

"He only wishes to tell Dali what a good job Dali has done." Dali considered the painting of the eye critically, fitting a hand under his jutting jawline. "Dali already knows this. Dali doesn't need to be told again." He brushed the canvas gently with his fingertips. A quirky smile twisted his lips. "Still, Dali doesn't mind being told what a genius he is. He will accompany you."

"Great." Sabrina glanced around at the other canvases, spotting one that was partially finished. On the canvas, melting clocks spread liquidly across a desert landscape. Excitement filled her. "Hey, I know you. You're Salvador Dali, the artist who did *The Persistence of Memory.*" She'd seen a print of that painting in art class. Dali was one of Mrs. Singer's favorite painters. His paintings always presented a twisted and weird view of the world.

"Of course you know Dali," the painter said with a smile, gesturing magnanimously. "Everyone knows Dali." He rearranged brushes and paints on the caddy on the table. "All artists wish they were Dali."

Now, there's an ego, Sabrina thought. Still, she thought it was a quirk of fate that she was facing the millennium countdown and had met the man responsible for all the surrealistic images of melting clocks.

"Let us go," Dali said, turning quickly. "One must not keep adoration waiting too long. Otherwise it sours like milk and guests who overstay their welcome."

Sabrina remembered from Mrs. Singer's class that Dali had a temper to match his ego. She trailed after the painter, following him through the narrow alleys in the warehouse. "Can I ask you a question?"

"You already have," Dali said. "Ask another. Dali doesn't mind being questioned about his brilliance."

Asking the artist about his paintings wasn't exactly what Sabrina had in mind. "Why do you paint the melting clocks?"

Dali waved carelessly. "Dali replies, 'Why not?' "

A deep philosophical issue, obviously, Sabrina thought. "You know about"—she hesitated a moment—"the accidents that have happened on the set?"

"Of course. Dali sees much more than anyone else, and much more deeply." The artist opened a freestanding door in the center of the room and strode through.

Noticing how the door wiggled uncertainly, Sabrina was hesitant to walk through it, but she did anyway. A flash of light filled her vision. When she could see again, she was standing on a familiar starship bridge.

The captain and first officer jerked and moved across the bridge as if they were caught in the grip of a massive earthquake. The rest of the crew did the same, acting as if they were holding on to their seats and consoles.

"Bridge to Engineering, I need more power," the young captain ordered.

"Captain," a man replied in a thick Scots burr, "I'm givin' 'er all I've got!"

Sabrina watched in wonderment. She'd seen all of the episodes of this first generation of the popular television series, and the spacequake effect helped her narrow down which episode this was.

"Cut!" someone ordered. A director stepped through the missing wall of the bridge. He pointed at Sabrina. "Where'd she come from? She just spoiled the shot."

All the actors and actresses turned to Sabrina. "Oops," she said. "Gotta go." She turned and stepped back into the turbolift. The bright light blurred her vision again for a moment; then she was back on the *Spellbound* stage. She glanced at Dali, who'd never broken stride but apparently hadn't made it onto the starship. *More weirdness,* she thought. "Do you believe those mishaps on the set were really accidents?"

Dali snorted.

"I'll take that as a no," Sabrina said.

She heard the muted voices of Hitchcock and his crew echoing in the distance. She knew from looking at the script that they were planning to shoot the scene in which Norman Thompsen's character was about to have a breakdown in the operating room. It was going to be a tense scene.

Sabrina concentrated on the questions she wanted to ask Dali. "Do you know Mr. Gellman very well?"

"Dali knows *of* him," the artist answered. "And Dali has spoken to this man upon occasion. Dali's work is very valuable, and Gellman is in charge of seeing to the protection of the pieces here. Dali has had the opportunity to point out discrepancies in Gellman's security services."

"He doesn't seem to care for his job very much."

"The man likes his job," Dali said. "It's the stars that he doesn't like. Dali thinks he's a very jealous and bitter man. The security chief is like most of those who are envious of gifted people around them. Dali believes that artists like himself and Mr. Hitchcock are mirrors of creativity that reflect only the emptiness that lurks within people like Mr. Gellman. They seek out those brilliant people to associate with in the hope that some of that brilliance will rub off, but in the end the Gellmans of the world cannot stand those reflections."

Lost in thought, Sabrina followed Dali to the set. Dali went to talk with Hitchcock while she stood with the film crew. On the set the actors gathered around the operating table and talked about the scene they were about to shoot.

Gellman stood near one of the real walls, holding a cup of coffee and watching the action. He didn't look happy.

Too bad they're not making Snow White, Sabrina thought. *They could cast Gellman as Grumpy.* Still, her sense of humor didn't last long when she remembered the straight razor on the movie poster. She resolved to keep a closer eye on the security chief.

A few minutes later, Hitchcock gave the order to get ready. He spoke softly and briefly, setting up the scene and the emotions he wanted to wring out of it. Despite his seeming inflexibility, Sabrina had to admit the director was a master at what he did. Even though she'd read how the scene was going to turn out, she found herself captivated by the mood and atmosphere the director established on the set with the actors.

In the story, one of the patients had tried to commit suicide by slashing his own throat. Thompsen and Ingrid Bergman labored to save the patient but it was no use. In the middle of the rescue attempt, however, Thompsen's character was overcome with emotion and suffered a breakdown.

Just as the actor started freaking out, the lights on the soundstage went out.

"What is going on?" Hitchcock demanded. "Someone get those lights back on. I'm trying to shoot a motion picture here."

Sabrina froze, a chill creeping up the back of her

neck. She wished she had Salem with her: he could have been her seeing-eye cat. She whispered quickly.

Eyes bright, darkness and light,
Help me see in the night.

Her vision erupted into a purple explosion; then it cleared off and she could see the shadowy figures milling around on the set. Voices demanded to know what was going on.

Sabrina glanced at the wall where she'd seen Gellman and noticed that the security chief was missing. A sudden scream yanked her attention back to the set.

Without warning, the lights came back on, bathing the set in harsh illumination. The red-haired actress stood against the back wall of the set, her hands raised in front of her face. Her hospital gown was slashed in two places.

A scalpel stuck out of the wall beside her, only inches from her face.

Police officers came to the set and asked questions. However, since the lights had been off at the time of the attack, no one had seen anything. Sabrina suspected that Hitchcock was sincerely annoyed about the involvement of the police.

Ingrid Bergman, however, was a nervous wreck. Once the investigating detectives had finished with her, the actress returned to her trailer in back of the soundstage.

Sabrina stood in the shadows surrounding the set, lost amid the tall cameras on dollies and tracks. *Who had made the attack?* The question kept rattling around in her mind, and she kept coming back to the security chief. So far Gellman had remained out of the way of the questioning, but he lurked in the background.

She decided to check on the actress and offer whatever support she could. Something like this had to be scary—maybe even as scary as thinking about the problems in the Other Realm. Sabrina wished Salem had come with her. The cat probably could have figured out what was going on and who was to blame. After all, Salem Saberhagen had once planned to take over the world.

Some of the stars had trailers behind the soundstage. Sabrina let herself out into the cooling breeze of approaching evening. The western sky had turned a deep indigo and night was starting to cover Hollywood.

She approached the small trailers, which looked like silver bubbles. They still retained their wheels, but they were up on bricks. The breeze twisted among the close-set trailers. Each trailer had the occupant's name on it. The first two belonged to other stars in the movie. The third belonged to Norman Thompsen. Ingrid Bergman's trailer was parked nearby.

Sabrina climbed the three wooden steps to the actress's door.

Then she noticed the figure in the trench coat lurking near the rear of the trailer. He was almost hidden in the shadows of deep evening, but her spell to see in the dark was still working. She saw the man clearly enough to know he was there but not to know who he was.

Sabrina thought quickly. The police were still on the grounds, and she did have her magic—maybe. If the man in the trench coat was Gellman, the security chief, she hoped she could catch him and turn him over to the detectives.

She raised her hand as if to knock on the trailer door, then hesitated as if reconsidering. "No," she said out loud, for the lurker's benefit. "She probably doesn't want to be bothered now." She turned and walked back down the steps.

Continuing on past Norman Thompsen's trailer, Sabrina stepped into the shadows and headed back toward the actress's trailer. The trailer windows were too tiny for someone Gellman's size to slip through.

But what if the security chief had already been inside?

The thought left Sabrina's blood cold. She made herself go forward. She dashed through the gap between the trailers, trying hard not to make a sound. She listened, but she didn't hear anything except voices from Thompsen's trailer.

Sabrina eased alongside the actress's trailer, her dress whispering against the metal. Then she heard a shoe scuff against the pavement, and suddenly there was no time to turn around.

Muscular arms closed around Sabrina. She tried to scream, but a hand clapped over her mouth. She raised her finger to point, but there was no one to point at, and there were no guarantees that her magic would have worked. Time was running out for all magical beings everywhere; maybe it was just running out early for her.

"Easy, kid," a familiar voice said. "Just take it easy and you won't get hurt."

Sabrina relaxed. She knew that voice, and it didn't belong to the security chief. She twisted her head, and her captor allowed her to turn around.

Humphrey Bogart held her in his arms. There was no mistaking that craggy face and those sad eyes. Sabrina could remember the first time she'd seen him—as Rick in *Casablanca,* dressed in a white jacket as the camera had closed in on him. Sabrina understood then why Aunt Hilda had always talked so fondly of the actor.

Bogart wore a rumpled trench coat and a sharply creased fedora at a rakish angle. His dark liquid eyes regarded her suspiciously. "You're the new girl on the set."

Sabrina nodded.

He kept his voice at a whisper. "What're you doing out here, kid?"

Sabrina tried to talk but couldn't with his hand over her mouth.

Bogart shook his head, seemingly at himself. "I've been acting long enough I should know better than that. When I take my hand off your mouth, no funny business. Got it?"

Sabrina nodded. She felt certain Bogart wasn't up to anything bad. He was a good guy—unless, of course, he was playing a bad guy like Duke Mantee.

Bogart took his hand away. "Talk fast, sweetheart," the actor whispered. "We may not have much time."

"I came out here to check on Ingrid Bergman," Sabrina replied. "What are you doing here?"

Bogart jerked a thumb over his shoulder. "She called me. Said she was having trouble on this set. We worked together on a picture called *Casablanca.*"

"I've seen it," Sabrina said. "It's a great movie. I couldn't believe you just let her fly away at the end. I was mad at you for days."

Bogart grinned and rubbed his chin. "Couldn't believe it myself. But the movie just didn't play right any other way."

"You should make a sequel," Sabrina told him. "One where Rick and Ilsa get back together."

"Maybe we will," Bogart said. "There's a little talk going around."

Sabrina started to tell him that he wouldn't, but

she caught herself just in time. "So Miss Bergman called you."

The actor raked the gathering gloom with his eyes. "She's a swell kid. I wouldn't want anything to happen to her, so I thought I'd nose around, maybe see what I could see."

"It was you I saw earlier today," Sabrina said, realizing now whom she'd seen. "At lunch."

Bogart grinned ruefully and rubbed the back of his neck in embarrassment. "Maybe I ain't so good at this private-eye business as I play it on the big screen."

"You're *very* good," Sabrina said, feeling bad. "I don't think Gellman saw you."

Bogart's eyebrows arched. "Gellman?"

"Sure. You think he's the one causing these accidents, don't you? I mean, he doesn't like his job, doesn't like the people he works with."

Bogart shook his head. "You really like Gellman for this, kid?"

The question threw Sabrina off-balance. "You don't?"

"No. Gellman's a pain in the—" Bogart stopped himself. "He's a pain, but he's no killer. He's unhappy because no matter how hard he tries, he can't make enough money to support his gambling habit—or at least that losing streak he carries around."

"Then who's to blame for these mishaps?"

"I don't know, kid. I'm out of ideas."

Sabrina was grateful to have someone to talk to about the mysterious doings. And he was the most classic private eye on the silver screen. "Sam Spade would know. So would Philip Marlowe."

Bogart grinned at her, his teeth very white in the night. "Sam Spade had a script, and I don't know this Marlowe bird."

Oops, *The Big Sleep* was still in Bogart's future. Sabrina glanced around. No one else was in sight. "What about Salvador Dali? I mean, have you seen the kinds of pictures he paints?"

Bogart shook his head. "Nah. Dali's a flake, an attention-seeker, but he wouldn't do something like this."

"Then who do you like for it?" Sabrina found herself dropping into the speech patterns of the old noir movies that Hilda liked so much. Even Zelda would often drop what she was doing to sit in on those.

"I don't know, kid. I was trying to wrap my head around that while I was watching Ingrid's trailer. I moved to the other end of the trailer because Norman Thompsen's argument with his mother kept distracting me."

Sabrina nodded and wrapped her arms around herself. The night had brought a drastic drop in the temperature.

"You cold, kid?"

"Yes."

Bogart shrugged out of his trench coat and

wrapped it around Sabrina. He wore a black suit underneath. "That's this town for you. All lit up, she's warm and toasty, but you crawl around in her shadows, and you can get chilled to the bone."

Sabrina snuggled inside the trench coat. Then Bogart's words struck her. She stared at the actor. "You said Norman Thompsen was arguing with his mother?"

"Yeah."

"You're sure it was his mother?" Sabrina asked.

Bogart leaned back against Ingrid Bergman's trailer, arms crossed over his chest. "How many people is he going to call Mother? Yeah, I'm sure."

"What were they arguing about?" Sabrina gazed at the single square of yellow light filling one window in Thompsen's trailer.

"I don't know," Bogart replied irritably. "I don't pry into other people's business."

A knot of apprehension filled Sabrina's stomach when she remembered what Gellman had told her at lunch. She started moving slowly toward Thompsen's trailer.

"Where are you going?" Bogart demanded.

"To Thompsen's trailer."

"You're interested in the argument he's having with his mother?"

Sabrina gazed at the actor. "Thompsen's mother died a few weeks before they started shooting *Spellbound.* Gellman told me that today at lunch."

The irritation drained from Bogart's face, replaced by a persimmony grimace. "Then why's he talking to his mother?"

"Exactly." The thought didn't sit well with Sabrina either.

"Maybe you ought to stay back, kid." Bogart's hard gaze locked on Thompsen's trailer. "I'll drift over there and ask ol' Normie if everything's jake."

Sabrina felt relieved when Bogart took the lead, but she couldn't let him go by himself. She stayed close behind.

Bogart went through the darkness without a sound. Only the thrumming of the fans in the windows of the trailers echoed across the darkened lot. Sabrina got more tense as she watched Bogart ease up the narrow wooden steps leading to Thompsen's trailer door. Bogart's hand closed on the knob and twisted.

"Locked," Bogart whispered.

Inside the trailer, Sabrina heard two distinct voices.

"She's a bad woman, Norman," an old woman's voice declared. "She's not right for you."

"I think she's lovely, Mother," Thompsen said. He sounded as if he was holding his anger back, till his voice came out as a whine. "She's a good girl. I know she is."

"She doesn't care anything about you."

"She will."

"No!"

Listening to the two voices, Sabrina felt more

fearful than ever. She leaned closer to Bogart. "Maybe we should get the police."

Bogart shook his head. "They got all kinds of rules about suspects." The actor surveyed the lighted window beside the door. Only one shadow was moving around inside, silhouetted against the drawn window shade. "They have to have evidence on a guy before they can take him downtown and beat the truth out of him."

Now, there's a cheery thought. Sabrina watched the pacing shadow on the window shade. This person was the same size as Thompsen, but the hair was in wild disarray. "What are we going to do?"

Bogart bared his teeth in a wolfish smile that reminded Sabrina of Sam Spade. "We're gonna get inside, have a little chat with ol' Normie."

"She's not good for you, Norman," the old woman screeched.

"She could be."

"What are you going to do? Let her take you away from me?"

The conversation was threatening to shred Sabrina's nerves, especially since she knew Norman was talking to his dead mother. She wanted to be anywhere but there, but she couldn't leave Bogart on his own. Also, the item she needed for the clock might be inside Thompsen's trailer. What if she couldn't get it? Here she was in Hollywood, really close to being abandoned there forever without her magic.

Could she make a living in Hollywood? She wasn't a movie star, or even movie star material, despite what the cabby had said. Still, if she took care of herself, she could live to see her aunts again, right? Of course, by then she'd be older than they were.

And Harvey would never be interested in someone old enough to be his grandmother.

Desperate, she pointed at the locked door, hoping her magic would work.

Doors are locked
And doors are barred.
Unlock this lock
Before all time is marred.

"What?" Bogart asked.

Sabrina looked at him innocently. "I said maybe we should try the door again."

"It's locked," Bogart protested. His fingers curled around the edge of the tiny trailer window.

"You'll never get through there." Sabrina moved beside the actor and twisted the doorknob. It moved easily.

Bogart's eyes gleamed like a cat's in the darkness. "Step aside, kid. I'll handle it from here."

Sabrina tried, but the steps were narrow, and when she stepped backward, her heel caught on the trench-coat tail. She fell against the door and tumbled into the room. She glanced up just in time to see Thompsen whirl around. "Oops."

The actor had on a dark wig, and his face was heavily made up. His lips were ruby red. He spoke, but it wasn't his voice. "Norman, look out! See? That woman has betrayed you! She's told others about you!" Without another word, he launched himself at Sabrina.

"Gotta go," Sabrina said to herself. She rolled away from Thompsen's attack.

Then Bogart was there, coming between her and Thompsen. "End of the line, pal," the actor said gruffly. Bogart swung his fist and caught Thompsen on the point of the chin.

Thompsen stumbled back against the wall in the narrow confines of the tiny trailer. He stood dazed for a moment.

On her feet now, Sabrina pointed at a vase of roses on a shelf near Thompsen.

I'm here to save the future,
I'm here to save time.
So if you could,
Be my Valentine.

She'd hoped the vase would drop on Thompsen. Instead, a heart-shaped box of chocolates popped into her hands. She gazed down at the red package tied with pink ribbon. "Like I really need a box of chocolates. With magic like this, you never know what you're going to get." Still, she moved quickly and threw the candy heart toward the shelf with the vase on it.

The vase slid off the shelf and landed on the man's head with a loud crash, knocking him out cold. Thompsen slid to the floor.

Bogart looked at the shattered fragments of the vase, and the flowers spilled across Thompsen. He yanked a cord from the nearby lamp. He rolled the unconscious man over and tied his hands behind his back.

Bogart glanced at Sabrina. "Call the coppers, kid. I think we got this one all wrapped up."

"Something to drink?"

Bleary-eyed, Sabrina glanced up at Bogart. He held a blue ceramic cup out to her. She shook her head. "I don't drink coffee."

Bogart smiled. "Didn't figure you did, kid. I got a flatfoot to run down a cup of hot cocoa for you."

The smell of warm chocolate filled Sabrina's nose. She inhaled it gratefully and accepted the cup. As she drank, she glanced around the set.

Most of the Hollywood detectives and police officers had gone now, taking Thompsen with them. The ones left were taking statements from the cast and crew.

Alfred Hitchcock, looking as impeccable as ever, drifted over to join them. He glanced up at Bogart.

"So Norman Thompsen thought he was conversing with his dead mother?"

Bogart nodded. "In between grilling sessions with the bulls," he said, referring to the detectives, "I made a couple calls to a gossip columnist I know. Frannie tells me Norman had a real controlling mother. She broke up both of his marriages, but that fact was kept quiet. The studio didn't want that stuff leaking out for fear it might hurt his leading-man image." He shrugged. "Norman was such a nice quiet guy that nobody had a problem with the divorces. But this . . . this is going to get out."

"Talking with his dead mother," the director repeated, a gleam in his eye. "Fascinating, truly fascinating."

"If you think so," Bogart said.

Well, Sabrina thought as she watched the director walk away, *now we know what inspired Hitchcock to direct the movie* Psycho. She looked at Bogart. "How's Ingrid Bergman?"

"Resting. She's a tough gal. She's going to be okay." Bogart looked at her with his hooded eyes and nodded. "Maybe she wouldn't have been if you hadn't put it together."

"You were there."

"Maybe. But you did the sleuthing on this one, kid. You did good. I owe you. If you ever need anything—"

"Just whistle?" Sabrina asked.

Bogart grinned. "Something like that, I guess."

"How are they going to finish *Spellbound* now that they've lost their leading man?"

"I talked to Hitch earlier. He said they're going to go with a young guy named Peck—Gregory Peck. This role needs an actor with kind of a soft touch, not a guy noted for ham-fisted roles. I think Peck will do fine."

Sabrina nodded, knowing Gregory Peck would be wonderful. That was what she had been trying to remember when she'd first seen the *Spellbound* poster. Norman Thompsen hadn't been the male star of the movie; Gregory Peck had been.

"Take care of yourself, kid," Bogart said. "Hollywood's big and she's rough, just candy-coated on the outside. See you." He put his hands in his pockets and walked way.

"Ah, child, Dali is proud of you."

Sabrina turned to look at the painter, surprised he'd come up on her so quietly.

"You showed such bravery in confronting that man," Dali said. "Dali doesn't think such bravery should go unrewarded." He handed her a package. "You showed great interest in Dali's clocks. Dali thinks you should try painting your own clock."

"Painting my own clock?" Sabrina looked at the package of paints in her hands. *Of course! That's what I'm supposed to get here!* A smile spread across her face. "Thank you. Thank you very much."

The painter waved the thanks away. "Dali knows

you will put these to good use. Now if you will excuse Dali, he must go paint. These events have inspired Dali very much." He turned and left.

Excitement filled Sabrina, pushing away the tiredness that filled her. She finished her cocoa and made sure no one was watching her. Then she walked from the light surrounding the soundstage into the shadows that hid her from view. She held the paints tightly as she noticed the freestanding door Dali had used earlier.

Sparkles circled the door, and she was certain when she stepped through it this time she wouldn't be on the set of a science fiction series. She held on to the paints, walked through the doorway, and reappeared in her bedroom.

"Back so soon?" Salem asked. The cat was curled up on her bed.

"Maybe for you," Sabrina told him. "Some of us have been working. If Humphrey Bogart hadn't helped me this time, I don't know what I would have done."

Salem's eyes flew open. "You saw Bogie? *The* Bogie? Play it again, Sam? When I was in Hollywood, he never returned . . . I mean, my agent was never able to get us together."

"He's a nice guy," Sabrina said. She added the paints to the other items she'd collected. She had accumulated quite a few items, but she had no idea what she was going to do with them. "Have you talked to Hilda, Zelda, or Vesta?"

"No," Salem grumbled, "I'm just the family cat. No one tells me anything or takes me anywhere."

Sabrina ignored the cat's complaint. She could see, through her open bedroom door, that the linen closet had started to glow. She walked toward it anxiously, wondering where the Timekeeper would send her this time and what she was supposed to bring back.

How I Discovered North America
By Mark Dubowski

"In the world of cats," Salem told her, "we have a saying: Friends don't let friends wear anything that would put their self-esteem at risk by exposing them to ridicule by insensitive onlookers."

"That's a saying?" Sabrina Spellman asked, turning this way and that to check out her outfit.

"It loses something in the translation," Salem admitted. "It sounds much more clever when spoken in Cat."

Sabrina frowned. "What you're really telling me, Salem, is that you think my outfit isn't cool." She was wearing knee-high, fake walrus-hide boots, a simulated weasel-pelt tunic, a metal vest, a plastic bone necklace, and a cone-shaped helmet fitted out with faux antlers.

"The hat's acceptable," he told her hopping up on

a rock beside her to admire the harbor below them, "if your plan is to be shot, stuffed, and mounted on a wall."

"This isn't my prom dress," she pointed out. "We're trying to get on a Viking ship, remember?"

"How could I forget?" Salem replied. Their orders had come directly from the Timekeeper. Salem and Sabrina had been sent back in time to Norway in A.D. 999 to find a Viking explorer named Leif. According to the Timekeeper, Leif had something for them—an ancient measuring wheel that looked like a modern pizza cutter. The Witches' Council and Hilda and Zelda were working on the Great Clock of the Other Realm, but Justin Time was working with Sabrina on their own solution.

Salem wasn't afraid of the Timekeeper, but any command that had to do with the Witches' Council gave him a shudder. The last time he questioned the council's judgment they had changed him from a warlock into a cat. *And I'm not going any lower down the food chain than this,* he thought.

"You gotta have job skills if you want to sail with the Vikings," he told Sabrina. "I hate to tell you, but you don't look like much of an oarsman."

"There must be something else I can do."

"Perhaps you have experience pillaging or plundering?" he suggested.

Sabrina thought for a minute. "Not exactly. But once I returned a perfectly good sweater just because I changed my mind about the color."

Salem shook his head. "That's not nearly fiendish enough. Think cruel. Like what cats do to mice."

Sabrina's eyes shone at that. "Great idea, Salem!"

"Me and my big mouth," Salem moaned nervously. "I've given you an idea, haven't I?"

"I'm going to offer our services as a *team*. We can be in charge of keeping everything shipshape"—she patted him on the head—"including rat removal."

"Yuck," Salem said. But he doubted that would be enough to land them a job. "You're forgetting the main problem," he said. "The fact that you're a girl."

Sabrina smiled at that. "Girls were Vikings—and pirates too," she told him. "Leif Ericsson's own daughter was a famous pirate captain."

"I feel seasick already," Salem moaned.

Sabrina promptly located a big red-bearded Viking near the gangplank leading to a long ship decorated at the prow with the carved head of a blood-red dragon. He hired Sabrina and Salem on the spot.

"I can't wait to meet the cruise director," Salem quipped. "Shuffleboard, anyone? No? How about Walk the Plank?"

"No talking!" Sabrina warned him as they headed up the gangway. "You'll get us fired."

"I wouldn't worry about that," Salem told her. "It's a thousand years ago, and according to my calculations that would make the minimum wage about two cents a day. Good help must be extremely hard to find."

The main deck of the wooden Viking ship was divided down the center by a long walkway. Built along the sides were benches from which the sailors could row the ship with long oars. When the wind was up, a single square sail could be unfurled from a center mast. Storage and sleeping areas were below the main deck, in the hull.

Salem and Sabrina headed straight down the companionway to clean, hunt vermin, and search for the measuring wheel belowdecks.

"Above all," Salem pointed out, "we must avoid manning the oars. That looks way too much like actual work."

After a few minutes' fumbling Sabrina whispered, "Have you seen anything that looks like a pizza cutter?" Talking was okay as long as they were alone—the rest of the crew was busy topside, rowing out to sea.

Salem raised his head from an open barrel. "No, but I found plenty of anchovies," he reported, raising a salted cod for her to see. The ship was heavily stocked with food, clothing, and tools. "I think we're going on a long voyage," he predicted.

The Timekeeper had given Sabrina a sketchy itinerary. "I know this ship is going to Iceland to pick up Leif's dad, Eric the Red," she said. "That's where the name Ericson comes from, you know.

They plan to explore some land they've heard about to the west of Iceland."

"Ye gads!" Salem gasped. "They wouldn't be thinking about visiting Massachusetts, would they?" The thought struck terror in his heart. "I can't bear the thought of anyone we know seeing you in those antlers."

"Calm down, Salem," Sabrina said. "It's a thousand years ago. North America hasn't been discovered by Europeans yet. That's what Leif Ericsson is going to do."

"It's all coming back to me," Salem said. "When I was a warlock, my plot to conquer the world included overthrowing a place called Vinland."

"That was Leif Ericsson's name for it. We call it Canada."

Salem's eyes flashed. He had an idea. "You know, Sabrina, if this is a thousand years ago and we're headed for America, you and I should think about going into real estate." To the warlock-turned-cat, it seemed like a golden opportunity. "We'll buy the entire East Coast, subdivide it, and when the Pilgrims arrive, we can sell lots! We'll make a fortune!"

He was interrupted by a sound like that of a football team rushing into the locker room at halftime. Actually it was the Viking crew. They were on the open sea now. They had unfurled the square sail, and the sailors were coming down the companionway for a break from rowing.

"Look busy!" Salem hissed. But the crew wasn't interested in the progress of the cleaning team. They had come belowdecks for a game of Plunder.

Plunder was a Viking betting game, and its existence on board raised Salem's opinion of the ship. "A casino!" he said. "I had no idea."

Salem watched the game carefully, learning the rules and ranking the players. "Forget what I said about real estate," he told Sabrina after a few rounds. "I see your future in this little game of chance. With luck—and magic, of course—you could clean up! And I don't mean by doing time on kitchen patrol."

"Using magic to win a game would be cheating," Sabrina argued.

"These men are Vikings," Salem pointed out. "Pirates! A little cheating is expected and encouraged."

She saw some logic in that. But there was another problem. "It's against the rules to use witchcraft for monetary gain," she insisted. "The Witches' Council would get mad."

"You're whining, Sabrina. We need that pizza wheel at any cost. What if we have to fork over cold, hard cash to get it?"

"I've got a few dollars," she said.

Salem rolled his eyes. "I hope you're not counting on using anything with George Washington's picture on it. He won't be born for another 733 years."

Sabrina gritted her teeth. Salem was right. "I'll

need to watch them for a few minutes to figure out the rules," she said at last.

The game was embarrassingly easy. Any idiot could play—a fact that explained its popularity with the Viking crew. All you needed was a shield and some rocks. You put the shield on the floor and piled all of the rocks in the center except one. To play, you threw that one remaining stone at the pile and scored one point for each rock you could knock off the shield. The game was stupid, it was point-less, and you didn't need an Internet connection to participate.

"Someday they'll call this marbles," Salem pre-dicted.

For each point scored, the player collected one coin from each of the other players.

"This is going to be too, too easy," Sabrina said. She soon proved she was right. By the time the lookout yelled "Land ho!" she had a new nickname: Spellman the Lucky.

"Do you think there's shopping in Iceland?" Sa-brina asked Salem as they watched the rock-pile coastline rise in the distance. The heavy load of Viking coins she'd won playing Plunder was al-ready burning a hole in her fake walrus-hide shoul-der bag.

"I've heard tell the Vikings have a mall," Salem replied. "Except I think they mean *m-a-u-l*. Regard-less, we need to focus on our quest, don't you think? Business before shopping, I always say."

Sabrina agreed. "Problem is, I have no idea how much a pizza cutter costs. Do you? I probably have enough money, but we should look for a kitchenware store or something."

"Remember, the mysterious object we seek only *looks* like a pizza cutter," Salem pointed out. Suddenly there it was, a pizza wheel—whatever. Captain Leif had one in his hand.

"What *is* that thing?" Salem whispered.

"There's only one way to find out," Sabrina said, "and that's to ask. Watch me play dumb."

"You're wearing the right hat," Salem said. "But watch the horns, will you?"

"Don't worry. I'll be blunt," Sabrina said.

In Old Norse she told the captain she had noticed the instrument in his hand. "I'm a landlubber," she confessed. "But I've been studying for my SATs— my Sailing Aptitude Test."

"This is called a bearing wheel," Leif told her, handing it over. "We use it to determine our position by the stars."

So that's what that Viking pizza cutter is, Salem thought. *A bearing wheel.* In Sabrina's time, sailors found their way across the open sea by following signals from satellites. Before that, they used the sextant, which was sort of like a telescope. The bearing wheel was used before that. It was better than nothing, but just barely. It was why Vikings got lost. It was why they had seen North America many times, by accident, before Leif Ericsson landed there on purpose.

"Did you get it?" Salem asked eagerly when Sabrina came back from her discussion with the captain.

Sabrina shook her head. "He won't give it up voluntarily. It's too important."

Salem growled. "He'll get another one. We'll liberate it while he's at his dad's house."

"Oh, right," Sabrina said. "His dad is Eric the Red. From what I hear, there's only thing worse than an angry Viking, and that's *two* angry Vikings. Anyway, I'm worried about interfering with Leif's ability to navigate. What if he can't get another bearing wheel? What if he doesn't discover North America?"

"Hey, no problem," Salem said. "Christopher Columbus will come along eventually."

The captain was the last to go ashore, except for Salem and Sabrina. To their dismay, he took the bearing wheel with him.

"He carries that thing around like it's his cell phone or something," Salem griped.

"I told you it was important," Sabrina said. They followed Ericsson all the way to the home of Eric the Red. When Salem saw the fierce-looking pair together, he changed his mind about simply "liberating" the wheel.

"I say we switch to Plan B," Salem said. "Let's get a new bearing wheel."

"The Timekeeper sent us to Leif Ericsson," Sabrina pointed out. "I have a feeling he wants us to bring back the original."

"Fine," Salem said. "We'll give the new one to Leif. We'll all come out ahead."

It sounded like a good idea until they actually went shopping. Although Sabrina found a lovely bracelet made of lava beads and Salem located a stash of battle-axes they could get at wholesale prices, when it came to bearing wheels, they both came up empty-handed.

That was when one of their shipmates—a toothless, shifty-eyed sailor named Lars—stepped in. He'd heard about Sabrina's inquiries, he said. He wanted her to meet an Icelandic friend of his named Thig.

"Thig can get you a bearing wheel," Lars cackled. "Cheap!"

"We don't care how much it costs," Sabrina said. "We really need a bearing wheel, and we need it right away."

Salem winced. He didn't want them to seem too eager.

At least Thig wasted no time finding them. He literally came running.

"I can get you this thing," he said, panting. "It costs . . ." He paused a moment before asking, "How much did you say you had?"

Sabrina shook her heavy bag of Plunder winnings, making a huge impression on the pirate. "Meet me at the dock before you sail tomorrow morning," he said, and loped off.

* * *

That night, while the Vikings prepared the ship to sail, Leif's father fell and sprained his ankle. The injury wasn't serious, but nonetheless he concluded that it was a bad omen and decided to stay home. To make up for his absence, he threw a farewell party for the crew. Everyone in the settlement came aboard, had fun, and slept where they fell until dawn's early light.

The first one standing on the main deck at sunup was Thig. As promised, he had a bearing wheel, and it looked just like the captain's.

"Perfect," Sabrina said, handing over her entire bag of money.

Salem coughed up a hair ball.

"You want me to give you some advice, Sabrina?" Salem said once the ship was under way. "Thanks to Thig, we've got a very good copy of Leif Ericsson's pizza cutter in hand. I can't tell the difference between it and the original, and I'll bet the Timekeeper won't be able to, either. Let's scram while the scramming's good."

But Sabrina wasn't so sure. "What if this one doesn't fix the clock? What if it absolutely has to be the one from Leif Ericsson? We have to make the switch."

Salem rolled his eyes.

"Let's sit back and enjoy the cruise," Sabrina said. "I want to help discover North America. Wouldn't this make a super report for history! 'How I Discovered North America.' Oh, and by the way, you haven't caught a single rat, Salem."

She was right, he hadn't. But he felt he'd met one—a big one named Thig. Just how big Salem discovered an hour later, when they were called to a meeting with the captain.

"Bad news," Leif Ericsson said. "My bearing wheel is missing." He was sure it was somewhere on the ship. He'd probably misplaced it during the party. It was up to the cleanup crew to find it.

Sabrina thought about the wheel in her pocket— how remarkably like the captain's it was. And she knew in her heart that it *was* the captain's.

"Thig stole it and sold it us!" Sabrina said after the meeting, and there was steam coming off her words.

"Used equipment, and he charged full price," Salem griped. "Talk about a rip-off." Then he smiled. "Good thing I'm known for seeing the bright side of things. We've got the correct wheel, haven't we? C'mon, let's split while the splitting's good."

Sabrina gave him a look of disgust. "You've been hanging around with the crew too long," she told him. "That would be stealing, and we're not that kind of pirate!"

"What other kind of pirate is there?" Salem shot back. He was thinking about Lars now, the shipmate who'd referred them to Thig. Had he known Thig was a thief?

"Just because one person is mean to you isn't a reason to be mean to everybody else," Sabrina said.

"This is no time for wisdom," Salem said. The

men were reefing the sail; the sky had darkened; the wind was singing in the lines, and the boat was pitching and rolling like a bathtub toy. "We have to leave sooner or later, and I vote for sooner."

"Not until we make sure Leif Ericsson discovers North America," Sabrina told him. "We have the bearing wheel, and the responsibility that goes along with it for making sure that things go according to history."

Salem's heart sank like an anchor. "That'll take weeks!" he protested. "We have a clock to fix, remember?"

"This is the past," Sabrina said. "Maybe since it's already happened, we're not using up any time."

"But we're doomed," Salem sobbed. Lightning cracked and rain poured from the heavens. "Doomed!"

"The next time I want to see water act like that," Salem wheezed the next day, "I'll take four quarters to the Laundromat and watch it through a little round window."

All night the storm had raged, throwing the crew around like stones in a game of Plunder.

"You're right," Sabrina croaked. "It's not easy being green."

It took a little time, but eventually the crew recovered and managed to unfurl the sail. After consulting with Spellman the Lucky, Leif Ericsson set a westward course. As only Sabrina and Salem knew, as long as they kept to it, North America was impossible to miss.

The days went by. The fair winds blew. Salem played Plunder.

Yes, the crew let him in the game. Designed to be easy enough for sailors, it surprised no one to see that even a cat could play.

After a week, the ship touched land. Vinland, Leif called it.

America.

"There's no place like home. Right, Sabrina?" Salem whispered.

"I can take a hint," Sabrina said. "Now that Leif Ericson's job is done, you're ready to go back—I mean, forward—in time. I am, too, but I feel like a thief for taking the ship's only bearing wheel."

"These men are Vikings," Salem repeated from earlier. "Pirates! A little cheating is expected and encouraged. Anyway, you paid for it."

"It's still not right," she said. "This wheel is stolen merchandise."

Then Salem played his trump card. "You're honest, Sabrina. I gotta hand it to you." Then he did hand it to her—another bearing wheel that looked just like the one they'd bought from Thig.

"Where did you get this?" Sabrina said. "And how?!"

"Plunder," Salem replied. "The game? Remember Lars, the sailor who introduced us to Thig? I found out his last name's Thigson."

"You mean like Eric and Ericson?"

"Exactly," Salem said. "Thig is his dad. I started playing against Lars at Plunder, just for revenge. It was sweet; when he ran out of cash, I made him put up the farm. Well, not the farm, exactly, but something else he had that was just as valuable—bearing wheels. He's got quite a stash, it turns out. The Thig family's been hoarding them for months."

"No wonder we couldn't find one when we were in Iceland," Sabrina said. "That's mean!"

"No, that's business," Salem explained. "What's mean is the trail of evidence I left for Captain Leif to find, leading directly to Lars's stash."

"You're a bad cat, Salem, did you know that?" Sabrina teased.

Salem purred. "Now would you mind giving that wheel to the captain so we can go? Please? Pretty please?"

"No problemo, to quote my favorite cat," Sabrina replied. Belowdecks the captain's eyes widened as he spotted something under Lars Thigson's bunk. Sabrina waved a pinkie, and in the next instant she and Salem were back in her bedroom.

"That worked out perfectly!" Sabrina said.

"Except for the hat," Salem admitted. Sabrina was still wearing antlers.

"Bear with me," she said, waving the little wheel.

This Magic Moment
By Nancy Holder

On Sabrina's desk, the brilliant crystals continued to drain into the bottom of the hourglass.

One more hour and twelve seconds. When am I supposed to have time to put the Great Clock together?

Sabrina held her breath as she stood in the center of her bedroom, waiting for her twelfth adventure to begin. She looked at Salem, who was lying on her bed. "Aren't you coming with me?" she asked.

"I think I'll sit this one out," he said. "I've reached my limit. I'm just too nervous and worn out to be any help."

He rolled over and immediately began to snore.

"Harrumph," Sabrina said. "Thanks a lot."

She waited.

Nothing happened.

She cleared her throat and said, "Mr. Time? I'm ready to go." Expectantly, she closed her eyes.

Still nothing.

She opened one eye. "Timekeeper?" she called over Salem's snoring. "What's going on?"

There was no answer.

She opened both eyes and looked around. Nothing had changed. Justin Time was nowhere to be seen. She and the loudly snoring black cat were the only ones in the room.

Did that mean *this* was the magic moment?

Listening to Salem snore?

Frowning, Sabrina crossed to the hourglass and held it up, as if it might present a clue. Uninspired, she put it down and paged through her magic book. She looked up "Magic Moment" and read the entry: " 'This Magic Moment,' a song written by Doc Pomus and Mort Shuman, originally performed by the Drifters in 1960, covered by Jay and the Americans in 1969."

"Well, that's useful," she groused. She closed the book. "Let's try something else."

With that, she gave Salem a gentle shake. "Salem, wake up. It's time to take some action."

Salem said, "Wha, we need reinforcements!" His eyelids fluttered. He yawned. Then he smacked his lips and said, "Oh, hi. I was having the nicest dream."

"Let me guess. It was either about food or taking over the Mortal Realm."

"The answer is *B*," he replied with a wistful yawn. "I was king of all I surveyed. Including the fish markets. So I suppose the complete answer is both of the above."

Sabrina gave his head a pat. "Poor Salem. Those certainly were your glory days."

"Which I *shall* reclaim, thank you very much," he retorted.

Sabrina sighed. "Not unless we can figure out what the twelfth magic moment is and put the new clock together. If we fail, you'll be a cat for the rest of your nine lives."

"Gulp." Salem looked stricken. "That could be bad, especially if tuna as we know it ceases to exist."

"Who can say?" Sabrina murmured. "Who knows what this realm will be like without magic?"

"We've got to think this through," Salem urged. "I mean, losing all hope of regaining my magical powers would be bad enough, but to be deprived of tuna . . ." He groaned. "We must be missing something. Something obvious."

Sabrina slumped "Well, I have no idea what it is."

She looked down at the pile of magical souvenirs on her desk. There were eleven of them:

Queen Elizabeth's locket
A moon rock
Thomas Jefferson's pen
Harry Houdini's secret key

L. Frank Baum's pencil
A flint from the cave people
Cupid's arrow
The cauldron of the Lancashire witches
A dinosaur tooth
Salvador Dali's paints
Leif Ericsson's bearing wheel

How on earth could all these things make a Great Clock? And if I don't know that, how am I supposed to figure out what to look for next?

Then she remembered what Salem had mumbled as he awoke from his dream: "reinforcements." Thoughtfully, she pointed a large woven basket into existence. Then, one by one, she guided each magical souvenir into the basket, being careful not to break the arrow or tip over the paint.

A last-minute addition to the basket was the hourglass, since it was the only timepiece she could actually trust. Or so she had assumed. *What if it's wrong? What if it's later than I think? Or too late?*

She levitated the basket and walked out of the room. The basket floated magically behind her.

"Where are we going?" Salem asked, following.

"To the Other Realm," she told him. "For reinforcements, just as you said. I think it's time to get some help."

"Just as I *dreamed*," Salem corrected her, "but okay, I'll go with that. And may I point out that the

Timekeeper said we couldn't get assistance from any other magic users?"

Sabrina sighed. "I know. But we're not getting zapped anywhere, so maybe we'll find our last magic moment in the one place where's there more magic than anywhere else. And who knows? Maybe we can persuade someone to listen to us and help us—my aunts, for example."

"Good thinking." Salem gulped again. "But what happens if we're over there when the Great Clock stops? Will the Other Realm cease to exist, or what?"

It was Sabrina's turn to gulp. "I really, truly have no idea," she confessed. "But I don't know what else to do."

"And I'm fresh out of creative and innovative solutions, amazingly enough," Salem admitted. "At least, when I'm awake. I think it's because I haven't had anything to eat in so long. Low blood sugar."

Sabrina opened the linen closet. Taking a deep breath, she crossed the threshold. Salem hopped in after her.

Sabrina shut the door.

"If this doesn't work, I . . . I want to thank you for that dish of tuna cat food you zapped for me," Salem said with great feeling. "That was a personal magic moment. One I hope to repeat, may I add. At least four or five hundred more times—"

Crash! Flash!

Before Sabrina could respond, they were in the Other Realm. Her basket of magic souvenirs floated behind her as she looked up and down the street. There was no one around.

"They're probably down at Great Clock Central," Sabrina said, "trying to fix the old clock."

"Fools," Salem muttered.

"They don't know what we know." She looked at the conglomeration in the basket. "But I'm not sure what we know, either, except that we have to create a new clock."

"Maybe you're right about trying to convince them," Salem said. "Maybe that's part of the magic moment."

Sabrina shrugged. "I have no idea." She took a breath. "Well, here goes nothing." She started down the street.

"Think positive," Salem urged. "After all, what do we have to lose—except just about everything we hold near and dear?" He shuddered. "Including the hope of ever dating Jennifer Love Hewitt in my handsome warlock form."

Just then, the loud *tick-tock-tick-tock* of the Great Clock echoed around them. But then it slowed, going *tiiiiiick-tooooooock.* Salem and Sabrina gasped.

"Forget *walking* there," she muttered, and chanted:

Hickory, dickory, dock!
Let's go to the clock!

Toil and trouble,
On the double!

"Ka-ching!" Salem exulted, as they were magically deposited on the outskirts of a huge crowd gathered around the Great Clock. Everyone in the crowd was staring up at a group of about a dozen witches, including Hilda, Zelda, Vesta, and Drell, the head of the Witches' Council, an equal number of warlocks, a sorcerer, a Druid, a Hawaiian kahuna, a Gypsy fortune-teller, and several packs of pixies and brownies. They were standing on a platform directly in front of the clock face, arguing and gesturing at each other and the clock.

Drell held the clock hands Sabrina had obtained from the wicked witch. He was trying to attach them to the Great Clock, but something was wrong.

Sabrina tapped the shoulder of the Australian shaman standing beside her. Dressed in a loose, short robe, he was barefoot and carried a long stick. His hair was burnt sienna and his skin was very brown.

He looked at her and said, "Yeah? Can I help you, miss?"

"What's going on?" she asked him.

The man shrugged. "A last-ditch effort by the sub-sub-subcommittee to save all of magicdom," he replied simply. "Drell keeps trying to put those new hands on the Great Clock, but that clock's having none of it." He sighed heavily. " 'Struth? It ain't looking good."

"Well, I know how to save it," Sabrina said.

"How's that?" he asked.

"I had a visit from Justin Time, and—"

The man's brows lifted. "Father Time's son-in-law? He's a likable mate. I've had occasion to talk things over with him now and then. You see, we Australians putter about in the Dreamtime, which is another magical realm. Time is very different there."

"Yeah, well, it's been pretty different where I live, too," she said dejectedly. "I had to fail the same test four times in a row."

He shook his head. "What's this realm coming to?"

"That was in the Mortal Realm," she explained.

"Too right." He leaned against his long stick. "Well, ah, Miss . . ." He looked at her expectantly.

"Sabrina."

"Miss Sabrina. I'm Peter Weird. Please tell me how you propose to save all of magicdom."

Her eyes widened. "So you'll listen to me?"

He pointed to the conference on the platform. "Better'n listening to that pack of dingoes yipping on without doing anything."

"Mr. Time told me that we need to build a new clock," she said in a rush. "It's like the Y2K problem, you see. The programmers didn't fix the old stuff. They made all new stuff."

He nodded. "Go on."

"I was supposed to go to twelve magical moments in time and collect something from each moment." She made the basket dip. "Those are the things we're to build the new Great Clock from. But I only have eleven, so far."

She glanced at the hourglass. "Yikes! And I only have thirty-one minutes to go! We've got to hurry!"

He held up a finger. "Too right. I believe you. And I'll help you."

He clapped his hands together. Instantly he, Sabrina, and Salem were catapulted to the platform where the sub-sub-subcommittee stood. She figured maybe Peter Weird's magic was working well because they were so close to the clock.

"Sabrina," Zelda said, looking worried. "Where've you been?"

"Aunt Zelda," Sabrina began. She looked at her other two aunts. "Please, I need your help. I don't have time to explain, but you've got to help me. It's time to build a new clock."

The three aunts exchanged looks. "What do you mean, Sabrina?" Zelda asked.

"Think about it," Sabrina pleaded. "The Y2K problem? Did they fix the old stuff that was broken? No. They created new stuff. Well, we need new stuff. We need a new Great Clock!"

The kahuna shook his head. "No way, little *wahine*. We do things the way our forewitches and forewarlocks set them down."

"No, you don't understand! We have to start over," Sabrina said urgently.

Zelda patted her arm. "Sabrina, slow down just a little, please, dear."

"Okay." Sabrina talked fast. "I tried to repair the Great Clock with a spell," she began, "but instead of Father Time, I got his son-in-law."

"Justin." Hilda made a face. "We used to date. Long story. Go on."

"He told me the Great Clock couldn't be—"

A loud *bongggggg* shook the platform. Someone cried, "It's the end of the world!"

"No," Sabrina said, as the sound died down. She picked up the hourglass. "We still have twenty-seven minutes and twelve seconds!"

"Oy, so soon it's all over," the wizard said. He turned to the sorcerer. "Hey, Moishe, it was great working with you and your apprentice. Such a nice young sorcerer, he could have become. Well, next year, Jerusalem."

"We'll probably have to fly to Israel in an airplane," the wizard replied. "Which could be all right. I've always wanted to leave the driving to someone else, *nu?*"

Teary-eyed, they nodded at each other.

"Being a witch has been so wonderful," an elderly lady moaned, dabbing her eyes with a handkerchief.

Someone in the crowd started crying. A violinist began to play a sad song.

Hilda turned to Zelda and whispered, "Don't ever let go."

"You guys, this is not the *Titanic*," Sabrina said impatiently. "We can fix this!"

Bonnnnnggggggggg.

"Donnnn't try to get help," a formless voice said.

"I think that's Justin Time," the Australian told Sabrina. "Are you under a gag order? You're not supposed to tell anyone about this?"

She nodded with great reluctance.

He pursed his lips. "Well then, you'd better zip your lip, eh?"

"But I was able to tell you," she pointed out.

"I've got that *in* with Justin I was telling you about," he suggested. "He probably did it as a personal favor to me."

"Will you help me, if you can?" She gestured to the floating basket. "I need to use those things to construct a clock."

He walked over to the basket and surveyed her souvenirs. "I'll do what I can." He smiled at her. "Let's get to work."

With a snap, he transported her, the basket, and Salem to a spot about twenty yards away—and about two hundred feet above the ground.

"First, something to hold us up," he said and let go of his stick. It grew into a huge wooden pillar and anchored itself to the ground.

Salem said, "Ooh, I have an intense fear of heights."

"Since when?" Sabrina asked.

"Since it occurred to me that I might not survive

a fall," he replied. "Mortal cats are amazingly fragile."

"You aren't mortal yet," Sabrina pointed out.

"No, but if this pillar changes back into a stick in"—he checked the hourglass—"twenty minutes. Me-*ow!* I'm not sure I could land on my feet from this height!"

"Sure you could," Peter Weird soothed. "But you won't have to find out, mate. We'll get this clock built in no time."

"Which is a good thing, since that's almost as little time as we have," Salem muttered.

Peter looked at Sabrina. "What does each of these objects represent to you?"

Sabrina took a deep breath. "Well, let's see." She gestured at Houdini's key. It rose from the basket. "This stands for the wonder of magic, at least to me."

"Good. Then that will be the clockworks," he announced. He said, "You need to invent a spell to make it happen."

"Okay," she said, flexing her finger.

"One, two, three. Go, Sabrina," Peter encouraged her.

Sabrina stared at the key and said:

Every timepiece has a heart.
Magic is the place to start.
Houdini's magic is the key
To extend our history!

The key rose and twisted itself into gears and cogs and springs and all kinds of things Sabrina couldn't identify. She figured that didn't matter. As long as it worked, she didn't care what the parts were called.

"All right, what next?" Peter asked her.

She hesitated. "Well, the dinosaur tooth stands for the importance of preserving history."

"The tooth will become the weights," he suggested.

"Okay," she said. "Weights."

Minutes, seconds, go so fast,
Once gone, they become our past.
Weigh it down and make it stay,
So we'll make history, day by day.

The tooth transformed itself into three long cylinders that appeared to be made of brass or bronze. They hung from the clockworks on three substantial chains of the same material.

Peter looked satisfied. Sabrina smiled. She was really getting into this.

Just then, Hilda and Zelda popped over. Zelda said, "We decided we should try to help you, dear. We aren't sure what you're doing, but we're happy to pitch in."

"Where's Aunt Vesta?" Sabrina asked them.

The two Spellman sisters traded worried glances. "We don't know," Hilda admitted. "She went to the

Other Realm Public Library to get some books on time, but she never came back."

"We're afraid she got caught in a time change," Zelda added. "We're worried."

"We zapped the books on over here," Hilda added. Then she frowned. "Not that they did any good."

The five of them looked over at the other platform, where Drell was still fiddling with the clock hands.

"We're with you to the end, Sabrina," Hilda said.

"Thank you." Sabrina smiled uncertainly. "I have no idea whether this is going to work or not."

"Well, nobody seems to have a better idea."

"But she has to do the actual spell-casting herself," Peter said, wagging his finger. "Or so Sabrina told me."

I did? I'm so nervous, I can't remember.

"Then take it away, Sabrina," Hilda said.

"Okay. Next souvenir." Sabrina looked in the basket. "How about Cupid's arrow for the pendulum?" She smiled at the others. "Because time heals all wounds? Or love makes the world go around? Or something like that?"

"Pendulums look like arrows, too," Hilda observed.

"To be honest, that's why I thought of it," Sabrina confessed.

"It's a great idea," Peter put in. "And, actually, that part of the clock is more accurately called the pendulum rod."

Sabrina thought fast, to come up with an appropriate spell:

Love is timeless,
So it seems.
It keeps us moving
Toward our dreams.

"Oh, that's nice," Salem murmured. "Very sentimental, but not hokey."

Sabrina nodded. "Thanks."

The arrow rose from the basket and hung suspended from the clockworks, behind the weights.

It looks exactly like a pendulum. Maybe this will work!

"Okay, the locket." She held it as she considered what to use it for. It had belonged to a witchly mother who had passed it down to her daughter, the strongest monarch her nation had ever known. She had provided a firm foundation for England to become a great nation.

"This is what the rest of the clock sits on," she ventured.

"That's called the plinth," Peter Weird said. "Or you can call it the base."

"Okay." Sabrina thought for a few moments. Then she pointed at the locket and said:

A mother's locket for a lovely queen.
In olden days, she reigned supreme.

She used her wisdom, strength, grace.
The locket will be our firm, strong base.

The locket shimmered and stretched and became a golden square beneath those parts of the clock that had been assembled.

"Good job," Salem said. "Although you might have mentioned in there somewhere that I play a mean lute."

"What else have you got in there?" Hilda asked, rummaging through the basket. "Oh, look, Zelly! It's the cauldron of the Lancashire Witches!"

"You know what it is?" Sabrina asked in surprise.

"Sure." Hilda picked it up and inspected it. "We ran into the witches who donated it. . . . Oh, when was that, Zelly? 1600s? 1700s? We met them while we were cruising London."

"Cruising in a boat, down the river Thames," Zelda added hastily.

"Yeah, it's not like we were down on the docks or anything," Hilda added. "Even back then we were nice girls."

"Pardon me, but don't we have a bit of a deadline to worry about?" Salem interjected.

"Yes, such as"——Peter checked the hourglass——"thirteen more minutes."

"Yikes!" Sabrina cried. She pointed to the cauldron. "Clock face?" she suggested. "Because the passage of time can inspire people to be creative?

And outer beauty fades, but inner beauty never does?"

Everyone nodded. "Why not?" Hilda said. "Go for it."

To help us win this timely race,
The cauldron is the Great Clock's face.
Previously employed for drama so tragic,
We now erase its baked-on magic.

Poof! The black cauldron became a blank white clock face.

"Let's use the pencil to add the numbers," Sabrina continued. "It was used by L. Frank Baum to write his notes for the *Wizard of Oz*. He wrote about following the Yellow Brick Road. The numbers will mark the passage of time."

"Go, girlfriend!" Salem cried.

At that point, the head of the Witches' Council appeared in their midst. Adjusting his white wig and black judge's robes, Drell said, "I heard you're building a new Great Clock. Sounds reasonable. What do you want me to do?"

"Oh, wow, thanks!" Sabrina cried. "Maybe you could think up a spell to make the pencil write the numbers on the clock face?"

"Okay," the Witches Council head replied, rubbing his hands together.

"Excuse me, but Sabrina has to do all the spells alone. So she told me," Peter said again.

I really don't remember saying that. Nevertheless, she sighed, pointed at the pencil, and made up a spell.

Twelve, six, nine, three,
The wizard's a story of mystery.
Three, six, twelve, nine,
Show us when it's story time!

The pencil rose and began writing on the clock face. The numbers were truly beautiful, very elaborate and ornate, yet there was something that was very modern about them. Like the new millennium . . .

As soon as the pencil was finished, it became the 1 in the 12. Then, with a *zing* and a shimmer, all the letters turned to gold.

"Okay, what's left?" Sabrina asked. She looked in the basket. In it were the bearing wheel, Dali's paint, the moon rock, Thomas Jefferson's pen, and the piece of flint.

"Hurry," Drell murmured.

Sabrina realized that this important, powerful witch believed in what she, Sabrina, was trying to accomplish, and she felt a little dizzy. The fate of all magicdom depended on her!

"Well, a bearing wheel points the direction. Not that that helped me much," Sabrina added sheepishly. "So we'll make that into the hands, okay?"

"Good," her aunts and Drell chorused. Their eyes

were shining with excitement and hope. Sabrina swallowed hard.

What if I make a mistake?

Now I'll speak a magic rhyme.
Wheel, turn into hands that tell the time!
You once helped me discover new lands.
Now help others as time's own hands.

"Ooh, that's my favorite so far," Salem said. "It would make a great rap song."

Boonnnnnnnnnnnggggggggg.

The old clock chimed. The sound was weak and shaky, and all the assembled magic users groaned in dismay. Sabrina started to panic, but she took a deep breath and forced herself to stay calm.

TICKKkkkktttTTTTTOCKkkkkTttick. . . .

"Oh, no, it's going to stop early," Sabrina said anxiously.

"Just keep going, sweetie," Hilda said. "You're doing great."

"We've still got the flint, the moon rock, Dali's paint, and Jefferson's pen," Zelda observed.

"Well, Thomas Jefferson drafted the Declaration of Independence to create a new nation and to preserve liberty. So his pen will become the casing for the clock."

"Fair dinkum," Peter enthused. "And did you know he invented a clock that showed what day of the week it was? Parts of it ran up the walls, then down to the basement. He was a very clever bloke. Could have been Australian."

How does Peter know about the clock? Sabrina was impressed. *I'll have to study my history home-work harder.*

Assuming, of course, that she could get back to Westbridge if this failed!

She pointed at the pen.

*Let's stop the talk
And house the clock!
T.J. used you with style and grace.
Become the Great Clock's sturdy case!*

The pen rose and began to grow hundreds of feet into the air. It was larger than a cathedral. Then it quickly shaped itself into a massive grandfather clock. The dark grain of the wood shone and gleamed. Life-size carved figures appeared on the base, the trunk, and the portion that housed the clock face. All types of magic users were represent-ed—witches, warlocks, fairies, pixies, brownies, leprechauns, wizards, sorcerers, magicians, and all the others—and they appeared to be dancing all over the clock in a joyous celebration of magic.

The other parts of the clock expanded to fit the case, and then magically slid inside. Two exquisite-ly etched glass doors, showing planets, moons, stars, and comets, encased the pendulum, the weights, and the face.

"Great job!" Zelda said, clapping her hands. "Sabrina, it's just beautiful!"

Sabrina pointed to the paint.

Salvador Dali, an artist, I reckon!
His paint covers this clock in only a second!
Masterpiece, timepiece, work of art,
All will gasp when it does start!

The paint can rose, and suddenly all the figures were painted in incredible detail. And all the male figures sported a Daliesque mustache!

The witches chortled when they saw the mustache. Sabrina took time for a giggle as well.

Then she checked the hourglass. *Five minutes. Only five minutes left.*

"The Great Clock has a battery, right?" Sabrina queried.

Her aunts nodded. "Yes," Zelda said. "We thought for a while that we could keep the Great Clock running if we simply made it work with the pendulum and the weights and forgot about the battery, but it didn't look promising."

Sabrina pointed at the flint.

You started fire,
Now start time!
Become a battery
So fine!"

* * *

"Not your best work," Salem murmured.

The flint shaped itself into a large rectangular metal object and disappeared inside the clock.

"And the moon rock, to adjust it and keep it running," Sabrina said. "Because it stands for adventure and daring and the will to keep growing."

You watched mankind take a giant leap.
Such inspiration we'd like to reap.
Oh, rock from mortal outer space,
Make sure our magic clock keeps pace.

The rock became a large key that fitted into a keyhole in the back of the clock. Written over it in swirling gold letters were these words: "Turn me if the Hours Don't."

"I wish the other Great Clock had had a key like that," the head of the Witches' Council said. "We probably wouldn't be in this mess." He smiled at Sabrina. "Now what?"

"That was the eleventh souvenir. I still don't have a twelfth," she admitted.

Suddenly, without warning, they were all transported to an enormous ballroom flashing with mirrors and gold. A jaunty symphony orchestra of crocodiles, wombats, and possums played rollicking piece of classical music while animals and people dressed in costumes from all different time periods—animal skins to hoopskirts to futuristic silver jumpsuits—jumped and twirled.

"This is the 'Dance of the Hours,' by Ponchielli," Hilda cried. "It's got great violin parts!"

"But I need to finish the clock!" Sabrina protested.

Just then Vesta rushed up to them. She was dressed in an enormous white gown. The numbers 1 through 12 were embroidered around the hem in black and gold, and the ends of a black sash, which hung down from a large bow at her waist, resembled the hands of a clock approaching the twelve, with scant inches to go until midnight!

"Thank goodness you found me!" she cried. "Get me out of here! All these people and animals want to do is dance!"

"We're in some kind of time-space warp," Peter said. He shook his head of burnt sienna hair. "This is bad. Very bad."

I'm going to fail, Sabrina thought miserably. *Will we be stuck here forever?*

Bonnnnggggggggg.

Tiiiiiiiiiiiiccccccccccccckkkkkkkkkkkkk.

Vesta's sash edged closer to the twelve on her skirt.

Salem's ears twitched. "Sabrina," he said, pawing at her shin, "*do* something!"

Me? Why me?

Because I started this. I have to finish it.

As she tried to think up a spell, the dancers twirled toward her and the others.

"You must dance!" a frog in knickers, a vest,

and a green velvet jacket insisted, grabbing her hands.

He began to drag her to the dance floor. Sabrina said, "No, thank you. Really. I need to get back to the Other Realm."

"Oh, pish-posh, Hieronymus Bosch!" the frog chortled. "Ribbet!"

Bonnnnnnnnnnnggggg.

"I *demand* that we return to the Other Realm now!" Sabrina shouted.

Poof!

They were back where they'd started, in the Other Realm. They stood before the new clock. Vesta was there, and so was the dancing frog.

"Ribbet!" he cried in astonishment.

All eleven souvenirs had been used. There was nothing else to do, so far as Sabrina knew. But the clock wasn't ticking. It wasn't doing anything.

And everyone was looking at her.

She cleared her throat. "How much time do we have?"

"Four minutes," Hilda cried.

"And twelve seconds," Peter added.

Sabrina whirled on him. "You're the Timekeeper, aren't you? You're Justin Time . . . in disguise!"

He grinned at her. Then he snapped his fingers and there, in place of Peter Weird, stood Justin Time.

"How'd you guess?" he asked, in his normal voice.

"Nobody could help me until Peter Weird showed up," Sabrina pointed out. "And you knew so much about what I was doing." She smiled. "The 'twelve seconds' part gave you away, for sure."

He nodded in defeat. "Very well. Now I'm here, and I can lend you a hand, but you have to solve this mystery yourself. The fate of all magicdom rests on your shoulders."

She blinked. She was panicking. She couldn't think straight.

She looked across to the other platform. The Great Clock was still ticking.

"Three minutes," the Timekeeper said.

"I don't know what to do!" she cried.

She looked at her aunts, at Salem, and at the head of the Witches' Council.

Zelda said, "Well, the other clock is still running, so . . ."

Sabrina opened her arms. "So . . . ?"

"What's making it run?" Hilda asked.

"Something that will ring out the old and ring in the new," Salem said.

Sabrina thought a moment. Then she clapped her hands. "Salem, you're right! Magic! Magic is making it go!"

Drell raised his eyebrows. "Of course! Why didn't I think of that?"

"And it's magic that's centuries and centuries old. Our heritage of magic!" Sabrina continued.

"That sounds right bonzer." Justin pointed to the hourglass. "Keep going. You have two and a half minutes."

"We have to take the last bit of magic from that clock and transfer it to this one," she told the others excitedly. "That's the twelfth magical thing we need. The old magic."

She turned to Drell. "We need to transfer the magic at the precise last second of the old millennium. And we have to put the magic into the new clock—the Great Clock of the New Millennium."

"Yes," the Timekeeper said, catching on. "All magic users everywhere must concentrate on getting the new clock magically ticking." He waved a hand at the new clock. "That's the lesson you must all learn—that you still control your destiny. You are still the users of magic. Magic does not use you."

"Oh, how well said," Zelda said, impressed.

"And you have one minute and twenty-one seconds left," the Timekeeper added. "That's including your twelve extra seconds."

"I'll inform the others," announced the head of the council. "Zelda, Hilda, Vesta, you're with me."

Poof! They disappeared. The frog croaked, "Ribbet!" and he disappeared, too.

Salem, Sabrina, and the Timekeeper stood before the new Great Clock.

"Now, Sabrina, think up a good spell," the Timekeeper urged her. "This is the most important spell you have ever cast." He held out a calming hand. "Take a little time to think it through."

"A very, very little time," Salem muttered.

Sabrina took a deep breath. Her mind was whirling. She could barely remember her own name, much less think up a spell.

She thought about how hard it had been in the beginning to accept the fact that she was a half-witch with magical powers. It had frightened her a little—okay, a lot—and she had thought the powers complicated her life rather than made it easier.

Then she became accustomed to having them. Now she couldn't imagine being without them.

"Sabrina, you have one minute," the Timekeeper told her.

She steadied herself.

"Okay."

She pointed at the old Great Clock. In a hush, she whispered:

Through the sands of time we sift
With our most beloved gift.
Time will rush, and time will slow,
But we have magic wherever we go.

Magic is
    the smile of a friend,
    the gift of a flower,

the power of a storm,
an April shower.

Magic is
to know you helped,
'cause you knew you could,
and if you'd keep trying,
the world will edge closer and closer to
good.

Magic is
the stars in the sky,
the moon and the sun.
It's what you and I are.
Mortal or witch.
It's in everyone.

"Yes, Sabrina," the Timekeeper said reverently. "You really, truly know what magic is. Now if all magic users everywhere—and I mean *everywhere*— really, truly can believe that, if only for a second, magic will be safe for another millennium."

Sabrina pointed at the old Great Clock. "Show me the magic," she told it.

"Ten, nine, eight," Salem counted, staring at the hourglass.

Suddenly all the magic users in Great Clock Central began to chant, "We are the magic. We are the magic."

"Seven, six . . ." Salem murmured. "Me too. I am the magic."

"We are the magic," the Timekeeper said.

"Five, four, three, and so is tuna," Salem said. "Two . . ."

Sabrina added her voice. "And I am the magic."

"One!" Salem shouted.

At that precise instant a shimmering wisp of golden magic rose from the old clock and flashed into the new one. The old clock immediately stopped.

Sabrina bit her lower lip, her fingers crossed.

Tick.

The new Great Clock of the Other Realm began to work! As thundering cheers rose up, the pendulum swung and the minute hand moved one little notch, signifying the passage of a single precious second.

Everyone danced with glee. Everyone hugged for joy. Sabrina shouted, "Woo-hoo!" and picked up Salem. The Timekeeper lifted them both in the air.

"You did it, Sabrina!" he cried happily. "You saved magic!"

"Happy New Year!" the throngs of magic users cried, waving at Sabrina.

She waved ecstatically back. "Happy New Year! It's going to be a wonderful year! And the best new millennium!"

Woo-hoo!

About the Authors

Cathy East Dubowski has written dozens of books for kids and often collaborates with husband, Mark Dubowski, whose work can also be found in this anthology. She wrote the following Sabrina, the Teenage Witch books: *Santa's Little Helper, A Dog's Life,* and *Fortune Cookie Fox,* plus the Salem's Tails books *Salem in Rome* (with Mark) and *Psychic Kitty.* One of her books for younger readers, *Cave Boy,* illustrated by Mark Dubowski, won an International Reading Association Children's Choice Award. Cathy likes to dream about the past and the future as she writes on an iMac computer in an old red barn in Chapel Hill, North Carolina, where she lives with Mark, their daughters, Lauren and Megan, and their golden retrievers, Macdougal and Morgan.

Mark Dubowski has written and illustrated many books for young readers, including books for the Salem's Tails series, starring Sabrina's cat.

About the Authors

Diana G. Gallagher is a Hugo Award–winning artist best known for her series Woof: The House Dragon. Her first adult novel, *The Alien Dark,* appeared in 1990. She coauthored *The Chance Factor,* a Star Trek: Starfleet Academy: Voyager book with her husband, Martin R. Burke. In addition to other Star Trek novels for intermediate readers, Diana has written many books in series published by Minstrel Books, including The Secret World of Alex Mack, Are You Afraid of the Dark? and The Mystery Files of Shelby Woo. She is currently working on original young adult novels for the Archway paperback series Sabrina, The Teenage Witch.

Nancy Holder has written forty books and over two hundred short stories. For Archway she has written three Sabrina, the Teenage Witch novels: *Spying Eyes, Scarabian Nights,* and *Up, Up, and Away.* She has also written *Feline Felon,* a Salem's Tails book for young readers. In addition, she has worked on a dozen books about Buffy the Vampire Slayer, including *The Sunnydale High School Yearbook.* She lives in San Diego with her daughter, Belle.

Nancy Krulik has written more than one hundred books for children and young adults, including two *New York Times* best-sellers: *Leonardo DiCaprio: A Biography* and *Taylor Hanson: Totally Taylor.* Nancy's daughter was the one who turned her on to the magic of Sabrina, the Teenage Witch, and she hasn't gone out on a Friday night since. If the truth be told, though, Nancy is actually a bigger fan of Salem's than of Sabrina's—there's just something about his nasty streak that she likes! Nancy lives in Manhattan with her husband and two children.

Mel Odom spends as much time as he can in the Other Realm hanging out with Sabrina and her friends, because they have the coolest adventures. He's also the author of three Sabrina novels and a contributor to *Eight Spells a Week*. He also spends time in the magical world of the Internet and loves to receive e-mail from people who enjoy Sabrina as much as he does. You can write to him at *denimbyte@aol.com.*

Brad Strickland is an English professor and writer from Georgia who has written or cowritten nearly forty books. He and his wife, Barbara, collaborated on the Salem's Tails adventure *You're History!* and they have also written for the following book series: Star Trek: Starfleet Academy, The Mystery Files of Shelby Woo, and Are You Afraid of the Dark? Brad's favorite fictional witches are those created by the hilarious English writer Terry Pratchett, but Sabrina is his favorite TV witch!

YOU AND A FRIEND COULD WIN A TRIP
TO THE KENNEDY SPACE CENTER
VISITOR COMPLEX TO SEE A REAL
SPACE SHUTTLE LAUNCH!

Sabrina
The Teenage
Witch™

NO PURCHASE NECESSARY

1 Grand Prize: A 3 day/2 night trip for three (winner plus friend and a parent or legal guardian) to see a space shuttle launch at the Kennedy Space Center Visitor Complex in Florida. Prize also includes a Sabrina, The Teenage Witch CD-ROM, a Sabrina, The Teenage Witch hand held game, and a Sabrina, The Teenage Witch Diary Kit.

> *Alternate grand prize:* In the event that the grand prize is unavailable, the following prize will be substituted: An Overnight Group Adventure at Apollo/Saturn V Center for three (winner plus friend and a parent or legal guardian). Winner and group will sleep under the Apollo/Saturn V rocket after an evening of space-related activities, including a Kennedy Space Center Visitor Complex group bus tour, pizza party dinner, a visit with Robot Scouts, hands-on activities. Winner and group will get a special NASA briefing of upcoming launches, demonstrations of Newton's Laws of Motion, midnight snack, breakfast and 3-D IMAX film. Prize includes a commemorative certificate for each group and patch for each participant.

10 First Prizes: A Sabrina, The Teenage Witch Book Library consisting of: Sabrina, The Teenage Witch, Showdown at the Mall, Good Switch, Bad Switch, Halloween Havoc, Santa's Little Helper, Ben There, Done That, All You Need is a Love Spell, Salem on Trial, A Dog's Life, Lotsa Luck, Prisoner of Cabin 13, All That Glitters, Go Fetch, Spying Eyes, Harvest Moon, Now You See Her, Now You Don't, Eight Spells a Week, I'll Zap Manhattan, Shamrock Shenanigans, The Age of Aquariums, Prom Time, Witchopoly, Bridal Bedlam, Scarabian Nights, While the Cat's Away, Fortune Cookie Fox, Haunts in the House, Up, Up and Away, Millennium Madness, Switcheroo, Sabrina Goes to Rome, Magic Handbook, and Down Under

20 Second Prizes: A Sabrina, The Teenage Witch gift package including a Sabrina, The Teenage Witch hand held game, a Sabrina, The Teenage Witch diary kit, and a Sabrina, The Teenage Witch CD-ROM

50 Third Prizes: A one-year Sabrina comic books subscription and a Sabrina, The Teenage Witch Diary Kit

---

See back for official rules

ARCHWAY
PAPERBACKS

VIACOM

KENNEDY SPACE CENTER
VISITOR COMPLEX

Pastime
#1 IN KIDS FUN!™

Knowledge
Adventure

TIGER
ELECTRONICS, LTD.

Pocket Books/ "Sabrina, The Teenage Witch Space Launch Sweepstakes" Sponsors Official Rules:

1. No Purchase Necessary.

2. Enter by mailing this completed Official Entry Form (no copies allowed) or by mailing a 3" x 5" card with your name and address, daytime telephone number and birthdate to the Pocket Books/ "Sabrina, The Teenage Witch Space Launch Sweepstakes", 1230 Avenue of the Americas, 13th Floor, NY, NY 10020, or to obtain a copy of these rules, write to Pocket Books/ "Sabrina, The Teenage Witch Space Launch Sweepstakes" Rules, 1230 Avenue of the Americas, 13th Floor, NY, NY 10020. Entry forms and rules are available in the back of Archway Paperbacks' Sabrina, The Teenage Witch books: Sabrina's Guide to the Universe (12/99), Millennium Madness (1/00), Switcheroo (3/00), on in-store book displays, and on the web sites SimonSaysKids.com and archicomics.com. Sweepstakes begins December 1, 1999. Entries must be postmarked by April 30, 2000 and received by May 15, 2000. Sponsors are not responsible for lost, late, damaged, stolen, illegible, mutilated, incomplete, postage-due or misdirected or not delivered entries or mail or for typographical errors in the entry form or rules, or for telecommunication system or computer software or hardware errors or data loss. Entries are void if they are in whole or in part illegible, incomplete or damaged. Enter as often as you wish, but each entry must be mailed separately. Winners will be selected at random from all eligible entries received in a drawing to be held on or about May 25, 2000. The grand-prize winner must be available to travel during the months of September and October 2000. Winners will be notified by mail. The grand-prize winner will be notified by telephone as well.

3. Prizes: One Grand Prize: A 3-day/2-night trip for three (winner plus a friend and a chaperone, chaperone must be winner's parent or legal guardian) to Florida including round-trip coach/economy airfare from major U.S. or U.K. airport nearest the winner's residence, round-trip ground transportation to and from airport, double-occupancy hotel accommodations and all meals ($35/pounds per person, per day). Prize does not include transfers, gratuities and any other expenses not specifically listed herein. Travel and accommodations subject to availability; certain restrictions apply. Prize also includes a Sabrina, The Teenage Witch CD-ROM (approx. retail value $29.99) from Havas/SSI, a Sabrina, The Teenage Witch Hand Held Game (approx. retail value $14.99) from Tiger Electronics, and a Sabrina, The Teenage Witch Diary Kit (approx. retail value $16.99) from Pastime. (approx. total retail value of prize package $3,000.00 for travel within the U.S. & Canada; £4,000 for travel from the U.K.). Alternate grand prize: In the event that the grand prize is unavailable, the following prize will be substituted: An Overnight Group Adventure at Apollo/Saturn V Center for three (winner plus friend and a parent or legal guardian). Winner and group will sleep under the Apollo/Saturn V rocket after an evening of space-related activities, including a Kennedy Space Center Visitor Complex group bus tour, pizza party dinner, a visit with Robot Scouts, hands-on activities. Winner and group will get a special NASA briefing of upcoming launches, demonstrations of Newton's Laws of Motion, midnight snack, breakfast and 3-D IMAX film. Prize includes a commemorative certificate for each group and patch for each participant. If winner cannot take the trip on the specified date, the prize may be forfeited and an alternate winner may be selected.
Ten 1st Prizes: A Sabrina, The Teenage Witch Library (approx. retail value $150.00) from Archway Paperbacks published by Pocket Books. Twenty 2nd Prizes: A Sabrina, The Teenage Witch Gift Package including Hand Held Game (approx. retail value $14.99) from Tiger Electronics, Diary Kit (approx. retail value $16.99) from Pastime, Sabrina, The Teenage Witch CD-ROM (approx. retail value $29.99) from Havas/SSI. (approx. total retail value of prize package: $62.00). Fifty 3rd Prizes: A one-year Sabrina comic books subscription (approx. retail value $23.00) from Archie Comics and a Sabrina, The Teenage Witch Diary Kit (approx. retail value $16.99) from Pastime (approx. total retail value of prize package $39.99). The Grand Prize must be taken on the date specified by sponsors.

4. The sweepstakes is open to legal residents of the U.S., U.K. and Canada (excluding Quebec) ages 8-14 as of April 30, 2000, except as set forth below. Proof of age is required to claim prize. Prizes will be awarded to the winner's parent or legal guardian. Void in Puerto Rico and wherever prohibited or restricted by law. All federal, state and local laws apply. Viacom International, Archie Comic Publications Inc., and the Kennedy Space Center Visitor Complex, their respective officers, directors, shareholders, employees, suppliers, parent companies, subsidiaries, affiliates, agencies, sponsors, participating retailers, and persons connected with the use, marketing or conduct of this sweepstakes are not eligible. Family members living in the same household as any of the individuals referred to in the preceding sentence are not eligible.

5. One prize per person or household. Prizes are not transferable and may not be substituted except by sponsors, in the event of prize unavailability, in which case the alternate grand prize outlined on previous page will be awarded. All prizes will be awarded. The odds of winning a prize depend upon the number of eligible entries received.

6. If a winner is a Canadian resident, then he/she must correctly answer a skill-based question administered by mail.

7. All expenses on receipt and use of prize including federal, state and local taxes are the sole responsibility of the winners. Winners will be notified by mail. Winners may be required to execute and return an Affidavit of Eligibility and Publicity Release and all other legal documents which the sweepstakes sponsors may require (including a W-9 tax form) within 15 days of attempted notification or an alternate winner will be selected. The grand-prize winner's travel companions will be required to execute a liability release form prior to ticketing.

8. Winners or winners' parents on winners' behalf agree to allow use of their names, photographs, likenesses, and entries for any advertising, promotion and publicity purposes without further compensation to or permission from the entrants, except where prohibited by law.

9. Winners and winners' parents or legal guardians, as applicable, agree that Viacom International, Inc., Archie Comic Publications Inc., and the Kennedy Space Center Visitor Complex, and their respective officers, directors, shareholders, employees, suppliers, parent companies, subsidiaries, affiliates, agencies, sponsors, participating retailers, and persons connected with the use, marketing or conduct of this sweepstakes, shall have no responsibility or liability for injuries, losses or damages of any kind in connection with the collection, acceptance or use of the prizes awarded herein, or from participation in this promotion.

10. By participating in this sweepstakes, entrants agree to be bound by these rules and the decisions of the judges and sweepstakes sponsors, which are final in all matters relating to the sweepstakes. Failure to comply with the Official Rules may result in a disqualification of your entry and prohibition of any further participation in this sweepstakes.

11. The first names of major prize winners will be posted at SimonSays.com and archiecomics.com (after May 31, 2000) or may be obtained by sending a stamped, self-addressed envelope to Prize Winners, Pocket Books "Sabrina, The Teenage Witch Space Launch Sweepstakes", 1230 Avenue of the Americas, 13th Floor, NY, NY 10020.